Praise for Kennedy Ryan

"Kennedy Ryan pours her whole soul into everything she writes, and it makes for books that are heart-searing, sensual, and life affirming. We are lucky to be living in a world where she writes."

—Emily Henry, #1 *New York Times* bestselling author

"Few authors can write romance like Kennedy Ryan."

—JL Armentrout, #1 *New York Times* bestselling author

"Kennedy Ryan has a fan for life."

—Ali Hazelwood, *New York Times* bestselling author

"Ryan is a powerhouse of a writer." —*USA Today*

"Kennedy Ryan is a true artist."

—Helen Hoang, *New York Times* bestselling author

"Ryan is a fantastic storyteller and superb writer." —NPR

"Kennedy writes these gripping, touching, romantic, transporting books every single time."

—Denise Williams, author of *How to Fail at Flirting*

"The queen of hard-hitting romance books." —The Culturess

"Ryan always manages to ring her heavy stories with an aura of hope and a propulsive narrative that makes them impossible to put down." —*Entertainment Weekly*

"Every time I think Kennedy Ryan can't possibly raise the bar any further, she proves me wrong in the most delightful way possible." —Katee Robert, *New York Times* bestselling author

"Ryan creates characters who are deeply relatable, so compelling and lushly drawn that they feel like old friends." —BookPage

WHEN YOU ARE MINE

"*When You Are Mine* is exactly what I look for in a romance! Achingly beautiful with palpable, real characters you cannot help but completely fall in love with. I cannot wait for more!"

—A.L. Jackson, *New York Times* bestselling author

"Ryan's debut is rife with sexual tension, while her easy style and likable characters bring this unpredictable love triangle to life." —Karina Halle, *USA Today* bestselling author

WHEN *You* ARE MINE

ALSO BY KENNEDY RYAN

THE BENNETTS
Loving You Always
Be Mine Forever
Until I'm Yours

SKYLAND
Before I Let Go

ALL THE KING'S MEN
The Kingmaker
The Rebel King
Queen Move

HOOPS
Long Shot
Block Shot
Hook Shot

SOUL
My Soul to Keep
Down to My Soul
Refrain

GRIP
Flow
Grip
Still

STANDALONE
Reel

WHEN *You* ARE MINE

KENNEDY RYAN

FOREVER

New York Boston

Copyright © 2023 by Kennedy Ryan
Cover design by Daniela Medina. Cover copyright © 2023 by Hachette Book Group, Inc.

Forever
Hachette Book Group
1290 Avenue of the Americas, New York, NY 10104
read-forever.com
twitter.com/readforeverpub

Originally published as a print on demand and ebook by Grand Central Publishing in June 2014

First trade paperback edition: October 2023

Forever is an imprint of Grand Central Publishing. The Forever name and logo are trademarks of Hachette Book Group, Inc.

The publisher is not responsible for websites (or their content) that are not owned by the publisher.

Forever books may be purchased in bulk for business, educational, or promotional use. For information, please contact your local bookseller or the Hachette Book Group Special Markets Department at special.markets @hbgusa.com.

Library of Congress Control Number: 2023942543

ISBNs: 978-1-5387-6690-3 (trade paperback), 978-1-4555-5681-6 (ebook)

Printed in the United States of America

LSC-C

Printing 1, 2023

Acknowledgments

I could probably fill every page of this book with thanks for so many people. That is impractical, so I'll narrow it down to just a few, and hope that I've told everyone else at some point how very grateful I am. I have to thank my parents. My father for planting a love for words and excellence in my heart, and even when he was busy, finding ways to water them. My mother, who passed along a voracious appetite for reading, always reminded me I was a writer and always whispered destiny to me. To my first beta readers, my family who read this piece by piece, chapter by chapter, and encouraged me to continue when I assumed it was crap. To so many awesome writers I've met in this industry I'm pleased as punch to call friends.

And finally, to my best friend, champion, and the absolute love of my life, my husband. It has always been you. It will always be you.

Author's Note

Thanks so much for picking up *When You Are Mine*. It's a story of how life challenges and sometimes hurts, but also how we mend and heal and, ultimately, love. To help safeguard your mental health, I just wanted to let you know the content contains the death of parent, death of a child, cancer, and reference to childhood abuse (off the page and in the past). Please read with care, and know that Walsh, Kerris, and Cam's story continues in *Loving You Always*.

—Kennedy

Chapter One

All eyes were on him, except the bride's. Walsh hadn't looked at Kerris Moreton, his best friend's wife-to-be, for weeks. As two hundred wedding guests waited, Walsh contemplated his glass of champagne and the toast they expected from the best man.

"I met this scrawny, mean punk of a kid at camp thirteen years ago." Walsh pieced together his most charming smile around the words. "We pretty much hated each other on sight."

He paused for a ripple of polite laughter before focusing his attention on his best friend, Cam.

"But by the end of the summer, I had a best friend. I had a brother, and that's never changed. We've been through a lot together, and you deserve every happiness. I love you, man."

With a look, Walsh and Cam exchanged years of memories and emotions in a silent moment between them.

And then Walsh did what he had deliberately denied himself all day. He looked at the bride. Really looked at her, full on, and every word he had scripted fled his mind. His breath caught up in his throat at her beauty, illuminated by the kindness and compassion he knew lay beneath that gorgeous face. His tongue clung to the roof of his mouth for an extra second before he wrenched himself from drowning in her amber eyes.

Kerris met his stare, her expression not guarded enough to disguise the fear, the near-panic. He read the question in her eyes as if she had spoken aloud.

What are you about to say?

"And what a girl you've found," he said, unable to look away from her solemn gaze.

"I saw her before I knew she was the girl you'd been telling me all about. She was going out of her way to help someone. I knew then that she was different, and that she deserved a special man."

He raised his glass to toast the bride, swishing champagne and disappointment in his mouth.

He'd wanted to be that man.

* * *

Six Months Earlier

Walsh couldn't stop watching her. She stood too far away for him to see her face clearly in the dim light, but he suspected it would take his breath away. She peered up at the bus schedule, speaking with an elderly woman. Her bright red dress in the almost empty parking lot drew his eye like a silver lining in a dark cloud.

"Does it say when the B is coming?" The older woman's question carried across the space separating them, her white hair gleaming in the light from the street lamp.

"Oh, no. You just missed the last bus." The girl's voice was husky-hot and sweet. Honey burned to a crisp.

"Well, I only live a few blocks away. I'll walk."

"My car's over here. I'll take you."

"No, I couldn't put you out like that." It sounded like only half the lady's heart was in the protest, and the other half didn't want to walk in the dark. "You don't even know me."

"I know it's too dark for you to walk the streets alone. I won't sleep tonight wondering if you made it home. Come on."

Walsh wished she would turn around so he could see this Good Samaritan's face, but he only glimpsed a delicate profile and a flower behind her ear before she marched toward a battered Toyota Camry.

Walsh pushed the incident from his mind, crossing the parking lot and entering the hotel across the street. He was late, but his mother wouldn't care. She'd just be glad to have him home.

"Bennett!" a voice boomed as soon as he entered the beautifully decorated ballroom. "What the hell. I didn't know you were coming tonight."

"It's called a surprise."

Walsh warded off Cameron Mitchell's playful jabs before hooking an elbow around his neck.

Walsh watched his cousin Joanne approach, walking as fast as she could in her prized Manolos, weaving through the food-laden tables and well-dressed people. Her smooth skin glowed with health. The sleek, chestnut-streaked bob fell around her ears, a glossy frame for her oval face. Her full lips tilted up at the edges, hinting at the laughter she usually reserved for her tight circle of friends and family. Jo wedged herself between Cam and Walsh, throwing an arm over each man's shoulder. She had been fitting nicely between the two of them since they'd met Cam at camp thirteen years ago. Walsh had been fourteen and they had been thirteen. That slim age difference had been about the only thing separating them ever since.

"You didn't tell us you were coming." Jo nodded at Walsh's jeans and polo shirt, her gray eyes sparkling, a cheeky grin lighting her face. "Your mom will be so glad to see you. Even dressed like that."

Walsh gave Jo an affectionate squeeze and kiss, eyeing her brightly patterned halter dress and Cam's sports jacket and slacks. He *was* underdressed.

"She won't mind." Walsh cast a cursory glance around the ballroom. "Is Uncle James here?"

"Daddy?" Jo rolled her eyes, hand on the curve of her slim hip. "He was still at the office when I left, but he'll be here."

"Or Mom will have his head." Walsh shared a knowing look with his cousin.

Uncle James and Walsh's mother were not only siblings, but best friends. They had always been partners in crime in everything, including running the family foundation and raising their children.

Walsh spotted his mother working the room, trolling for donors.

"I'll see Unc when he gets here," Walsh said. "Going to go grab Mom now."

Cam laid a hand on Walsh's shoulder, his smile as broad as the Eno River, which snaked through the small town of Rivermont, North Carolina.

"Okay, but don't forget I want to introduce you to my new girl. She's amazing."

"Can you believe this?" Walsh nodded his head toward Cam, but looked at Jo. "The certified player, wanting one girl?"

"She is pretty amazing." Jo offered a wry smile, bumping Cam's shoulder with hers. "What's most amazing is that she wasn't running after him like the swarm of girls he's used to."

"It took me *six months* to even get a date with this girl." Cam waved his hand to indicate his olive-toned skin, blue-gray eyes, and dark, wavy hair. "Me!"

Jo rolled her eyes, shaking her head and setting her gold hoop earrings in motion. "She *is* something else."

"I'll meet her later." Walsh turned in his mother's direction. "Right now, I gotta go kiss the most beautiful woman in the room."

He snuck up behind his mother and covered her eyes.

"Who is this?" She starched and pressed the words.

"How many people did you give birth to?"

"Walsh!" She whooped and turned around to hug him as tightly as he had known she would. Her dark hair was pulled back in an elegant knot, showing off her smooth, still-unlined skin. "I didn't know you were coming tonight. Your room isn't even ready."

The ever-practical Southern hospitality. Kristeene Walsh Bennett had never lost it, even when she'd been married to his father, living among New York's most elite.

"I'll be fine." Walsh gave her an extra squeeze before pulling away. "Just as long as there's a bed. Feels like parts of me are scattered across three time zones. I just want to crash after this."

"But you will stay, right?" She rolled a threat and a plea into one tiny frown. "You have to meet our Scholar of the Year. She's overcome so much."

"Haven't they all?" Walsh thought of Cam and several of the other foster kids who'd come through the foundation over the years.

"Well, yes, but she's special," Kristeene said, something approaching pride in her voice. "She's driven and determined. Just a good girl."

"Let me guess. She has a great personality?"

"Well, yes, she does." His mother pressed her lips together, but Walsh knew laughter could spill from the sides at any minute. "Come on. Time to announce the awards."

Walsh took a seat across from Cam and Jo.

"Where is she?" Cam twisted around, scanning the crowded room. "She should've been here by now."

"She'll be here." Jo took a quick sip of her white wine and toyed with the studded bangle wrapped around her wrist. "She's probably just running late, and I'm sure there's an excellent reason for it. God forbid she'd do anything wrong."

"She did mention she was taking her mentee home after

school." Worry pulled Cam's dark brows together. "But that would've been hours ago."

Was this really Cam? Walsh couldn't believe all this concern. For a girl? Cam barely remembered the names of the girls he'd slept with over the years, usually referring to them by distinguishing characteristics.

The girl with the belly-button ring.

That chick with the tramp stamp.

The one who did that trick with her tongue.

Now Cam was worried because this girl was *late*?

"Thank you all for being here tonight," Walsh's mother said from the platform, her warm gaze skimming each table. "My great-grandfather married a girl who never knew her mother or father. A girl who lived in an orphanage throughout her childhood. Her story compelled my family to start the Walsh Foundation, and we've been helping kids without parents or homes all over the world ever since."

Polite applause from the donors. The college students who had grown up in foster homes and been able to attend college because of the foundation offered a less reserved response, cheering and whistling until Kristeene held up a staying hand.

"Speaking of all over the world." Kristeene turned a bright smile in Walsh's direction. "I'm going to have a proud mother moment and welcome my son, Walsh, home. He's finally back from visiting our orphanage in Kenya. Help me convince him to stay for the summer. Stand up, baby."

Walsh stood, offering a brief salute before quickly sitting, feeling as self-conscious as he had at six years old when she'd forced him to play the piano for company.

"We're so proud of him." Her eyes lingered on her only child. "He's been working with the Walsh Foundation ever since he graduated from NYU, and he helps out his father in New York when he can."

Walsh nearly smirked, thinking of how disgusted Martin Bennett would be to hear about his son "helping out" in New York. Like training to run a multibillion dollar enterprise was his side gig. His father wanted Walsh to work all of what he liked to call this "philanthropy crap" out of his system with his mother's do-gooder family.

"And that brings us to our final award, the Scholar of the Year," his mother said, regaining Walsh's attention. "This young lady has impressed us all. Not only did she graduate last week summa cum laude, but she also serves as a mentor at Walsh House in Raleigh, where we serve at-risk teens. I interviewed her myself for the scholarship last year. I was blown away by her strength of will, determination, and compassion. Please welcome Kerris Moreton, our Scholar of the Year."

Everyone applauded. After that grand introduction, Walsh wondered if this girl would ascend to the stage flanked by cherubim and seraphim and accompanied by harps. Walsh envisioned everyone genuflecting when this paragon finally decided to bless them with her presence. His hands stung from clapping, waiting for her to show up.

Where the hell was she?

His mother scanned the room, obviously looking for the

little scholar-cum-saint. She shielded her eyes against the glare of discreetly lit chandeliers.

"I guess promptness isn't one of her virtues," Walsh said.

Cam surprised him with an irritated look. What? Did the little saint have him under her spell, too? Wonder what his new girlfriend thought of that. Then Cam's face lit up.

"Here she comes."

She rushed through the door and down the aisle toward the stage. Walsh blinked, thinking she would be less lovely at a second glance. She was not less of anything. No less blinding. No less stunning. No less captivating. She rushed past their table, but not before he got a good look at her.

She was probably no more than an inch over five feet, and softly curved. He would stand more than a foot taller. Her hair waved around her shoulders and streamed down her slim back, dark brown, spiked with lighter red streaks, as if the tresses had trapped rays of sun. Her cheekbones curved high, a perfect setting for eyes that tilted a little, glinting with green, amber, and gold. And that mouth.

Damn, that mouth.

It was full and wide. Lush, like raspberries at peak season.

And damned if she wasn't wearing a scarlet dress and a flower behind her ear.

Chapter Two

He was a mountain. Insurmountable. Stark against the backdrop of the glittering ballroom like peaks against a feather-clouded sky. His unwavering stare scrambled her thoughts.

Kerris knew she should be used to the stares by now. People could never label her ethnicity. A little bit of this, a little bit of that. She'd never know what genetic cocktail had been shaken or stirred to get this face that made people take a second look, trying to place her. She'd always struggled to find her place. Hard to do when you were practically born on a doorstep and passed around like an old library book everyone keeps returning.

She got the impression this man wasn't used to waiting for people and things, but he didn't seem impatient. If anything, he was completely still. He seemed to be waiting for her.

After the awards had been given out, Kerris tried to focus on several well-wishers offering congratulations. With her undignified sprint to the stage, she was just glad to have made it. Old ladies and kids. She could never say no.

Kerris managed to nod and smile at Jenni, the Walsh Foundation's program coordinator, but she really just wanted to drag her weary bones home, wrap up in her thrift store kimono, and sip her Earl Grey.

"Excuse me, Jenni." His voice was dark and rich and strong like a shot of espresso.

"We didn't know you were coming tonight." Jenni's back straightened and her hand flitted to adjust an already-perfectly-straight collar.

"Surprise." He smiled, and Jenni couldn't seem to look away. Neither could Kerris. "I wanted to congratulate Miss Moreton personally. Would you excuse us?"

Jenni scurried off without a word. Had he been rude? Kerris couldn't tell. She wondered if charm like that wrapped around such a steely will left people feeling they should thank him when he stepped on their feet.

He watched her with the focus of a jaguar considering a particularly scrumptious prey. That look should have frightened her, but it wasn't fear unfurling inside. She didn't know this feeling, but she was certain she had never felt it before.

"Congratulations." He slid his hands into his pockets and cocked his head to one side, his casual stance belying the barely checked energy of a hunter. "I don't know which was more impressive. The award, or your good deed earlier taking the old lady home."

Kerris's jaw nearly gave in to gravity and dropped.

"How did you…when did you…huh?"

Wow. Stellar articulation. She gave her mental processes a second to catch up. Let's try this again.

"How did you know about the lady?"

"I was in the parking lot across from the hotel, running late for the awards ceremony, and overheard."

The room narrowed to the width of his smile, and Kerris felt herself leaning toward him, on the verge of toppling.

"Most people wouldn't have helped her out."

"She was a sweetheart. It was nothing."

One hand went to her throat. The other touched the silk orchid nested behind her ear. A succession of twitches she couldn't control. Butterfly wings brushed the lining of her belly. She willed the triple time tempo of her heart to slow, but he inundated her senses, and they would not be soothed.

Kerris watched him catalog every detail about her, his eyes surveying each limb and curve. Her fingers plucked at her thrift shop dress, a scarlet tunic with gold embroidery edging the sleeves and collar, stopping just above her knees. Under his scrutiny, her toes curled in the scarlet leather mules. She shifted her weight from one leg to the other. And then back again, like an uneven scale, grappling for balance.

She returned his inspection, noting the dark green eyes under thick, well-shaped brows. The sculpted blade of a nose. The high cheekbones jutting to create hollows above his jaw. His tanned skin stretched taut over the regal bones of his face. He wore jeans, a green polo shirt, and leather moccasins, but he carried an air of careless glamour only money could achieve. He was a slumming prince, and the strong male beauty of him snagged the breath in her throat. The rest of the room dissolved into a peripheral blur.

She wasn't sure if she was supposed to speak, or if it was his turn. She wanted to say something, make small talk, but speech and sense had fled. She was naturally reticent. Slow to share much about herself. Some might even call her shy. But somehow she knew this man could trample her defenses and dismantle her like a ticking bomb.

"So you two finally met." A familiar male voice a few feet away snapped the invisible thread tugging her closer by the second.

Kerris looked over her shoulder, coming back to herself and finally absorbing something beyond *him*. Cam walked up, making her smile. He made smiling an involuntary action, like blinking or sneezing. Something you just couldn't hold back.

Cam slid an arm around her waist, leaning down to kiss her cheek. She forced herself to give him her full attention, willing Mr. Mountain to drift away.

"This is the guy I've been trying to get you to meet for the last year, but he's been all over the globe saving orphans. This is my best friend in the world, Walsh Bennett."

Oh. Freaking. No.

Kerris's only consolation was that Walsh looked just as disconcerted before disciplining his features into a polite mask, as if that moment hadn't happened. Maybe it had been her imagination. Feeling a wordless, mindless connection that strong with your boyfriend's best friend would border on tragic.

"I was just congratulating Kerris on her award. My mom practically threatened to disown me if I didn't." Walsh split his glance between the two of them. "I had no idea Mom's star scholar was the girl you've been raving about."

Jo sidled up and slipped her arm through the crook of Walsh's.

"I'm just glad someone made Cam work for it."

"I finally found a girl worth working for." Cam's half-serious look rested on Kerris.

He placed a kiss on her unsuspecting lips, surprising her when his tongue made a quick foray into her mouth. She willed herself not to jerk away. Cam knew how difficult physical affection was for her in private, much less in a room full of people. Her discomfort deepened in front of *him*.

"I'm glad to finally have you both in the same state," Cam said. "This summer's gonna be great. The two people I love most in the world. Sorry, Jo. Make that three."

"Whatever," Jo said, her laugh good-natured. "Are we going to celebrate the scholar or what? The food at this reception looks delish."

"Um, remember I kind of had a private celebration planned for Kerris and me." Cam offered a sheepish grin, squeezing Kerris's hand.

"What'd you have in mind?" Kerris found a smile she hoped passed for normal.

"You'll have to wait and see." Cam's look asked Jo and Walsh to understand. "You guys don't mind if we skip the reception, right? I'll see you tomorrow."

"Tomorrow?" Walsh glanced at Kerris before looking back at Cam.

"Just some of us getting together at the river to kick off the summer," Jo said. "Grill some food. Swim. You in, Walsh?"

"Sounds like fun. If you don't mind me sleeping half the time. Jet lag's kicking my ass."

"Sleep as much as you want." Jo leaned her head against Walsh's shoulder. "We just want you around. We've missed you, man."

"Yeah, great having you home. Can't wait to catch up." Cam turned to Kerris. "But right now, we're gonna head on out. Ready, Ker?"

Kerris watched the interaction between the longtime friends. The feeling was finally returning to each body part Walsh had so closely inspected moments before.

"Oh, sure," she said. Cam pulled her toward the door, but she glanced over her shoulder one last time. "Nice to finally meet you, Walsh."

Before she turned away, Walsh's eyes held hers for an extra beat of her heart. That same jolt struck right down the middle of her soul. The intensity of that stare left her insides crackling.

* * *

Walsh watched until the crowd swallowed Kerris's scarlet silk. He felt like someone had shaken him from a coma, and he'd awakened disoriented in a world that was familiar, but changed in ways vast and indiscernible.

"Hellooooo." Jo waved a hand in front of his face. "What were you looking at?"

"Nothing." Walsh carefully hid his churning emotions beneath a protective layer of composure. The trick he'd learned over the years didn't usually work on his sharp-eyed cousin, but it was worth a try.

"I can tell when you're attracted to a girl, and the look you just gave Kerris was *way* beyond that. Forget it. She's taken. By your best friend, I might add."

"The girl's beautiful." Walsh did his best to look directly into the censure of Jo's eyes. "Can't blame a guy just for looking."

"Keep it that way." Skepticism twisted Jo's mouth, lifting one side and not bothering with the other.

"You think Cam's serious about this girl?" Walsh deliberately kept his voice casual and devoid of the rabid curiosity gnawing through his mind.

"Serious? That plan of his?" Jo paused as if giving Walsh time to prepare for what she'd say next. "Tonight he's asking her to marry him."

The word "marry" punched Walsh in the throat, the breath soughing through his nose. He had glimpsed a great prize behind the curtain, only to have it snatched away. A cruel sleight of hand. He reminded himself he had exchanged only a handful of words with the girl. His strong response to the possibility of Cam marrying her was because he didn't know her, and only wanted the best for Cam. For Cam to be happy. That was the reason.

A shame he couldn't convince himself.

Chapter Three

Cam and Kerris pulled up the cobbled driveway leading to his lovely, stacked stone cottage. A wide front porch with a swing looked like a holdover from a time long gone.

"You're so lucky to live here rent-free, Cam." Kerris pulled off her seat belt and eyed the charming house she fell a little bit more in love with every time she visited.

"Yeah, Ms. Kristeene won't take my money, which is fine with me since I don't have much." He angled a grin her way in the dim light of the car. "This cottage has been in their family for probably sixty years, but since they all live at the house closer to town, it works out."

Kristeene would have done a lot more for Cam if he'd let her. Kerris admired his fierce pride and determination to make his own way. She followed him to the front door and through the house, and couldn't help but be glad he'd at least accepted this beautiful cottage. He squeezed her hand and smiled over his shoulder every few seconds. Anticipation lit his eyes like it was Christmas morning.

A screened-in porch led to a well-manicured backyard. Small, sand-filled bags lit with votives marked a clear path on the ground, directing them toward the center of the backyard. Looking at the multicolored quilt spread across the grass, with lanterns at each edge to bathe it in warm light, another corner of Kerris's heart softened.

"Cam, how'd you do all this? It's beautiful."

"Jo definitely got involved. The Walsh family cook made the food." Cam smiled, shy and bold all at once. "I had help, but the idea for a candlelit picnic was all mine."

"It's absolutely perfect." So few things had been perfect for Kerris, and these moments, this gesture, was one of them.

"Sit down." He took her hand, settling her onto one of the overstuffed satin-covered cushions in the center of the quilt. "I'm glad you were fine skipping the reception. I knew this was waiting for us."

"I'm glad, too." Kerris lifted the silver domes covering the dishes to reveal roast chicken with vegetables, risotto, and snow peas. The aroma of freshly baked bread wafted from beneath linen napkins, luring her to dive into the feast.

They ate with only a few comments, laughter and the sounds of silverware scraping plates punctuating their companionable silence.

"I'm stuffed."

Kerris lay back on the soft cushion supporting her and patted her tummy. Eyes heavy-lidded, she listened to the crickets' chatter and the river's rumbling just over the hill. The late-night lullaby could have easily lulled her to sleep if Cam hadn't leaned down beside her, propped on one elbow. She peered up at him, smiling and wondering when he had become so dear. She traced the dark slant of his brows.

"Thank you." Kerris barely had the energy to raise her voice over the rush of the river.

Cam pressed warm lips to her eyelids and the lashes feathering her cheeks. His kisses wandered from her eyes, across the tilt of her nose and the curve of one cheekbone, before settling over her mouth. He skimmed her lips once, twice, and again before she opened her mouth, brushing her tongue against his. She hoped for a measure of the fire she could sense building inside of him, but it never came.

She had stopped believing in the lightning strike of desire. She had assumed that if this beautiful man with his lean, muscled body and sensually curved lips couldn't stoke a fire inside of her, no one could.

And she'd believed that. Until tonight.

Cam's hand wandered across the curve of her breast and slid over her hip, down her thigh, and moved in for a more intimate touch.

"Cam." Kerris placed her hand over his, halting his progress.

"Hmmmmm." The vibration of his groan hummed through her like a revving engine. He lay his forehead against hers, obviously working to regain control. "You're right. We need to talk."

"Talk about what?" She sat up, pulling the neckline he

had tugged aside back into place, tired from the mental paces tonight's encounter with Walsh had put her through.

"Kerris." Cam gulped with uncharacteristic nervousness before starting again. "Kerris, you know we both had really shitty childhoods."

With a laugh as bitter as it was short, Kerris nodded. She wasn't sure what was worse, her mother abandoning her on the orphanage steps or Cam's mother actually thinking she could pull herself together long enough to raise him. Fortunately, or unfortunately, Cam's mother had tried for the first twelve years of his life. He had only alluded to parts of it, keeping his deepest scars covered. Yet another thing they had in common.

"You know I love you." He stroked one finger over the full bow of her mouth. "I've never had a family of my own. I mean, the Walshes took me under their wing, and Walsh is the closest thing I have to a brother, but I don't belong to them. And they don't belong to me."

"People don't *belong* to each other, Cam. People love each other."

"No, baby, people *do* belong to each other." The conviction on his face glowed brighter than the candlelight. "We just don't know about it because we never had it. Don't you want that? To belong to someone? And have him belong to you?"

His words, though softly spoken, echoed her deepest desire. She could think of only one person who had truly loved her, and Kerris had been taken away from Mama Jess's foster home cruelly and abruptly. No one had looked at her with that much love in a long time, but it was there on Cam's face now.

"Marry me." The tremor in Cam's voice made her more nervous than the words he'd spoken.

Kerris struggled to even her erratic breaths, but could not. Heat rushed to her cheeks under Cam's probing, waiting stare. The blood thumped at her wrists and temples, reminding her that she was alive and not a statue-still shell frozen by his words.

"Cam, I just graduated, and it took me longer than most. Don't you think we need a little time?" Kerris ran damp palms along the fabric stretched across her legs. "I'm only twenty-five. Maybe we should—"

"Not now. I know you're not ready. I know we've only been dating six months, but I want you to think about it. And at the end of the summer, I'll ask you again." He tugged the orchid in her hair away and placed it in her lap, kissing behind her ear and slanting her a cocky grin. "And you'll say yes."

She raised her lashes, forcing herself not to look away from his hungry stare. He was so into her.

Please don't let me hurt him.

She smiled through her confusion, thinking of the friend Cam had been to her. Thinking of how comfortable she always felt with him. How patient he'd been with her abstinence. Maybe the night that haunted her had bankrupted her heart and stripped her body of its capacity for physical desire. She had abandoned love-struck delusions of butterflies and goose bumps. Perhaps what she felt for Cam was all she was capable of. It felt good. It could be enough.

The situation with Walsh had been her imagination. Or a fluke. After all these years of isolation and numbness, that rush of desire, that sense of…rightness…couldn't have been real. With a stranger? With Cam's best friend?

"Did you hear me?" Cam's eyes were fixed on the expression she had pulled into place to hide her thoughts. "I said you'll say yes at the end of the summer."

"Cam, I can't make any promises." Kerris toyed with a chunk of bread from the basket, tearing it into tiny pieces in her lap.

"Just promise me you'll think about it." Cam lifted her chin, gently compelling her to look at him.

She set her disturbing thoughts aside and laced her smile with all that she could promise.

"I'll think about it."

"That's all I can ask for." He dropped a quick kiss on her lips, its sweetness a thin veneer covering the passion she knew he carefully checked. "That's enough for now."

Chapter Four

Someone in this elevator smelled good enough to eat.

A sexy-sweet scent of vanilla and brown sugar titillated Walsh's sense of smell and taste. His mouth watered.

The heavy Tag Heuer watch wrapped around his wrist confirmed that he was late. Walsh bided his time in the packed elevator, revisiting every detail about Kerris from last night. Her face, her hair, her voice, the act of kindness he'd witnessed in the parking lot. Everything about her had haunted him since they'd left the scholars' awards.

By the tenth floor, everyone had filed out of the elevator. Walsh was startled to see Kerris's slight frame leaning against the wall, eyes closed. There was no flower in her hair today. Her dark jeans weren't tight, but still hugged the lean, curvy lines of her petite figure.

"Kerris?" Walsh asked, afraid his half-horny imagination had conjured her up.

She jerked here eyes open wide.

"Walsh, what are you doing here?" She wore a white T-shirt emblazoned with the Walsh Foundation logo. Her dark wavy hair was caught in two low ponytails at her neck.

He couldn't stop the smile that worked its way onto his face. Talk about oblivious. Here he'd been indulging in guilt-soaked fantasies about a woman not even five feet away from him.

"How'd you hide in an elevator?"

"There were a lot of people in here." She grinned back, and it felt like they'd had this conversation a thousand times before. "I don't have on my heels, so I guess I kind of got lost in the sauce."

His deep-rumbled chuckle and her husky laugh met in the space separating them. Walsh felt it again; that invisible thread stretching between them. Electricity zipped up and down his body like a current on a power line.

"Okay, this is my floor." Kerris smiled her good-bye.

"It's my floor, too."

He gestured for her to precede him into the children's ward, catching a noseful of vanilla and brown sugar. How had he missed that last night when every other detail had played over and over in his head?

"You visiting someone in the children's ward?" He paced his long steps to match her shorter ones.

"Actually, a few someones." She slid a hand into her back pocket over the subtle swell of her bottom. "I volunteer here. We do crafts, mostly making jewelry. Necklaces, bracelets. Nothing fancy, but it seems to cheer them up."

He nodded, searching his mind for something that would

make her linger. She saved him from asking something truly idiotic with a question of her own.

"Are you visiting someone?"

"Yeah. Her name's Iyani." Walsh looked up the hall toward the little girl's room. "She's one of the kids from our orphanage in Kenya. She has a brain tumor. We thought it had been taken care of, but it's back. The prognosis isn't good, but I wanted the medical team here to take a look."

"You really care about those kids, huh?" Kerris lobbed him an admiring glance.

"Of course. In addition to our own orphanages, there are several all over the world that we support. I'm involved with them all."

"So you have a thing for orphans, huh?" Kerris's smile drew him in and warmed him up. "Is that why you and Cam get along so well?"

"I don't know what Cam told you, but things didn't start off so smoothly with us." Walsh couldn't help but smile remembering his early years with Cam. "He was at one of our camps here in North Carolina. I was down from New York spending the summer with my mom. Cam and I hated each other immediately."

"He didn't tell me that part. Just that you guys ended up attached at the hip."

"I wouldn't say attached at the hip, but…" He scoffed with affronted male dignity. "But we were close by the end of the summer. A few fights, several pranks, and lots of trash talk later."

"I know he feels really lucky to have found you and your family."

"*We* felt lucky to find him. I always wanted a brother. He was it."

An awkward silence fell between them when they realized their destinations would take them in different directions. Walsh knew that he shouldn't, but he looked for an excuse to prolong…again.

"I know you have your crafts class, but do you have time to meet Iyani?"

"I'd love to." She glanced at the watch on her wrist. "I have a few minutes."

They entered the sterile room, both watching the little girl swallowed by the large hospital bed. Walsh made a note to brighten things up next time he came.

"Mr. Bennett!" Iyani stretched her IV'd arms toward him, like little wired pencils. "You came."

"I told you I would." He gave her a quick hug and a smile. "And I brought someone to meet you."

Walsh noticed Kerris blinking away tears at the sight of the little girl whose smooth, dark skin contrasted against the stark white sheets like coffee against milk. Soft, dark curls were just starting to grow back on her smooth scalp, but a scar streaked its way along one side of her head like an angry lightning bolt. The other side looked swollen, the growth below pushing against the skin. In contrast to the battle-scarred head, her bright smile and shining eyes glowed with simple joy.

"She's so pretty," Iyani said in her softly accented voice.

"Well, I was just thinking the same thing about you." Kerris's smile widened when Iyani brightened even more under the faint praise.

"How are you feeling today, Iyani?" Walsh leaned in to drop a kiss on her forehead.

"I am good, Mr. Bennett," she assured him with a vigorous nod. "A little tired from our long trip."

"Did you enjoy your first plane ride?" He brushed his hand across hers.

"It was a lot of fun!" Iyani shared a heart-melting smile with Walsh and Kerris.

"Well, I think your doctor will be coming through in the next hour, so I thought I'd come hang out for a little while until then," Walsh said.

"No more Uno." Iyani left her voice serious, but her eyes laughed.

"I thought you loved Uno." Walsh put on a mock-offended frown.

"Just so much…" Iyani scrunched her nose.

"We got bored on the plane, so we kind of played a little Uno," Walsh explained to Kerris.

"Sounds like more than a little." Kerris's eyes teased him. "Well, Iyani, if you have some time, I'm about to meet some other little girls down the hall, and we're going to make necklaces and bracelets and rings. Would you like to come?"

"Can I, Mr. Bennett? Please, please, please?" Iyani clasped her small hands together under her chin.

"Let me get this straight. You'd rather go make jewelry with a bunch of *girls* than hang out here with me and play Uno?"

"Yes! I mean…just this once?"

"I think it'll be fine." He laughed, hazarding a glance in Kerris's direction. "Lead the way."

"Oh, you're…you're coming with us?" Kerris's smile slipped a little.

"Well, I'm responsible for this young lady. I need to see what she's up to."

An hour later, Walsh watched Kerris flit from one small, drawn figure to the next, helping them bead strings and glue on sparkly ornaments. She showed that same compassionate heart to these desperately sick children that he'd glimpsed with the sweet old lady.

He thought of the childhood she'd probably had, similar to Cam's. This loving, generous, captivating woman had probably lived through hell and emerged like a butterfly with scorched wings. He wanted to pull his eyes away from the vibrancy of her, but he just couldn't.

"Okay, kiddos." Kerris passed her smile out to each of the girls. "I'll see you on Tuesday."

The gaggle of girls laughed and squealed their excitement, admiring their handmade treasures.

"Iyani." Walsh reached for her hand. "Come on, sweetie. It's time to meet Dr. Myer."

Her small face fell. He knew that, for a little while, she had actually forgotten her reason for being in this hospital so far from home. Then she brightened and turned in Kerris's loose embrace.

"Will you come again on Tuesday? We could make jewelry again." Iyani's eagerness and hope strained and stretched out of every pore.

"Sure will." Kerris gave her a gentle squeeze and bent down to whisper in her ear, just loud enough for Walsh to hear. "And maybe I'll see you before then. Would that be okay?"

Iyani offered a shy smile and nod, shuffling her feet under the stiff hospital gown.

"Iyani, we have to go," Walsh reminded his small charge, glancing at Kerris. "I guess I'll see you at the river later."

"Maybe." She pushed back a dark brown tendril that had slipped forward. "I have an appointment that could take a while."

"What could be more important than lounging by the river?" Walsh knew he should just let her go, but between his genuine curiosity and his desire for a few more minutes with her, he couldn't stop talking.

"Well, I'm opening a business."

"Didn't you just graduate last week?" His laugh provoked her to roll her eyes.

"Yes, but my roommate, Meredith, and I are opening a thrift store."

"A thrift store? Like a Goodwill kind of thing?"

"Think a step above." A defensive note entered her voice and pride tilted her chin. "Higher end, gently used stuff. Items that are excellent quality, and when first bought, were probably pretty expensive. When the wealthies are done with them, they pass 'em onto places like ours. And the wealthies' gently used is usually *barely* used."

"The wealthies, huh?" Walsh glanced down at his jeans, which probably cost as much as a small car payment, and figured he'd fall into that category. "That's your term?"

"Yeah, my term, but I don't mean it in a bad way." She offered him a smile that stole any sting from her words. "Your family's the best kind of wealthies. Not snobs. Always looking to help. I don't resent people who have money."

"I've never felt guilty about it. My grandpa Walsh taught me you shouldn't feel guilty about having money. You should feel responsible, and make sure you do the right things with it."

"He sounds like a very wise man."

"He was."

"Well, I'd better run." Kerris ran her hand over Iyani's hair as the girl waited, twisting the beads on her new bracelet. "We're scoping out a few locations, and I'm already late."

Walsh watched Kerris until she'd disappeared down the hall, but the images of her from the afternoon they'd spent together lingered in his mind. Laughing with the children. Patiently showing them how to make their precious jewelry. In his circles, most of the women had led a pretty privileged existence. Other than his mom and Jo, he'd never met one who gave as much as this woman, despite her having been given so little in life. The combination of her kindness, beauty, and sweetness filled his thoughts after he left Iyani and drove to meet his friends by the river.

When Walsh reached the riverbank, Cam, Jo, and even Sofie, his childhood friend from New York, along with the rest of their usual summer entourage, headed farther down the Eno River, looking for the rope they'd used to dive into the icy water years ago. Walsh passed, saying he'd grab a few winks and be ready to play when they returned. He spread out a blanket on the verdant grass, succumbing to the rest he'd been denying himself since he'd departed Wilson Airport in Nairobi two days ago. A dark-haired girl awaited him in his dreams, and she set his pulse pounding even in his sleep.

Chapter Five

Kerris pulled her ancient car half in one space and half in another, barely pausing to lock the doors before dashing across the street to the bungalow where she saw her best friend's Volkswagen. Something good was going to happen. She could feel it. Though you wouldn't know it from Meredith's face.

"Mer, you okay?" Kerris asked, thrown by the frown marring the delicate features of her usually optimistic friend.

"You're late, and I'm about as nervous as a cat ready to be spayed." Meredith held out one hand, loaded down with silver rings. "Look at my hands. They're shaking, Kerris!"

"Calm down." Kerris used the Zen voice she reserved for her friend's high-strung nature, nothing she couldn't handle. "We have a great concept. We have our business loan. And today, we'll get our space. I have a good feeling about it."

"We'd better." Meredith ran a trembling hand down her face. "I want my parents off my back."

Meredith's parents wished their first-generation Japanese-

American daughter had pursued one of the industries her siblings had obediently entered—computer programming, physics, or biochemistry. Meredith, to their dismay, had shown more interest in *Vogue* than the periodic table.

Freshman year, Kerris had been seeking work to pay her way through college when she'd seen the ad for hardworking, responsible students willing to clean. She'd been shocked to discover the owner of the cleaning business, Maid 4 U, was only two years her senior, and just as driven as she was. Now, between working together and sharing a small apartment not too far from campus, they were nearly inseparable.

"This will work, Mer. Your parents will be proud of you. I guarantee it."

"Like I care about that." Meredith rolled her eyes at Kerris's knowing look. "Okay, so maybe I care a *little* about that."

"Right. Just a little. Where's the agent? I was late and I still beat him here."

"Why were you late?" Meredith peered up the road, searching for the agent and rationing only half her attention for Kerris.

"Oh, I um, I had to go by the hospital, remember?"

Meredith's radar was infallible. She always knew when Kerris was not being completely forthcoming. With a childhood haunted by dark, shadowy corners, there were lots of things Kerris didn't want to discuss. Meredith had learned when to press and when to back away. Kerris's expression must have led her to press.

"Something held you up there?" Meredith tilted her head,

studying Kerris with telescopic intensity. Kerris always felt like the edges of her soul had been peeled back under that look.

"No, there was just this new little girl from Kenya." Kerris forced herself to stand still on the bungalow porch. Maybe she could slide past without piquing Meredith's interest further. "She's the sweetest thing, but she has a brain tumor. She was in the crafts class, and I spent some extra time with her. Sorry I was late."

"Kenya?" Meredith bit her bottom lip, a dangerous sign that she was working out a problem in her head. "How'd she end up here from Kenya?"

"Oh, Walsh brought her from the foundation's orphanage." Kerris leaned against a post, keeping her tone casual.

"Walsh? As in Walsh Bennett?" Meredith pounced, her dark eyes lit with speculation. She twirled a lock of the plum-colored hair she had dyed and hacked into a stylish, blunt bob. "You didn't tell me you were meeting him at the hospital."

"Well, I didn't go to meet him—"

"But he was there."

"Well, yeah." Kerris felt like a mouse lured into a trap by fake cheese. "He just happened to be there."

"Hmmm, I've never met him in all the years he's been coming to Rivermont."

Kerris narrowed her eyes at her friend, unresponsive to her fishing.

"He's hot, though." Meredith dropped the words between them, curiosity etched on her pretty face.

"Really?" Kerris stripped her voice of all intonation, feigning interest in the still-empty road. "I hadn't noticed."

"Oh, come on. You'd have to be dead from the neck down not to notice him."

That sounded about right. Dead from the neck down included the heart and all her arousable girly parts, which had remained stubbornly unresponsive over the years.

"He's Cam's best friend. That's all I need to know." Kerris peered over Meredith's shoulder at a car approaching, a Realtor logo on the side. "Hey, I think this is the agent. Ready?"

With one last assessing glance and a glint in her eye warning she wasn't done digging, Meredith nodded. Her features set into the familiar mask of consummate professional and driven businesswoman that Kerris had come to know and love.

* * *

The smell of vanilla lured Walsh from the warm cocoon of much-needed sleep. That perfectly sweet scent shimmied up his nostrils and brought him around. He rolled over without opening his eyes, surprised to encounter something soft and warm. His eyes popped open, widening at the sight of Kerris, asleep on his blanket.

She'd pulled her knees up to her chest, and her small hands curled under her cheek. He studied the woman, wishing she wasn't as spectacular as he'd remembered. He knew he should let her sleep. She'd been flagging even in the elevator this morning, leaning up against the wall dozing. But he couldn't resist.

"Kerris."

She blinked drowsily a few times before jumping when her eyes set on him, leaning over her.

"Walsh," she said, eyes still languid. "Hope you don't mind me plopping down here to wait for everybody to get back. I wasn't sure where they'd gone, and I was so tired."

"It's fine. You were obviously as done as I was. How'd it go?"

"Go?" She blinked, sitting up and taking the elastic bands from the ponytails at her nape. Running her fingers through the heavy fall of hair, she let out a relieved breath. "Sorry. Those were tight. How'd what go?"

Walsh watched the thick hair tumbling over Kerris's shoulders and down her back, forgetting that she'd asked a question. Her eyes slid away as she licked at that plump, raspberry-colored bottom lip, clearing her throat and squeezing her lips against her teeth. It finally sank in for Walsh that his extended silence was making her uncomfortable.

"Sorry. Um, how'd your appointment go?" Maybe his casual tone would distract her from the fact that he'd practically gobbled her up with one look. "Weren't you considering some space for your thrift store?"

Enthusiasm for the venture lit her up. She talked about the property, sketching pictures in the air with her hands, bringing the retail space to life with her slim fingers.

Cam's girl.

She stretched her pretty mouth into a wide smile, laughing through her description of the Realtor, who'd been late and eccentric.

Cam's girl.

She bit the corner of her lip, pleating her brows with her calculations of what it would take to whip the space into shape.

Cam's girl.

The reminder beat a guilty rhythm in his head, but he couldn't stop watching, couldn't stop wishing, couldn't stop wanting to know everything about her…for himself. Not for Cam.

He felt like a cryptologist facing a magnificent strip of code, determined to crack it and understand the secret language he read in her guarded eyes.

"So, let me get this straight," he said when she paused to draw a breath. "Instead of having professionals come in and do the remodeling work for your thrift shop—you said it's called Déjà Vu, right? You're asking for the money so you can do it yourselves?"

"They wouldn't stretch the allowance like Meredith and I will." Kerris's hands finally stilled, clasping around her denim-clad knees. "And the money that's going toward labor, we can use on our space. You know?"

"Can't say I do. I like professionals doing the things they're supposed to do, and me paying them to do it."

"Only one of the many differences between us, I'm sure." A wry smile tugged up one side of her mouth.

"What's that supposed to mean?" He sat up straighter on the shared blanket.

"No offense. It's just the kind of response I'd expect from someone who doesn't have to save money."

"Not that again. You do realize this is reverse snobbism, right?"

"Wait, *you're* calling *me* a snob?" She threw back her head and laughed, locking eyes with him. The sound of her laughter, raw and free, punched him in the gut.

The intensity simmering between them had knocked him over from that first glance. It was still there, right below the surface, coiled like a whip poised to crack at any moment. He felt it now, and knew the moment she felt it, too. The laughter withered on her face, replaced by the guard she'd probably never meant to let down.

"What's wrong?" Walsh knew. It was wrong for him, too, but he still had to ask.

"Nothing." She didn't look up from the simple floral pattern on the blanket. Apparently daisies fascinated her. "Just wondering if Cam said how long they'd be gone?"

Walsh looked up the riverbank, squinting against the sunlight. Their friends were walking toward them, laughing, with a few canoes hoisted on their shoulders.

"Here they come." He stood and reached down to help her up.

She ignored his hand, standing on her own and brushing imaginary grass from her jeans. He searched her face, silently questioning, but she ignored that, too. She gave him a brief smile constructed mostly of plastic, before taking off toward Cam, who sprinted forward, grabbing her by the waist and lifting her up. They shared a smile that twisted Walsh's stomach into a knot.

"Get everything done?" Cam kissed her lightly on the lips. "You feel good?"

"I feel better now that I'm with you." She smiled into the tenderness of his kiss.

"Hey, dude." Cam smiled at Walsh over Kerris's shoulder. "'Bout time you joined the living. I hope you won't be such a drag all summer."

Walsh returned his smile, watching Cam lower Kerris back to the ground. She was where she belonged. He'd only just met the woman yesterday. He refused to believe the signals his heart kept sending him. It wasn't real. Cam was the best friend he'd ever had. The bond they'd built over years of happiness and hurt—that was real.

A silver-blond goddess walked up behind Cam, looking like she'd walked off the set of an Abercrombie & Fitch shoot. Knowing his friend Sofie, she might have.

"Did you have a good nap, Walsh?" Sofie stepped close enough for him to smell her perfume mixing with the scents of the outdoors.

He'd known her since preschool. Her father had been right beside his, building the Bennett empire. Her recent success in modeling had landed her on an unwritten "It Girl" list, and she was starting a new role as celebrity goodwill ambassador for the Walsh Foundation. He knew, though, that he was the real reason she was in Rivermont.

She caught his hand. He sharpened the look he gave her to a fine point, hoping she knew what it meant.

Don't even think about it. It's never going to happen.

"Yeah, it was just what I needed." He freed his hand, deliberately and gently. "You ready to meet the Walsh Foundation board on Monday?"

"I think so." Un-Sofie-like tentativeness filled her bottle green eyes. "I just hope I'm what they're looking for."

"They're looking for someone refined, well-spoken, and who'll bring positive attention to our cause." He reassured her with his smile, forcing himself to keep his eyes trained on her, rather than straying to the couple still talking a few feet away. "And the fact that your dad is my father's right-hand man doesn't hurt. Plus, your good looks don't hurt."

"So you *do* think I'm pretty?" She slid a chunk of hair behind her ear and flashed a too-wide smile.

He had known since high school that he could have Sofie whenever he wanted her. Problem was, he just didn't see her that way. She was beautiful, with a cover-worthy body, but there wasn't enough beyond the shiny packaging to hold his attention.

"Look at you, fishing for compliments." He brushed a finger down her perfect nose, keeping his tone fraternal. "Does it really matter what I think when the rest of the world is at your feet?"

"It does to me," she said, no smile.

"Sof—" She stopped whatever he'd been about to say with the well-manicured finger she placed across his lips.

"When you're ready to give me a chance, I'll be waiting." She dragged him toward the riverbank, smiling like she knew what was best for him. "For now, let's show these country bumpkins what the captain of the rowing team can do."

"Is it a race?" He glanced past her to where their friends were lining up canoes on the river. He was nothing if not competitive, another legacy from his father. He felt a tiny thrill of anticipation. He hadn't rowed in years, not since high school.

"Yeah, it's a race," Cam said from his canoe, where Kerris had already settled in front of him. "And we're gonna kick your ass, Bennett."

Never one to leave a gauntlet on the ground, Walsh staked his claim in the canoe beside them, helping Sofie get situated. He and Cam had a time-honored tradition of competing. The more trash talking, the better.

"You gonna kick my ass, Mitchell? That'd be a first."

"Would you two just load in and stop with all the talking?" Jo laughed from her canoe. "I'm ready to kick some ass myself."

* * *

In the end, Sofie and Walsh triumphed, and rubbed it in mercilessly.

"Did we forget to mention that we were both captains of our high school rowing teams?" Sofie asked, hoisted on Walsh's shoulder like a trophy.

Kerris laughed like everyone else, not begrudging them their fair and square victory, but a knot of briars rolled around in her stomach at the sight of Sofie and Walsh together. They both looked so perfect. And she had no right to this feeling, whatever they were to each other.

"Disgusting, huh?" Jo settled on the ground beside Kerris.

"What's disgusting?" Kerris looked away from their good-natured gloating, meeting Jo's eyes.

"Them." Jo smiled and pointed her chin toward Sofie and Walsh. "I mean, it's not enough that they both look genetically engineered. They have to have the money, education, and athleticism to back it all up. What line were they standing in to get all that, huh?"

Kerris looked at the couple again. She'd noticed the way Sofie looked at Walsh, as if at any moment the sun would set on him.

"Have they known each other long?"

"Only since birth." Jo skipped a pebble across the river's surface. "If arranged marriages still happened, you'd be looking at one. Not formally, of course, but everyone knows that's where Walsh'll end up."

Kerris watched Sofie and Walsh splash water on each other at the edge of the river.

"Sofie's father is Uncle Martin's right-hand man. They've always been in the same schools. Hung in the same circles. And she's always loved him."

"And how does he feel?" Kerris wished she could retract the nosy question.

"Walsh may date other girls, sleep with other girls even, but everyone knows the deal. He may play the field, but Sofie's home base. That's where he'll settle down."

Kerris felt more than saw the speculative glance Jo flitted between her and the couple.

"A guy like Walsh has the world in the palm of his hand. He needs a woman who knows what to do with it. That's Sofie. They aren't people who can marry just anybody."

Not just anybody, and certainly not a nobody. Remember that, little girl, Kerris told herself. He's out of your league. He's gorgeous. He's been groomed to charm birds from trees. He flies all over the world, rescuing orphans just like you.

There were a million reasons she had responded to Walsh Bennett the way she had. And a million reasons she should avoid him. She would spend the whole summer making sure she didn't forget that.

Chapter Six

Over the next month, Kerris and Meredith put their shoulders to the plow readying Déjà Vu for its end-of-summer grand opening. In the mornings, they cleaned houses for Maid 4 U. They needed a comfortable financial cushion as insurance for the thrift store's potential slow start. Meredith had a nice little nest egg, and Kerris refused to touch the money she had won as Scholar of the Year.

They cleaned houses all morning, squeezed in a hurried lunch, and then resumed cleaning in the afternoons. From there, they would comb the city and surrounding areas for unique finds to stock the shop with the beautiful, unusual, affordable pieces they wanted to build their reputation on. They spent most evenings sanding floors, painting and wallpapering, staining, decorating—whatever it took to transform the space into what they dreamed it could be.

It was a bruising pace, but Kerris knew it was worth it, and in another month, they could have it all done. They didn't deny themselves little breaks here and there. When one of them received an invitation to a party, or a picnic, or even a game of volleyball, they gave themselves permission to take guilt-free advantage of it. These slices of leisure kept Kerris sane. Most of those times were spent with Cam and his friends, who were determined to enjoy the gorgeous weather and one another's company.

They were halcyon days filled with horseshoes, baseball games, outdoor concerts, and the river. That summer Kerris fell in love. In love with the water, sometimes placid and tranquil, other times rushing so violently that the banks alongside seemed barely able to contain it. In love with the lullaby of moving water whispering its promises to her as she drifted off to sleep under a canopy of trees. Cam's cottage was just over the hill, so the river became the centerpiece of that summer, her oasis from the commitments she balanced to make this new chapter of her life unfold.

It was the first day of July, and she and Meredith were close to being done with the space. Their goal was to finish by the Fourth of July. Meredith, however, had a prospect she couldn't ignore.

"His name is Sam Watanabe. He's five eight." Meredith grabbed her purse and prepared to leave for the date. "Finally, I found a first-generation, Japanese-American man who's actually tall enough for me. *And* he's a biochemist. *And* he's cute. Even my parents should approve."

"I would never ask you to pass up destiny." Kerris laid out her sarcasm along with a tarp for painting.

"I'm actually excited. I think Sam and I could hit it off."

"I can't wait to hear about it." Kerris adjusted the edges of the tarp, glancing at Meredith over her shoulder. "And you look really pretty, by the way."

"I'm not sure I can return the compliment." Meredith examined Kerris's cutoff jeans, white tank top, and work boots. Kerris's hair was caught up in a messy ponytail atop her head, dark tendrils escaping around her face and neck. "Will you get to freshen up at all before Cam comes with dinner?"

"It'll have to do." Kerris grimaced, glancing down at her paint-spattered hands. "He's been slammed, too, with this crazy deadline at the office, so maybe he won't look much better."

"He needs to be painting. His talent is wasted with graphic design."

"I know. It's in his plans." Kerris blew at a tendril of hair drooping over her eyes. "In the meantime, he's got bills to pay like the rest of us."

"I'm sure Kristeene Bennett would help, right?"

"If Cam would let her, yeah." Kerris glanced at her watch. "You better get outta here if you don't want to be late for your date with destiny."

"Thanks again for the pass tonight." Meredith backed her way toward the door.

"Just name your firstborn Watanabe after me!" Kerris flung the request after her friend dashing down the front porch steps.

Still laughing, Kerris slipped in her earphones. Her pop playlist got her through half a wall before her stomach growled like a stray dog. Her phone screen lit up with an incoming call from Cam.

"Hey." She sidestepped two buckets of paint. "You on your way?"

"About that." He colored his sigh with frustration. "This project is kicking my ass. I don't think I'll make it over."

Kerris swallowed disappointment, wishing it were a Big Mac. Her stomach growled more aggressively, echoing its displeasure.

"That's okay. I'll be fine. I think I have an apple left from lunch or something."

"Actually, Walsh said he could drop something off here for me on his way home, and I asked him to pick something up for you, too."

"No!" The word erupted from her mouth more violently than she had intended. "I mean, he doesn't have to. Call him and tell him not to do that. I don't want him going out of his way."

"It's not out of his way. It's *on* his way. Besides, he's already on his way over."

"Oh, how sweet." Kerris gnawed on her bottom lip and fiddled with the pencil securing her washed-two-days-ago hair.

"Okay, babe." She could hear Cam's attention already drifting back to his project. "Gotta get this done tonight. Love you."

"Love you, too." She tugged at the frayed bottoms of her cutoffs, glancing at her paint-stained shirt.

Walsh was on his way. She had tried to avoid being alone with him for the last month. They saw each other at least once a week at the children's ward for craft hour. Was it coincidence that he was usually there visiting Iyani? It probably just worked out that way, but she found herself secretly, guiltily looking forward to that hour.

Simply put, she had never met anyone like him. Self-assured, but not arrogant. Humble, but not wimpy. Appreciated the finer things, but didn't seem to need them. Compassionate. Generous. Driven. She wanted to stop, but the list went on.

Walsh could have anyone. She and Cam were made for each other; they could heal each other and build together. The future and family they'd never thought they'd have, they could have with each other. She was more and more sure that at the end of the summer, when Cam asked again, she would agree to marry him.

But there were moments, when she was drifting asleep by the river, when things were quiet and the day was done. In those moments, her vigilance sagged and the armor encasing her mind slipped. She'd think of Walsh and undo all her self-preservation.

She would eventually build up an immunity to the sheer magnetism of the man. If she didn't smother this insensible attraction, how could she move forward with the future she craved, the one where her children waited? And who better than Cam to share that future?

A tap on her shoulder startled her, cannoning her several inches off the ground. She whirled around to see Walsh towering over her, a large brown bag in hand.

"You scared me to death," she said, louder than normal because she still had in her earphones.

"Sorry, I didn't mean to. I called your name a couple of times, but…"

"No problem."

Kerris swallowed around the tumbleweed pushing its way up her throat and brushed suddenly damp palms over her ragged shorts. She needed to get him out the door as soon as possible. "I told Cam you didn't have to bring me anything."

"It was fine." His smile seemed more casual than what was in his eyes. "Your spot's not far from Cam's, and my mom was determined to feed him. Each Monday she cooks soul food."

"Soul food, huh?"

"Walsh Foods was founded on Southern cooking. Mom can make every one of those frozen meals right in her kitchen from scratch."

Kerris often forgot about the prepared foods business that had made the Walsh Foundation possible.

She sniffed appreciatively in spite of herself.

"I guess I could eat a little something."

"Big of you." His response had soaked in sarcasm overnight.

"Sorry." She had to laugh at herself, feeling some of the tension drain from her shoulders. "I really am starving, and would love to inhale whatever is in that bag smelling so good."

He looked around for a place to set the food, eyes widening at the gleaming hardwood floors, newly spackled ceiling, and freshly painted walls.

"This looks incredible, Kerris."

"Oh, you should have seen it before." She reached in her

pocket to grab her phone. "Look at these early pictures. See how far our little fixer-upper has come."

"Wow, you weren't joking about what you two could do."

"You ain't seen nothing yet." She knew she was bragging, but couldn't resist. "Come see the furniture and display racks upstairs."

She grabbed his hand and dragged him deeper into the shop, tugging him into the small bathroom. Instead of wallpaper or paint, a mural covered the walls, depicting the river that cut through the city of Rivermont. It included the covered bridge, the historic houses and cottages along its bank, leisurely fishermen with their rods extended, and even canoes meandering down the placid stretch of water.

"This is gorgeous. Did you do this?" Walsh traced a finger along the river on the wall.

"No, Cam did."

"I forget sometimes how gifted he is." Walsh looked down at their still-clasped hands.

"Oh!" She jerked her hand free and darted from the room like a skittish colt. "Come on. I'm starving."

* * *

Walsh followed at a more leisurely pace, trying not to notice the elegant muscles in Kerris's calves and thighs, clearly displayed by her cutoffs. Or the toned line of her arms and shoulders. He'd been concentrating on *not* seeing Kerris all summer, without much success. Tonight, he didn't have the will, and there was no way he could resist.

"Actually, I haven't eaten, either."

He kept his voice soft and even, free of the rebellious desire he usually subdued. He should head home and eat with his family. Instead, he let the silent request to share her meal dangle in the quiet of the room around them.

"Oh," Kerris said into the awkward moment he had created. "Would you...well would you like to stay and eat?"

"What a gracious offer." He chuckled with self-derision. Was he so desperate that he would stay when she so obviously didn't want him to?

"Sorry. No, of course you can stay," she rushed to say. "There's a kitchen just through here."

They sat at the small card table in the kitchen, lit by summer's late-setting sun, a wary silence insulating them. Walsh raised his head when Kerris scraped her fork across the plates their cook, Mrs. Quinton, had packed. She barreled through her food, head bent, shoveling forkfuls of macaroni and cheese and collard greens into her mouth. Walsh carefully placed his fork down on the table, raising his brows at the swift repetition of the fork to her mouth, broken occasionally by a quick bite into a drumstick.

His lips twitched, wondering if she felt the tension as thick between them as he did, making her eager to put an end to their impromptu meal. She'd pay for it later with indigestion, considering how fast she was eating.

"So nice to meet a girl with an appetite." He watched her eyes go round and her mouth drop open then snap closed. A delicate rose tinged the honey of her cheeks.

"Sorry." She dropped her fork with a clang, delicately wiping the corners of her mouth with a napkin. "Guess I was hungry."

"Hmmm." He added a smile to the monosyllable, popping open a Diet Coke. "You guess? I only ate one of those *four* drumsticks."

"Rude! You never point out something like that to a lady." She sat back with feigned indignation. "Just for that, I might burp."

He laughed out loud, locking eyes with her as he took a gulp of his soft drink.

"A girl who's not afraid to eat *or* burp. No wonder Cam's so whipped."

She became perfectly still under his consideration.

"Cam's not whipped." She gave a little smile that told him she kind of knew Cam definitely was whipped.

"Any girl who can captivate Cam, a true player, fascinates me."

"There's nothing…interesting about me." She leaned her chin into the palm of her hand. "I'm just a girl."

"Tell me about this girl."

"What do you want to know?" She lifted those crazy-long lashes to squarely face him.

Everything. Anything.

"I know you were in foster care. How many homes?"

"Five total." She barely moved her lips to let the words out, signaling that this was a topic she usually guarded closely. "The last one I was in from age ten to eighteen, though. The Murphys."

"They never considered adopting you?"

"No, they didn't want kids of their own." She origamied the napkin between her fingers.

"Why'd they keep you all those years then?"

"I guess I was extra cash." She fixed her eyes on the wall behind him.

"I'm sorry." He made sure he didn't leak any pity in his voice. "Were they good people? Did they treat you well?"

"They didn't abuse me, if that's what you mean. They just didn't love me." Her lips thinned and tightened around the admission. "I'm not even sure they loved each other. The only thing I can say with confidence is that they loved church."

"Religious fanatics?"

"Not fanatics. They just had definite rules I had to follow." Her laugh was too tight to leave any room for real humor.

"Like what?" He watched her features settle into the hardness of cement, so at odds with its usual soft lines.

"Like not dating, not listening to secular music, not wearing makeup, not drinking, not cursing. Going to church three times a week—"

"Whoa!" He sliced into her litany, holding up a hand to stem the flow of rules that had governed her life for eight years. "What *could* you do?"

She tilted her head to the side, seemingly giving it serious consideration.

"I made jewelry. Read a lot. I spent a lot of time alone."

"Lonely or alone?"

"Maybe both." He wanted the thoughts her eyes shrouded.

She pulled her bottom lip between her teeth before continuing. "It was okay. I've always enjoyed my own company."

He couldn't blame her. Her company intoxicated him, hitting his bloodstream like a four-hundred-dollar bottle of vodka. Every sip of her felt like a reckless indulgence. She was a decadence he could ill afford but—God help him—couldn't resist.

"What about you?"

Tables neatly turned.

"What about me?" He tipped his head back, prepared to confess like she was his high priestess if it would buy him another five minutes with her. "My story was written before I was even born. All laid out for me."

"I don't believe that." She sipped her own Diet Coke, eyes getting tangled up with his over the can.

"It's true. My mom knew what she wanted for me, and so did my dad. They've been pulling me in opposite directions, fighting over me since the divorce when I was thirteen years old."

"Boo hoo hoo." He tasted a little sarcasm sprinkled in with her teasing. "Poor little rich boy had parents who wanted him so badly they fought over him."

"It wasn't like that."

He knew his tone was defensive. She was teasing him, but everyone made assumptions about him because of the privileges he'd been born into. He didn't want her to do that.

"I would have given everything if my parents had been able to work it out. If we could have been a family. I don't really care about the stuff."

"I believe you." The look she gave him knew more than it

should. "Your parents had to do something right, in their own way, for you to turn out like you have. I've heard your mother brag more than once that you're the best of them both. Can you see that?"

"Can you?" He wasn't sure what he meant by the question, but he felt certain she would know how to respond.

"Yes." She didn't look away. He could not.

He was the son of Martin and Kristeene Bennett in every way, constantly living in the dichotomy of that, dwelling between the warring factions of his heredity. And for the first time he really believed someone saw him in his entirety.

"Kerris," he began, but the buzz of her cell phone interrupted.

"'Scuse me." She glanced at her phone and back to him, her other hand wandering up to the knot of hair secured on her head. "It's Cam."

She answered, and he blew out the breath his chest had been holding hostage.

"Hey, baby. Yeah, Walsh dropped the food off. It was delicious. He stayed to eat with me."

Walsh stood to scrape the remnants of their meal into the garbage disposal, grinding the food and the intimacy they'd shared with the flick of the switch. He rinsed and dried the plates, packing everything up.

Her voice dipped lower. He couldn't make out what she was saying, but he sensed the ease that existed between her and Cam. Easy, not the fierce knot of urges and compulsions he wrestled to the ground every time he was around her.

"Sorry about that." She slid the phone in her back pocket. "Cam was just checking in."

"Everything good?" He distracted himself with one final sweep of the kitchen to make sure he hadn't left anything.

"Yeah." She tossed their soda cans into the recycling bin against the wall. "He was just finishing up. He'll swing through on his way out."

"Cool. I'll get going then."

"I'll see you tomorrow at the hospital." She looked at him with wide eyes. "I mean, I assume…you've been coming…"

So she *had* noticed.

"You're right. I always go on Tuesdays to see Iyani. I like to see her having fun with the other girls. It's become her favorite thing here in the States."

"She's precious." Kerris's smile played tug-of-war with her sad eyes. "Have they scheduled her surgery?"

"Yeah. She had an infection so they had to postpone it, but she's ready now. It's set for this Friday."

Walsh drew a roughened breath around the brambles crowding his chest. The procedure could save or end Iyani's life.

"Worrying won't do any good." Kerris grabbed his hand, squeezing comfort into his tensed fingers.

He glanced from their clasped hands back up to her face, watching the sweet tension that always sprang up between them draw her brows together and tighten her full mouth into a line. She pulled her hand free.

"I'd better get back to work."

She rushed back out to the front room and picked up

her paint roller. Walsh recognized a tactical withdrawal when he saw one.

"You want me to stay and help?" He started rolling up the sleeves of his mint green Brooks Brothers shirt.

"No, you go on home. I've got maybe thirty more minutes. Cam's on his way."

She faced the wall for a few moments without moving, head bent. Walsh willed her to look at him one more time. As if the tensile string that always seemed to snap between them had pulled her inexorably into it, she glanced at him over one slim shoulder.

That steamy awareness wafted between them again, agitating his insides until his breaths slipped over his lips like puffs of smoke.

She looked like snared prey.

"You'd better go," she finally said. "It's getting late."

"Yeah, I'll see you at the hospital tomorrow."

She offered no response and he didn't wait for one. Just turned and left.

Chapter Seven

Brightly colored blankets dotted the riverbank, crowded with picnic baskets and sun lovers on the Fourth of July. Kerris and Cam approached an empty patch of grass, swinging their clasped hands. They spread the blanket, shared a smile, and unpacked their picnic basket. Cam stretched out on the blanket, recapturing her hand to leisurely stroke her slim fingers. He considered their hands together, a small smile teasing the corners of his mouth.

"What's this?" He lifted the leather strap encircling her wrist.

"That's the bracelet Iyani made for me."

The bracelet held block letters spelling Iyani's name. The smile Kerris pushed onto her lips felt like a too-tight sweater.

"Her surgery is tomorrow. She wanted me to have it, just in case. I hate that she has had to even consider the possibility of dying. It's so unfair."

"Baby, if anyone knows about unfair childhoods, it's you and me. You learn to roll with whatever punches come your way. No matter what."

"What punches came your way?" She squeezed his hand, inviting a confidence she wasn't sure she was ready to reciprocate.

"Punches?" Cam boarded up his usually open face.

They'd both known so much pain at an early age, but had ironically shared few details with each other. She thought of the night she and Walsh had eaten at the bungalow, of how he had effortlessly drawn her out. She so rarely discussed her time in foster care, choosing to put one foot in front of the other and move forward as quickly as possible, leaving the past behind.

"Don't you think the woman you've asked to marry you should know about your past?"

"Is she going to share hers?" Cam stroked the hair back from her face.

"If you want to know." She braved a quick glance at his solemn face.

"I've only ever talked to Walsh about that stuff." His fingers continued to twist the block letters on Iyani's bracelet. He couldn't seem to look at her. "He has a way of getting shit outta you that you swore you'd never talk about."

She had experienced firsthand the truth serum of Walsh's irresistible, probing concern.

"Is there room to join you guys?" Jo asked from a few feet away, agilely weaving her long, lean limbs between blankets. "I think we can fit in right here beside you."

We?

Kerris looked past Jo, dismayed to see Walsh and Sofie headed their way, both loaded down with blankets and picnic baskets. Kerris's heart twisted. She knew a marriage between Sofie and Walsh was a certain eventuality, but she just couldn't see him with her. There was something at the girl's very core that seemed cold; cold and hard and not worthy of him.

"Are we interrupting?" Walsh spread out a blanket and set down a basket.

"You can only be interrupting so much out here in the open. Ker's not into public displays of affection." Cam laughed when Kerris's eyes stretched with embarrassment. "I'm only teasing you, baby."

Kerris leaned her cheek into his kiss, her smile as hard and stiff as drywall. Her eyes dropped from the intensity of Walsh's. He looked away, too, occupying himself with getting set up. They all dug into the food they'd packed, reaching across the blankets to share and sample one another's feasts.

Kerris glanced at Walsh's wrist, touched to see that he wore the bracelet Iyani had given him. She looked up, finding his sober eyes on her bracelet, too. She knew tomorrow's risky surgery caused him the same fear, anxiety, and hope.

"Walsh." She raised her voice just enough to be heard over the music and the crowd.

Walsh didn't hear, but the other three did. Their stares rested heavily on her.

"Walsh," she repeated, erecting a firewall against the icy, wintergreen eyes Sofie leveled her way.

"Yeah?" He turned his head in her direction.

"Um, would it be okay if I come to the hospital tomorrow for Iyani's surgery?" She pushed the words past the self-consciousness drying out her mouth. Her heart beat a furious tom-tom in her chest. She twisted a blade of grass between busy fingers, refusing to look away.

"Of course," he said, eyes serious. "I'd like the company."

* * *

Walsh looked away from Kerris, hoping he wasn't betraying himself to the other three, all of whom had known him long enough to detect his discomfort. A clenched fist, a tightened muscle in his jaw. Small things, but they were the physical responses he always seemed to have around Kerris. How was it that he'd known Jo, Cam, and Sofie his whole life, and yet it was Kerris to whom he felt most connected?

He hated this. Hated keeping this growing attraction to himself. Hated deceiving Cam, letting him believe he was barely aware of his best friend's girlfriend, when in reality he could think of little else. And most of all, he hated seeing Cam's hands on Kerris.

Touching her arm. Pushing the soft, dark cloud of hair away from her face. Raining kisses down the graceful line of her neck.

Walsh balled his hands into impotent fists and leaned back on his elbows, watching the couple surreptitiously. He had no right to this jealousy, this sense that Cam should keep his damn hands off her. It was unreasonable. He knew it, but he had to physically restrain himself from snatching her away from Cam.

This was only getting harder. He needed to get away. He'd be returning to Kenya soon, either taking a recovered Iyani back to the orphanage, or...He couldn't complete that thought even to himself. He had grown to love that little girl's boundless spirit. He glanced down at the bracelet, thinking of how somberly she had presented the identical bracelets to him and Kerris Tuesday at the hospital. Kerris had been taping one of Iyani's drawings to the wall when the child had called her over to sit on the bed with her and Walsh.

"Just in case," Iyani had whispered, fear-soaked tears in her dark eyes. "So you won't forget me."

"I could never forget you, sweet girl." Kerris had leaned down to kiss the jagged scar covering one side of Iyani's scalp, a reminder that she had survived one skirmish with death already. "I won't need this bracelet to remember you because you'll be here with us, but thank you so much. I love it."

Walsh looked at Kerris now, eyes closed as Cam played with the soft tendrils of hair flowering around her forehead. He knew Cam would ask her again to marry him at summer's end. Walsh wasn't sure he could allow it. The ancient instincts of a hunter swelled in his chest, the primeval nature of a warrior demanding that he fight for her, win her. Could he do that to Cam?

He watched Cam run his finger down the smoothness of Kerris's cheek. Cam had never been this way with anyone before. Either he was running from some woman who wanted to have sex with him, or he was chasing some woman he wanted to have sex with. It really had never gotten more complex than that for Cam with women. But he recognized the tenderness, the concern, the genuine affection and admiration his friend held for Kerris.

"Cam, did you see the elephant ears they're selling?" Jo stood to her feet and stretched one summer-gold arm down to him. "Come on. Let's go grab some."

Cam looked down at Kerris, uncertainty on his face.

"She's knocked out." Jo scrunched her brows, obviously a little irritated. "She'll be fine. Walsh and Sofie are here, and we'll be right back."

Cam allowed Jo to pull him to his feet, casting one more glance over his shoulder at his sleeping girlfriend before walking off, his arm hooked around Jo's neck.

"Sofie!" Walsh recognized a local reporter from a few feet away. "Could we get those shots of you we talked about? With the kids?"

"I forgot, there's some foundation kids here tonight, and the *Rivermont Herald* wanted some pictures of me with them." Sofie groaned softly. "Do you mind?"

"They don't want pictures of me." Walsh laughed, deliberately looking away from the fast-approaching reporter. "I'm off today."

Tossing a mildly reproachful look his way, Sofie stood and met the reporter halfway, allowing him to guide her toward the photo op. Walsh crawled over to Kerris, kicking himself for not being able to stay away from this woman for thirty seconds. He leaned down toward her ear, drawing in her sweet smell. Sun-toasted vanilla poured over her clean skin.

"I know you're not asleep," he whispered in her ear, grinning as her eyelids flickered.

"Well, not now," she whispered back, eyes still slammed shut.

"Not before, either." He laughed and sat up beside her.

She leaped to her feet and started toward the river. Walsh hesitated, not sure if she was seriously peeved about her nap, or if she was teasing. He stayed seated on the blanket, watching her. Her hair was loose today, hanging down to the middle of her back, blowing back like a dark banner in the light breeze. She wore a cotton candy pink calico skirt that belled out, hanging to just above her knees. A sea green tank top tucked into the skirt showed off her tiny waist.

"You coming, or what?" She looked back over her shoulder, mischief in her grin.

"I'm coming." He almost tripped over his feet.

"Are you getting in?" He noticed for the first time that she was barefoot and heading toward the water.

"Not exactly." She laughed up at him, eclipsing the splendor of the setting sun behind her. "I'm just wading in at the edge to gather a few rocks."

"Gather rocks? For what?"

"Ah, grasshopper." She bowed slightly with clasped hands at her chest. "The pupil becomes the teacher. I'm gathering rocks for a little business venture I have in mind."

"Pardon me for stating the obvious, but you haven't started your first business venture yet, have you? A little ambitious to already be 'gathering' for the next one."

"You've got some nerve talking to me about ambition." She angled a sweet smile his way.

"Point taken." He watched her lean forward to scoop an oblong rock from beneath the glassy surface of the water. "So, what exactly are you doing?"

"Some of these rocks are so beautiful." She smiled, holding the rock in her hand, rubbing the excess water away. "I think they'd look great as jewelry."

He looked at the smooth, crystalline stone in her hand, swirled with black, red, and green.

"Once Déjà Vu is up and running, I'll focus on learning the technique I need to know and figuring out how to do it. For now, I'd just like to find a pretty rock for Iyani."

"You're something else, you know that?"

The crowd teeming around them, the children's laughter, the kites billowing overhead—it all went into soft focus. The world had sharply narrowed to this river princess with rocks bundled in her skirt. Walsh watched the teasing laughter in her eyes die. Her pupils dilated and her breath quickened, making him wonder if her world had narrowed down to him, too.

"Walsh," Sofie called from the riverbank, her strident tone snapping them to attention. "I need you. The reporter wants shots of both of us with the kids."

Walsh stepped back. "See you later."

"Come on!" Sofie snapped, stepping down to grab his hand and pull him farther away from Kerris. "The kids are waiting."

* * *

The sight of them holding hands, towering over her like ruling monarchs, looking perfect together, made Kerris feel so ordinary—insignificant, like one of the pebbles under her feet. She was glad Sofie had walked up. She had to be imagining that Walsh felt the same intimate pull that she had. Sofie was Walsh's reality. And Kerris's reality was walking toward her with a smile, proffering an elephant ear.

"You're awake. Want one?" Cam eyed the departing couple speculatively. "Gotta give it to Sof. That girl is determined to catch her man."

"Seems like he's not running too hard." Kerris bit into the sweet fried dough.

"I dunno." Cam frowned and wiped powdered sugar from the corner of her mouth. "I know everyone thinks they're made for each other, but not sure Walsh sees it that way. Or at least he didn't used to. I always thought Walsh would fall in love with some girl no one saw coming. He's a closet romantic."

"What makes you think that?" Kerris tried to rein in her stampeding heart.

"I know him better than everybody else." Cam tugged her hand to help her out of the water. "I think Walsh will want to marry a girl he loves. I just don't see him ever loving Sofie."

"Maybe someone should tell Sofie that." Kerris ran her fingers over the few rocks she had collected.

"Someone has." Cam gave a short laugh. "Walsh has, in every way he can think of, but she keeps coming like a tank. A beautiful, sexy tank. I'll give her that, but I don't know if she's gonna land him."

"Jo thinks she will."

"Really?" Cam raised both eyebrows, obviously surprised. "She must know something I don't."

"Look, the fireworks are about to start. Let's go watch."

She changed gears with no clutch, not wanting to spend another minute talking about Walsh and Sofie.

Chapter Eight

W hat's taking so long?" Walsh asked the question for probably the hundredth time.

Kerris watched him pace back and forth in the small hospital waiting room, wanting to comfort him, to give him answers she knew they would have to wait for. Iyani had been so brave going into surgery, clutching the rock Kerris had brought her like a talisman with mystical powers of courage.

Kerris fingered the leather bracelet encircling her wrist, blinking back tears. It had been seven hours. Walsh had been on his laptop working for a good part of the day, staying connected to Walsh Foundation business, and, to her surprise, Bennett Enterprises. She hadn't realized until today how involved he was in his father's business affairs.

She had brought her laptop as well, glad that Meredith had installed the business software package so she could do some preliminary accounting and inventory work for Déjà Vu. She had also brought her sketch pad to capture ideas for her river rock jewelry. They both had plenty to occupy their time and attention, but that awareness of each other remained. From time to time, she would glance up from her laptop or from doodling on her pad to find his eyes resting on her. He wouldn't look away immediately, but held the look before returning to his own task, unnerving Kerris.

No sign of Dr. Myer bearing news, good or bad. Kerris felt completely helpless; useless. She hadn't wanted to go anywhere, even to the bathroom, in case she missed Dr. Myer coming out of surgery. At this point, her butt was numb and her leg had fallen asleep where she had it curled under her.

"I'll go grab you some hot coffee." She stood up, stretching her arms out like a clothesline.

"No, stay." Walsh reached for her wrist, pulling her back down to the seat beside him. "If I have any more coffee, I'll piss my pants."

She smiled for the first time in hours. Walsh twisted their fingers together in his lap. The smile shriveled on her lips. Her palms moistened and her foot started a *tap tap tap* on the wax-slick waiting room floor.

"I just want her to be okay, Ker." The deep assurance she had become accustomed to was completely absent from Walsh's low voice. "If she dies…"

"If she dies, you did everything in your power to help her." Kerris ignored the assault he was on her senses, tightening her fingers around his. "All we can do is—"

"Were you gonna say pray?" The question was soft and serious.

"I was gonna say hope." She lowered her lashes to cover the shadows of unanswered prayers her eyes harbored. "But you can pray if you want."

"That's what my grandmother would have said we should do."

"Oh, not the praying grandmother." Kerris hoped her comment would distract him and lighten the sober mood.

"Don't hate on MawMaw," he said, lips twitching.

"MawMaw!" She didn't even try to hold back her laugh. "Could you be more stereotypically Southern than having a praying grandmother named MawMaw? And let's not forget that you brought me collard greens, macaroni and cheese, and fried chicken for dinner."

"What are you saying?" He fake frowned, lips still twitching.

"That you try to front like you're some big city boy—"

"I'm from New York." His voice rose with citified indignation.

"I'm just saying—"

Jo walked toward them, looking pointedly at their still-clasped hands on Walsh's leg. Kerris jerked her hand back and put a few more inches between them.

"I can hear you guys all the way down the hall." Jo dropped her Yves Saint Laurent clutch on one of the seats. "I assume, based on the party I walked in on, that we're celebrating? Iyani's okay?"

Kerris and Walsh both sobered, exchanging worried glances. For those few moments they had forgotten why they were here, but it came rushing back with emotional force. Walsh shook his head, standing to his feet and resuming his pacing.

"Not yet." A frown settled on his forehead.

"Here comes the doctor." Kerris fought back her anxiety and kept her tone hopeful.

"Dr. Myer, how's Iyani?" Walsh turned to the physician, who was pulling his surgical mask down. "Did the surgery go okay?"

"Is she gonna be all right?" Kerris stepped toward the doctor, too. "When can we see her?"

"Give the man some space." Jo placed a restraining hand on Walsh's arm.

"It's okay." Dr. Myer tugged at the mask hanging around his neck. "Iyani came through just fine."

"Thank God." Walsh reached for Kerris's hand, gripping it tightly.

Kerris collapsed against his side, turning her head into the strength of his arm, limp with relief. Walsh brushed a gentle hand over her disheveled hair, long loosened from the elastic bands she'd started the day with. Kerris felt Jo's eyes resting on them, but was too elated to care.

"You have to understand how very delicate this surgery is." Dr. Myer measured his words into a recipe of warning. "This is the second aggressive growth removed from Iyani's brain. The fact that she survived the first time was a miracle. We're not out of the woods yet."

Kerris drew a relieved breath, letting the doctor's words float over her head. The surgery had only removed many of the tumor cells, but some cells remained inoperable. Radiation and chemotherapy were the next step. The doctor felt confident those could be administered in Kenya. Going home was going to be the best medicine for the homesick little girl.

"She's still recovering, and will be out of it for a while," Dr. Myer said. "I suggest you two get a few hours out of here, grab some dinner, get some rest, and come back a little later."

Kerris figured her face looked as implacable as Walsh's. Dr. Myer obviously wasn't going to convince either of them to leave until they had seen Iyani. The doctor looked to Jo for help.

"Here's a compromise," Jo said. "I'll go grab something for you guys to eat, and bring it here. That'll be better than hospital food, but you can still be here to see Iyani as soon as possible."

They both nodded, looking at each other to share a slow smile. Iyani was going to be okay. They seemed to release the breath they'd been holding together all day.

"Thank you for staying." Walsh gave her hand a quick squeeze.

"Are you kidding? I can't wait to see her."

* * *

Hours later, Iyani was still groggy, but seemed almost surprised to be alive.

"Am I in heaven?" Her eyes slitted open. Anesthesia thickened her accent.

"Not yet, sweetie." Relief threaded Walsh's laugh. "You can't get rid of us that easy."

A weak smile was Iyani's only answer before drifting back into a drug-induced slumber. Walsh stood by the bed, almost afraid to move. He felt like he'd been through battle, emotionally battered and worn down. He couldn't have gotten through the ordeal of waiting without Kerris. He was about to tell her that when Cam walked in. He saw Cam before Kerris did, since he approached from behind her. Cam's expression lightened at the sight of her. Walsh hoped he hid more than Cam, or else the whole world would know of his deepening feelings for the woman who had gone into battle with him today.

"Hey, babe." Cam looped his arms around her waist from behind.

"Hi." Kerris turned in the circle of Cam's arms and gave him a smile that invited him into their joy. "Iyani's gonna be okay. She came through fine."

Kerris was leaning against Cam with obvious fatigue. Guilt stabbed Walsh in the gut. He knew she still cleaned houses with Meredith, and was working all hours of the day to ensure Déjà Vu was ready by the end of August. Iyani was his responsibility, not hers.

"Cam, why don't you take your girl on home?" Walsh already missed having her to himself. "She's exhausted."

"Yeah, baby." Cam ran a gentle thumb over the shadows under Kerris's eyes. "Let me take you home."

"No, I want to be here when Iyani wakes up again." Walsh ignored the look Kerris shot his way, rich with confusion and accusation.

"Walsh and Cam are right, Kerris," Jo said from one of the chairs by the hospital bed. "You should let Cam take you home. You've been here all day."

"So have you, Walsh." Kerris narrowed her eyes at him.

"I'll be leaving soon, too," Walsh lied, planning to charm the floor nurse into letting him crash in the chair here in Iyani's room. "Go on home. Come back tomorrow."

Walsh turned away, walking over to the window to adjust the blinds. He hoped she'd take the hint and go. He was not above begging her to stay if she kept biting that bottom lip, looking torn.

"All right." Her mouth conceded, but Walsh could still feel the rebellion of her eyes hurling darts at his back. "You can take me home, Cam, but I want to know if there's any change. Okay, Walsh?"

He nodded without turning from the window, studying the suddenly fascinating parking lot.

"I'm gone then." He knew she was giving him one more chance to offer any other response. He nodded, stuffing his fist into the pocket of his jeans.

"See you tomorrow." He freed his voice of inflection, leaving it flat and disinterested. "I'll be fine."

A lie, of course.

He was getting good at those.

Chapter Nine

Kerris almost danced off the elevator and down the hospital corridor in her lemon-colored sundress, short, fitted denim jacket, and worn cowboy boots.

"Morning, Dr. Myer," Kerris greeted the tall, fair-haired physician who rounded the corner with head bent and hands buried in the pockets of his lab jacket. "I'm glad I ran into you. I wanted to thank you again for all you've done for Iyani."

"Kerris—"

"No, really." Kerris rushed the words, excited and steadily plodding her way to Iyani's room, in step with the doctor. "I know I'm not family or anything, but she's special to me. And we were so worried that something would go wrong during surgery."

"Well, if you remember, Kerris, the time after surgery was just as crucial," Dr. Myer said, his eyes just shy of meeting hers.

"Yes, but she got through that, too." Kerris refused to

entertain any negative possibilities. For once things were working out as they should. "I know she's anxious to get back home, but I'll miss her. Selfish of me, huh? If you feel confident, though, that radiation and chemotherapy will be fine administered in Kenya, who am I to—"

"Kerris." Dr. Myer's tension-filled voice sliced into her cheerful chatter like a serrated knife. "I don't know a better way to tell you this than just to say it."

"Say…say what?"

Kerris's smile wobbled. The doctor's eyes softened, but Kerris didn't like the straight line he disciplined his mouth into.

"Iyani died about an hour ago."

"No. No, but…what happened? I just saw her yesterday. She was fine."

The world stopped making sense. Pain sank its fangs into her fast-beating heart. She felt it physically and clutched the soft denim jacket covering her chest. Tears burned behind her lids and stung her nose.

"Her brain began hemorrhaging this morning. It was an unavoidable complication. We couldn't save her. I'm so sorry."

"Oh, I…I…thought…"

Kerris didn't know what to say, to do. She only knew what she felt, and it was an oppressive grief for a young warrior angel she had known for only a few weeks, but who had left an indelible imprint on her heart.

"I suppose Walsh has been notified." She spoke into the silence Dr. Myer was affording her to process the news.

"Yes, I believe he's in her room now. As you can imagine, he's having a pretty tough time with it." The doctor's eyes drifted to the left and then to the right and then down to his watch. "I'm sorry, Kerris, but I have a patient waiting."

Kerris brushed past him, heading toward Iyani's room. She watched Walsh for a moment from the doorway. He'd settled his leanly muscled length in the middle of Iyani's bed, long legs pulled into a loose criss-cross, forearms resting on his knees. She crossed to him without thought, slowing her steps the closer she got, until she was standing directly in front of him sitting on the bed.

"Walsh, I'm so sorry."

For a moment he didn't acknowledge her presence, but continued to stare down at his fist, clenched around Iyani's bracelet. She covered his hand with her own.

"Just in case." The heavy fist of grief flattened his voice.

"I'm so sorry." Saying it again didn't help, but she couldn't hold back the useless words.

"I just," he started and stopped, a muscle flexing in his jaw before he continued. "I just don't get it. She came through the surgery fine."

"I know." Kerris reached up to stroke the back of his head.

"I ended up spending the night, sleeping in the chair. I went downstairs to grab a muffin and some coffee. I was gone for only a minute, and when I came back in the room, all hell had broken loose." His brows snapped together. "And they said…they said…"

"Oh, Walsh." Tears soaked her words. She leaned forward to hug him awkwardly, the edge of the bed separating them.

He pulled her closer, forcing her to climb onto the edge of the bed on her knees. She pulled his head into the crook of her neck. His tears wet the shoulder of her denim jacket and her own tears trekked down her cheeks. She wanted to tear down the childish drawings on the walls. To pop the cheery balloons floating above them. To knock over the vases holding flowers from those who'd been pulling for Iyani. Instead, she just rocked back and forth as Walsh held her, for how long she didn't know. His tears stopped, but she knew he was drawing as much solace from her as she was from the warm surrounding strength of his arms.

"Are you okay?" She finally drew back just enough to see his face.

Even though he sat in the center of the bed, legs crossed, and she was on her knees in front of him, his superior height left her only a few inches above him. Her arms hung loosely over the muscles of his broad shoulders. She stroked the closely cropped waves at the back of his head, soft and cool beneath her fingers. He dropped a thick fan of lashes over his grief-darkened eyes and lowered his forehead to her shoulder, turning into her neck. He inhaled.

"Vanilla." His warm breath misted her neck with that one word, inciting goose bumps across the skin. "You always smell like vanilla."

Her smile shook, and she started to pull away, but his hands tightened on her waist. He leaned up, tilting his head and brushing his firm lips across her slightly open mouth. At the brief contact, liquid fire rushed down her nerve endings. His kiss was a feather and a flame, raising goose bumps and heating her skin. Something blossomed in her chest, unfurling and straining toward him. She pressed closer, defenseless against sensations she'd never experienced with anyone before. One of Walsh's strong hands left her waist, reaching for her chin to bring her face closer. The velvet of his tongue traced the still-drying tears on her cheeks before returning to her mouth, now clamped closed against the temptation of his.

"Open." Walsh gave the gentle command. An intimate invitation. An irresistible dare.

Sanity was a fugitive on the run from reason. Her mouth fell open. He wasted no time, plunging in to plunder, devouring her with unchecked hunger. He groaned, sending the hand at her waist on an expedition across the curve of her hip to grip the firm sleekness of the bare thigh beneath her dress.

"Kerris." His voice seemed to have fallen octaves, its deep timbre inspiring her to shudder. "Tell me to stop."

"Stop." Her hands made a lie of the weak plea. She pressed them to the strong vein in his neck. Urging him to continue. Pulling him closer.

"Not very convincing," he whispered, pulling her head down to hover over his open lips, luring her to close the space between their mouths.

Heat crawled up between them, their lips and tongues tangling. Walsh reached up, fingers fumbling at the buttons of the denim jacket Kerris wore over her dress. The jacket fell open. Walsh reached one hand behind her to press the softness of her back, almost spanning the narrow expanse of it. His fingers slid under the spaghetti straps of the dress, caressing her shoulder, trailing down to stroke the soft curves beneath her dress. Her breasts tightened with a pleasure so acute it bordered on pain. Kerris gasped, pulling back abruptly. They both panted, his breath heavy and hot on her kiss-swollen lips, rising from the dying flame of that kiss.

Her passion-clouded eyes slowly cleared. Sanity made a belated reappearance.

"Oh, gosh." She scooted back to put distance between them, and then slid off the bed altogether.

"Um, that was bad. It was…an accident." Her hand covered the throbbing fullness of her mouth.

"It's an accident when cars collide." The remnants of desire hoarsened Walsh's voice. "When lips collide it's a kiss. That wasn't an accident, and we need to talk about it."

"No, we don't." She fumbled through rebuttoning her jacket, fingers shaking. She closed her eyes for a few erratic heartbeats, struggling to rein in her body's response. She was a running engine slowly cooling down. "We have to forget that happened. It was…Iyani, and we were comforting each other, and the emotions got out of control and…misplaced."

"Is that how you'll explain it to Cam?"

"Cam!" Panic expelled the name from her mouth with the report of a bullet. "You absolutely *cannot* tell Cam. He wouldn't understand."

"I wouldn't, either." He stretched out one arm to pull her to him by the front of her jacket.

"No, Walsh." The words stilled in her throat when she

realized he was simply redoing the buttons she had misfastened in her clumsy rush. "Oh, thanks."

"So, you don't plan to tell Cam?" Walsh's hand fell away, his mouth a straight and narrow line. His fist clenched on his knee, making his calm tone a lie. His eyes never strayed from her cowboy boots.

"No, and neither can you. Look at me."

He met her eyes head on.

"Neither can you, Walsh." That bore repeating. "Cam seems mild-mannered, but he's so…"

"Possessive?" He paired the word with a frown.

"I guess, but most of all because it would hurt him unnecessarily. You have to see that."

"Do I?" A skeptical brow lifted. "I don't think that's the right way to handle it. I think we should be honest with Cam and with ourselves."

"What do you mean by 'with ourselves'?"

"Kerris, I can't promise it won't happen again." His voice was sandpaper. Rough. Abrasive. "This is serious. Cam's asked you to marry him."

"And you don't think I should? Is that it? Am I not good enough for Cam?"

"What?" A storm cloud gathered on his face. "I never said that. I don't *think* that. Don't try to smokescreen me by putting words in my mouth. If you marry Cam, and this doesn't go away…"

"What doesn't go away?" She directed the soft words to her boots, unable to meet his still-steaming eyes.

He lifted her chin with one thumb, caressing the line of her jaw with his index finger.

"Kerris, can you deny there's something between us?"

"An attraction?"

"Okay, if that's what you want to call it, yeah. An attraction."

"Walsh, you're an attractive guy. These were difficult, emotional circumstances, and we got carried away."

"I don't know. I just…"

"Do you love Cam?" she asked, stowing her emotions behind an impassive face. Walsh's friendship with Cam was her trump card. Maybe her *only* card.

"Of course. You know he's the brother I never had."

"Do you want to put a strain on that relationship over a kiss that meant nothing?" She poured all her nervousness into the fingers plucking at her dress, but kept her face placid.

"Nothing?" His narrowed eyes locked on hers. "You're telling me what just happened meant nothing to you?"

"That's exactly what I'm telling you." She nodded vigorously, one long braid slithering over her shoulder.

"Then you're right. There's nothing to tell."

"Great."

"Right."

"Okay."

"Okay."

"All right." She shifted her weight from one boot to the other. "I'm gonna go then."

She headed toward the door, stopping at the sight of Iyani's brightly colored papers taped to the wall by the light switch.

She had drawn herself between Kerris and Walsh, holding their hands. Kerris looked back over her shoulder at Walsh. He sat in the same spot on the bed. He had pulled the leather bracelet onto his strong wrist and was tracing the wooden blocks spelling Iyani's name. She pressed her lips together to stem the trembling, swiping at the one hot tear that streaked down her face.

"I really am so sorry, Walsh." She blinked back fresh tears. "About Iyani, I mean."

Kerris wasn't sure if he didn't hear or ignored her, but he didn't lift his eyes again. She didn't know if that kiss had begun one thing or destroyed another. The attraction between them, an undercurrent all summer, had broken the surface with violence and heat. She'd never forget the feeling that exploded inside of her, his touch tripping an invisible wire only he had discovered. Those sensations had been hidden treasures in her own body, and her insides still hummed and buzzed. No matter how good it felt, what happened could never happen again. Should never have happened at all.

Chapter Ten

Walsh stepped out of the elevator, adjusting his tie and checking the shine on his shoes. His father's suite of offices took up the entire twenty-first floor of a New York skyscraper. He had come here with his mother as a child, awed by this inner sanctum from which his father ruled. He hadn't understood then exactly what his father did, but he knew it was important, and that Daddy was powerful.

Now he knew what Daddy did.

Daddy was a pirate. A swashbuckling tycoon who preyed on the dismal circumstances of corporations too weakened to fend him off. Acquisitions. Takeovers, amicable or hostile. It really didn't make a difference to Martin Bennett. If he wanted a company, he would have it.

It took something like acquisitions to stretch his father to the outer limits of his intelligence and ambition. He was a raider. A marauder. And Walsh, God help him, was sitting at his feet to learn everything he knew. One day, this company would be his. He was determined that it would be on his own terms, but for now, he had to live with his father's.

Unmitigated adoration had burned bright for his father until Walsh was twelve years old and seen the man's feet of clay. He'd never forget the angry exchanges through the walls of their brownstone, or his mother's wrenching sobs after his father's infidelity.

Walsh checked his watch, shoving those emotions aside. Martin Bennett didn't deal in emotions. He dealt in power, results, and cash. Eyes incessantly trained on the bottom line and his ever-expanding interests, his dad had missed a lot of the smaller details of life, like his wife and son. In the grand scheme of things, though, did it really matter?

Not to Walsh. Not anymore.

"Morning, Claire."

Walsh greeted his father's assistant with genuine pleasure. He'd always liked her. He remembered the strange feeling of relief he'd felt the first time he came to the office and saw the staid, older woman who had replaced Laura, Martin's previous assistant.

Laura had been blond, voluptuous, condescending, and rude when his father wasn't around. The affair with her had destroyed his parents' marriage. The marriage had been unsalvageable, but at least Walsh hadn't had to look at Laura's smug face every time he came here.

"Walsh." Claire smiled, standing to give him a quick peck on the cheek. "How have you been?"

"Pretty good."

He hoped her usually omniscient glance missed the lines of fatigue around his mouth and eyes. It had been a long month, between making arrangements for Iyani and overseeing some additions at the Kenyan orphanage. He had only returned yesterday, per his father's summons. He had intended to head straight back to North Carolina, but Claire had called asking that he come to New York first.

"So why does he want to see me? I know you know."

Claire smiled a tiny bit, cracking her professional demeanor just enough to reveal her affection for him.

"You'll see." She studied him over her fashionable tortoise-shell glasses. "Go on in."

"Is my tie straight?"

He backed toward his father's office door, using his old standby—the boyish grin. She rolled her eyes and shooed him into the office.

"Unacceptable," Martin Bennett snapped into his cell phone. Walsh pushed the door open wider.

The opulent office always made Walsh feel like its luxury was closing in on him, from the expensive Persian rugs to the clean lines of the mammoth desk, set in front of the breathtaking view like a crown jewel. There was only one comfortable chair in the whole office, and his father kept that for himself. All the other seats were beautiful, but hard and unyielding, keeping you slightly on edge. Walsh knew this was just one layer of his father's design to maintain every advantage he could, no matter how small.

The office overlooked the crowded New York landscape.

Seeing the breadth of the city made his father proud of the patch of urban jungle he'd subdued with the machete of his relentless ambition.

"I don't pay you to 'think' you know things." Impatience pierced his father's every word. "I pay you to know, unequivocally without a doubt, what to do. Action, Miller. Not excuses. I want that company, and don't come back until you have it."

His father hung up without a good-bye. The weight of his considering look fell on Walsh like a steel beam. One Walsh had learned not to buckle beneath.

"Walsh."

"Dad."

"How's your mother? She has a birthday soon, doesn't she?"

"Um, she's fine." Walsh mentally scrambled to orient himself to this new tactic. One of the unspoken terms of his parents' armed truce was that they never asked him about each other. "Yeah, her birthday's tomorrow. I'm flying back today for the party."

"Hmmm. Still seeing that old man?" Martin picked up a heavy hourglass on the edge of his desk and flipped it over, setting it down with a thud before the sands could settle.

"Sam Whitby?" Walsh frowned, taking his eyes from his father's face only long enough to watch the sands' rapid fall in the new direction. "He's only five years older than you, Dad."

"He looks fifteen years older." Martin riffled through his catalog of disdainful expressions before settling on a sneer for Kristeene's suitor. "Don't know what she sees—never mind.

None of my business. So you're back from another one of your little mission trips, huh?"

"It's not a…never mind."

Walsh couldn't be bothered to explain again why the orphanages were so important to him. Philanthropy was another planet to his father, a strange land where people actually cared about the well-being of others.

"There was a little girl from the orphanage who had a brain tumor. I took her to Rivermont for surgery. She didn't make it and I flew her back to Kenya to be buried there."

"Sorry about that." It sounded like Iyani could have been a goldfish Walsh had flushed down the toilet as far as his father was concerned. "I have my eye on a new company."

"Oh?"

Walsh kept his tone neutral. He approached each of these paternal conversations with tactical precision, careful not to volunteer too much information, but to wait for his opponent to make the first move, revealing how to best defend.

"Merrist Holdings." Walsh recognized the predatory gleam in his father's eyes, savoring the taste of coming conquest. "You familiar?"

Walsh kept his posture deliberately languid, but his mind executed a rapid-fire retrieval of any information he could recall about Merrist Holdings. It never paid to reveal excitement about any venture. He had learned early that his father invariably viewed emotions as leverage. For him to know you wanted something was to give him a weapon to use against you.

"I know very little about Merrist, Dad. Enlighten me?"

"You must know something." His father fired him a know-ing look.

He always made it his business to know his father's next move. Part of the stratagem he employed to negotiate their relational minefield.

"I think Merrist was a family-owned operation. Medium-size logistics firm based in Burlington, New Jersey." Walsh lifted his Charvet tie to study the medallion pattern. "Recently went public. Established a Chicago branch about a year ago, which hemorrhaged profit. Now they find themselves with little cash flow. In addition to carrying some hefty debts they took on to open the new plant. Am I close?"

"So you are familiar." His father smiled, the closest thing to pride Walsh ever got to see in his eyes. "I want that company."

"And you want me on the team?"

"You *are* the team." Martin held his son's eyes captive for an extra moment before turning to survey the city skyline. "Can you handle it?"

"Of course I can handle it." Walsh made sure he didn't sound defensive or, worse, eager. "I've just never taken the lead on an acquisition before."

"Neither had I until I did it the first time." Martin challenged Walsh with his best alpha male look over his shoulder. "It's like sex. Grab your dick and figure it out."

"I'll be fine." Walsh stood, not giving his father the chance to dismiss him. "I'll have Claire send me any pertinent infor-mation we already have."

"Of course, you'll need to spend more time here, and less

time in North Carolina." His father picked up that damn hourglass again, his face in its usual hard lines, but his eyes alert and careful on Walsh.

"Of course." Ah, the end game. Always control and manipulation. "The summer will be over soon anyway."

"You can't wait until the summer's over to pursue this." Out of his father's face, Walsh's own eyes stared back at him with iron in the irises. "I need you on this now."

"I said I've got it." Walsh stiffened his back and calcified his tone. Martin Bennett only understood aggression; he only respected the kind of mental brawn he employed himself.

"You'll need an assistant."

"I'll ask Claire for recommendations."

"I've already selected someone." Martin turned to face Walsh wearing a younger man's wolfish grin. "Trisha McAvery."

"Hmmpph." Walsh grunted, refusing to blink, trying to decipher what his father was up to. "Okay, Trisha should be fine."

"That's a mild response. Most healthy, red-blooded males would jump at the chance to work with a woman who looks like Trisha."

"I hope that most healthy, red-blooded males would appreciate how highly unprofessional and unwise a relationship with an employee would be." Walsh's voice was a stone wall he dared his father to scale.

"Who said anything about a relationship?" Martin laughed like a rogue.

"Not interested." Walsh strode to the door, eager to get out of his father's presence. His soul needed a shower.

"You and Sofie practicing a little premarital monogamy?"

Walsh turned back toward his father, his hand on the door.

"Dad, I'm not marrying Sofie."

"Of course you are." Martin cut his hand through the air, a dismissal. "Everyone knows that."

"I don't know it."

"Sofie believes it."

"Sofie can believe in the tooth fairy and Santa Claus." Walsh sifted grit into his words. "I'm still not marrying her."

"You can't marry just anyone. One day Bennett will be yours, and you need the right kind of woman on your arm when you walk through certain doors."

"Maybe I'll wait for someone I love." Walsh faced his father fully now, matching his aggressive stance.

"Love," his father said, somewhere between a laugh and a hiss.

"Yeah, Dad, some people marry for it. You wouldn't know about that, though, would you?"

Anger made reptilian slits of his father's eyes.

"You don't think I loved your mother?"

"I think you broke my mother's heart." Walsh snapped the words before firming his mouth and smoothing the scowl from his face. "I think you cheated on her. Guess that was just part of grabbing your dick and figuring it out."

"Son, I—"

"I have a flight to catch." Walsh turned on his heel to leave before his father could offer excuses for the inexcusable.

Chapter Eleven

When she'd first started working with Maid 4 U, Kerris had thought there was nothing more cathartic than cleaning bathrooms. Give her an old toothbrush, a can of Comet, some moldy tile grout, and she was happy as a tick on a dog. Unfortunate comparison, but somehow it fit.

She had often lost herself in contemplation over a freshly scrubbed toilet or a sparkling sink and mirror. She had convinced herself in a particularly dirty bathroom to accept Cam's invitation for a date after six months of asking. By the time that bathroom was sparkling, she had decided she was waiting for something that would never happen. She shared a deep friendship with Cam. He was good to her, understood her issues, and wanted what she wanted more than anything as much as she did—a family of her own making. They'd had their first date the next day.

Kerris flung her sponge into the claw-footed tub, leaning her forehead against the cold rim. She closed her eyes, but the memories that had assailed her ever since that kiss at the hospital played on the backs of her lids with 3-D vividness. Inescapable images. Pleasure she had only imagined, never tasted.

She'd been haunted by a misplaced sense of rightness between her and Walsh as they'd touched. It had frightened and enchanted her. It was the thing she had stopped believing was possible, but with a man who could never belong to her; could never commit to her or give her the children she wanted. They were from completely different worlds. She couldn't ever breathe the rarefied air in the world Walsh inhabited, much less share his life.

And he was Cam's best friend. There was that.

If only she could delete the memory of him; the sweet brush of his lips and the desperate hunger of his hands. She closed her eyes tighter, tasting him again, hearing the hitch of his breath at that first touch. Smelling the intoxicating scent of him, a glorious male animal in heat.

She banged her head against the tub, willing the memories to shake and dislodge.

In the two weeks he had been gone, she had revised her opinion of herself. She wasn't a frozen river, iced over and immune to a man's touch. In those stolen moments in Iyani's room, redolent with death, the ice had cracked, and she was rushing water threatening to overflow her banks. The passion she had believed was a myth, she now craved.

How would she hide it from Walsh?

"You almost done in here?" Meredith asked from the

doorway, pulling the bandanna from her hair. She, like Kerris, wore cutoff jeans and a Maid 4 U T-shirt.

"Yeah. Just a few more minutes."

"You okay? You haven't been yourself lately."

"I'm cool." Kerris relaxed the muscles of her face one by one, avoiding Meredith's don't-shit-me eyes. "Just tired."

"Okay. If you're sure." Meredith leaned against the doorjamb. "Well, what'd you think of the mayor's house?"

"Beautiful, but not my style. Too stuffy." Kerris picked up her sponge to finish the tub.

"Did you get to meet his daughter, Ardis?"

"No. She lives here?"

"Yeah, I think she came in after you." Meredith rolled her eyes. "She's a real peach."

"What does she do?"

"Well, college was a hobby for her. Now she's having a lay-over until she finds the perfect man to take care of her and set her up as a professional socialite."

Meredith, a card-carrying worker bee, derided anyone who didn't see the value of gainful employment.

"She graduated a couple of years ago, but I haven't heard of her lifting a finger for anything but one of her committees. What a waste."

"If that's what the lady wants to do. It's her life, right?"

"I just don't get it. At least Sofie models."

"Sofie?" Kerris squeezed the sponge till water poured from it. "Why'd you mention her?"

"Oh, she's with Ardis. Apparently their families have been

friends forever, and Sofie's been staying here during the summer when she comes to visit Walsh. I overheard them talking about Mrs. Bennett's birthday party tonight, so I guess she's in town for that."

"Oh, yeah." Kerris ran both hands over her face, a weary gesture that smelled of Clorox. "That is tonight, isn't it?"

"Will Walsh be coming back for it?"

Kerris felt Meredith's eyes locked and loaded on her face with the focus of a sniper. She willed herself not to squirm under the eye of her friend's scope.

"Um, I wouldn't know." Kerris leaned into the tub to reach a spot, conveniently hiding her face. "Cam said he was scheduled to be back a couple of days ago. I doubt he'll miss his mother's birthday party."

"Well, I'm sure Sofie will be waiting with open arms."

"Yeah, you're probably right." Kerris reached up to tighten the bandanna wrapped around her head, needing to occupy her hands. "Well, let me finish up in here."

Meredith rightly interpreted that as the dismissal and No Trespassing sign that it was, and let it go.

"I'll wait on the porch then. See you in a few."

Kerris resumed her scrubbing, biting her lip against foolish tears. She chided herself. Walsh was off-limits. He might be attracted to Kerris, might have great chemistry with her, but he wouldn't be settling down with someone like her. And what about Cam? He was the surest thing in her life right now. Not only did he love her, but he accepted her. He saw the damage her past had done and wanted her anyway. Wanted a life with her. Wanted a family with her. She couldn't allow one kiss with a man she really barely knew to ruin that, could she?

"I'm pretty sure I left it in the bathroom," a voice said from behind her. "Oh! I didn't realize your maid was in here. Does she speak English?"

"Yeah, she does." Kerris threaded as much outrage and dignity into the response as she could before she saw who it was. "Oh, Sofie."

Kerris glanced down, not sure if the rags on her body were much better than the rags in her bucket. Of course, it *would* be Sofie. It was just that kind of day.

"Kerris?" Sofie ventured, as if surely no one of her acquaintance would be cleaning a bathroom. "Is that you?"

"No, it's my domestic doppelgänger." Kerris tacked a smile onto the quip. "Hi, Sofie. How are you?"

"Doing well." Sofie fiddled with the belt of her designer dress and looked like she was afraid menial labor was contagious.

"Did you find it?" a pretty brunette, just as well dressed as Sofie, asked from the doorway. "Oh, hi. *¿Hablas inglés?*"

Kerris gritted her teeth. She should be used to it by now. All her life she'd had people walk up to her speaking Spanish, French, whatever—assuming she was one of them. She wished it were that simple. She was a mutt, a mix of things, that was for sure. And right now both ladies looked at her like she'd just peed on the rug.

"I speak English." Kerris rose to her feet and gave both ladies a pseudo-sparkly smile.

"Ardis, this is Kerris." Sofie recovered her manners. "She's Cam's girlfriend."

Ardis looked at Sofie blankly, mouthing "who"? Did she think she was invisible? *I can see you,* Kerris wanted to yell. Wealth doesn't give you superpowers.

"Cam." Sofie raised her "you know" brows. "Walsh's best friend."

"He's adorable." Ardis looked at Kerris with new eyes. Probably wondering what he saw in a cleaning urchin.

"Yes, I hear he's pretty serious," Sofie said in a singsongy voice to Kerris. "Heard he's popped the question."

"Where'd you hear that?" Kerris asked, raising her brows into the bandanna covering half her forehead.

And what business is it of yours?

"Jo told me. They're thrilled that Cam has found someone so...compatible. I think your similar backgrounds make you a perfect match."

Kerris squeezed a dry sponge with unnecessary force, not bothering to respond.

"I just want you to know how much I admire you," Sofie continued.

Kerris gathered her bucket of cleaning supplies, careful not to brush against either woman's finery on her way into the hallway.

"I mean, you've worked so hard to pull yourself out of miserable circumstances." Sofie's private-school-educated voice followed Kerris onto the landing of the stairs. "And now I hear you're opening your own business. It'll be a real rags-to-riches story one day. Don't be discouraged that right now it's just, well, rags."

Kerris's anger throbbed in her temples. Her teeth gated the spiteful responses she wanted to hurl at Sofie. Her jaw ached with the restraint. Obviously Sofie wanted to put her firmly in her place.

"I'm gonna do one more walk through to make sure we didn't overlook anything," Kerris finally said. "It was nice meeting you, Ardis. Nice seeing you again, Sofie."

Chapter Twelve

Kerris leaned back in the small boat Cam had rowed out to the middle of the river, closing her eyes against the brightness of the August sun. After cleaning the mayor's house all morning and breathing those fumes, Kerris appreciated the clean summer air. She slitted her eyes open, realizing Cam had stopped rowing.

"You okay?" She sat up, searched the somber lines of his face. "You look so serious."

"For once, I am serious."

"What's up?" She trailed her fingers through the cold water.

"Remember what you said on the Fourth of July? That the woman I want to marry should know everything?"

Kerris's fingers went limp in the water. For the first time in the August heat, she felt sweat break out under her arms and between her breasts. She wasn't ready for another proposal. There were too many unresolved issues, too many questions she didn't have the right answers for yet. She was still sorting through what had happened with Walsh. Could she actually marry Cam, knowing she didn't feel as deeply for him as he felt for her? He said he'd take whatever she had to offer, but what if some day down the road, it wasn't enough?

"Do you remember that?" Cam's frown pressed her when she looked at him without responding.

"I remember."

"I want you to know everything." He swallowed loud enough for her to hear. A gulp telling the story of his anxiety. "I've never shared this shit with anybody except Walsh, but I want you to know."

"Okay." She watched her reflection in the water, giving him space to tell her in his own way.

"My mom was a crackhead." He looked at her from beneath his straight, silky brows. "You know that, right?"

Kerris nodded, feeling like a voyeur about to look on a past possibly more obscenely painful than her own.

"She started tricking before she had me, I guess to get the drugs. I know my mom was biracial, half white, half black. Her name was Sarah. My old man—who knows. One of her Johns." He chopped the words up finely, pushing them to the side to make room for more. "I'm guessing he wasn't Black because of how I look. Maybe white or Hispanic. Guess we'll never know."

Even with such gaps in his identical mosaic, Kerris envied him the knowledge of his mother. The vital pieces of the puzzle she had been. Her face, her hands, her hair, her smile. Even her vices, the mistakes she'd made that set his life on the course it had taken. Kerris didn't have even that.

"We lived in a hellhole. It was rough."

By the look on Cam's face, Kerris felt pretty sure that was an understatement. She recognized the painful thought of that place twisting in his eyes; eyes that were no longer seeing her, but looking back along a darkened corridor of memory.

"I mean, my mom was a crackhead who whored for money, so yeah, it was bad, but bad is relative. It could've been worse. It *did* get worse."

He let his last words settle around them and drift away with the river's strengthening current before drawing a shallow breath and continuing.

"My mom met this guy, Ron MacKenzie, when I was about nine. He became her pimp and drug dealer, and then it got…much worse." Cam paused, running his eyes down the river before starting again. "We shared a room, me and my mom. I slept on the floor. She slept on the bed. Well, not just slept. That's where she did business."

Kerris closed her eyes against the horrific images invading her mind. A young boy subjected to the filth of that lifestyle. The sounds, the smells, the sights of adult moral squalor robbing him of his innocence.

"I saw it all. It was bad enough having to listen to my mom fucking some stranger, blowing guys off while I was doing my homework or whatever." A perverse smile played around Cam's mobile mouth. "Sounds pretty fucked up now that I say it out loud, but I got used to it."

"Mac was a real piece of work." Cam pulled his brows down

around something Kerris wasn't sure he wanted to share. "He would beat my mom some, but not too bad, if she kept him happy. You know, brought in enough cash and other stuff that he wanted. He, um, he liked boys."

Kerris's breath stilled in her throat, her eyes glued to Cam's shuttered face. She could see the red crawling up his neck, but wasn't sure if it was shame, anger, embarrassment, or some witch's brew that stirred them all together until one was completely indistinguishable from the others. Dread filled her.

"He liked boys." Cam said it again and looked at her without flinching or hiding. "He liked me, Ker."

The summer sunshine toasted and dried Kerris's tears before she realized they'd slid down her cheeks.

"It was about a year." He plowed on, looking at his reflection in the water before quickly looking away like he couldn't stand what he saw. "For about a year he…you know, molested me. He had me and my mom both hung up. Told her that if she didn't let him have me, he'd cut off her drugs. And he told me that if I fought him, he'd kill my mom. And I knew he would, so I stopped fighting.

"We got lucky," Cam continued in a voice as flat and dead as his eyes had become. "He died."

Kerris remembered the relief she'd felt when the man who had hurt her died in prison. Like she could breathe easier just because he was no longer in the world.

"What happened?"

Cam looked over her shoulder, his face hiding secrets.

"He got what was coming to him." Cam's eyes, cold as

a corpse, shifted back to Kerris. "Live by the sword, die by the sword."

Kerris shivered in the sun. The Cam sitting across from her was not the man she knew. Rough around the edges, but tender and quick to smile. This man had granite for eyes and turned the air around him deadly. Kerris remained quiet, fingers floating in the water, until Cam's face softened and he returned to her. Cam rubbed his eyes, wiping away the last vestiges of that hardened stranger.

"After that, Mom got arrested when she approached some undercover cop posing as a john. I saw her only one more time after that. She signed all her parental rights away and I got tossed into foster care."

"And how was foster care?" Kerris was afraid to unearth anything worse than what he had already revealed.

"Not bad." He shrugged like a man who knew what bad really looked like. "In the first one, there was this guy who liked punching on me, but nobody was ever gonna have me by the balls again like Mac did. I told my social worker, and she got me out of there. Put me with these really sweet folks I stayed with until I graduated high school. They moved to Florida my freshman year of college, but we still talk from time to time. They're the ones who found out about the Walsh Foundation's summer camp."

She smiled at how his face relaxed when he talked about that first summer. How he and Walsh had rubbed each other the wrong way, only to become best friends. How Jo was the sister he'd never had.

"And Ms. Kris." His features softened in a way reserved for Walsh's mother. "I hadn't ever met anyone like her. Walsh has no idea how lucky he is to have her."

"They're like family to you."

"They're not family, though, Kerris." He leaned forward in the small boat, capturing one of her hands still floating in the water. "I love them, but they're not my family. That's what I want with you. Even with them, I didn't belong to them. My mom was the only person I ever belonged to, and she sold me out for crack."

Kerris understood parental betrayal, when the person everything in nature dictated should preserve and protect you had abandoned and hurt you the most.

"I want you to be my only." Cam stripped every barrier away from his eyes, leaving them wide open and vulnerable. "The only other person on earth I belong to, and who belongs to me. And then we can start a family from scratch. Something we never had."

If she'd never met Walsh, never gotten caught with him in an electric storm, she would have told Cam yes with no hesitation. She had resigned herself to a marriage where the greatest fruit would be their children, expecting no real pleasure, no rush of emotion at the sight of her spouse. What a bitter irony that the man who cracked open the emotion she dammed away could never be hers.

Cam's phone ringing jarred her, pulling her eyes to meet his considering stare. He didn't look away even when he reached in his pocket for his phone.

"Yeah." He listened and released a short breath, squeezing the bridge of his nose. "Okay, I'll be right there. Gimme a few minutes. I'm at lunch."

He ended the call and started rowing swiftly back toward the bank.

"Everything okay?"

"Just a glitch with that project I thought was wrapped." Cam's strong shoulders flexed with the force of his exertions. "I think fixing this thing might take the rest of the afternoon. This client keeps making changes."

"It's okay. Drop me off at my apartment. Do you need me to meet you at the party?"

"No way. I'm picking you up and we're riding together. I want to be the first to see you. I know once you're there and all dressed up, I'll have to fight 'em off."

"I doubt that. All those women tonight will be dressed up in couture. I'll be in dime vintage. No comparison."

"You got that right." Cam's smile, so tender and open, jerked her heart around like an errant kite with a guilty tail. "I can guarantee there won't be any comparison."

They zipped over to her apartment on his Harley. She pressed her cheek against Cam's back and wrapped her arms around him.

He was a good man. His edges were rough, his mouth was foul, and before he met her, he'd been a player. But when he looked at her, he made her feel that everything he'd ever wanted in the whole world was standing in front of him. If she had still been a praying woman, she would have asked God if He could please, please, please make her feel the same.

Chapter Thirteen

Walsh glanced around the room, searching for one petite woman who could easily be lost in the crowd assembled for his mother's birthday. The large room sparkled, the crystals of the chandeliers overhead vying for shine with the overdecorated women laden with diamonds. The room had been cleared of all furniture, giving everyone room to mingle and preparing them for later, for the dancing his mother loved so much.

He would have preferred a barbecue out back in the yard leading down to the river, just family and a few close friends. Not his mother. Not for her fiftieth birthday. She had turned this special occasion into a charity extravaganza, packed wall to wall with big spenders who'd trade their cold, hard cash for the chance to rub up against the high-profile partygoers Kristeene Bennett could bring together.

Jo walked up beside him, wearing high-waisted black satin tuxedo pants and an emerald green blouse that molded the sleek muscles of her arms and peekabooed her generous cleavage.

Walsh looked frighteningly like his father, but Jo could easily be Kristeene Bennett's daughter. Same dark hair, streaked with burned chestnut. Same impossibly high regal cheekbones. Dark brows arching in her creamy skin. Two things set Jo apart. Where his mother's eyes were hazel, Jo had Uncle James's startling gray, nearly silver eyes. And though Jo was tall and lean like his mother, she curved more, especially in the hips and butt. Walsh glared at some guy he caught staring at his cousin's ass.

Jo flashed Walsh a knowing grin.

"Leave the poor man alone."

Walsh frowned, grabbing her hand and folding it over his forearm.

"I'll never get used to guys eyeing you like a piece of meat."

"At least someone does." Jo twisted her lips and slid him a sideways glance, moving on before he had a chance to probe. "So who were you looking for?"

And just like his mother, Jo had a way of disarming him. Lulling him into forgetting just how damn sharp she was.

"No one in particular." Walsh made his face as bland as beige. "You?"

"No one in particular." Jo looked up at him, the silence making him uncomfortable before she relaxed her mouth into a smile. "Your mom's in heaven. All this money in one room, all locked, loaded, and aimed at her favorite cause."

"I was thinking the same thing." Walsh pulled her close enough to drop a kiss on her forehead. "I was also thinking how much alike the two of you are. You look beautiful tonight, by the way."

Some hybrid of surprise and disbelief flitted across Jo's smooth features. He leaned in closer, considering for the first time that Jo, his fortress during his parents' tumultuous divorce and his rock in the madhouse life he led now, might not know how awesome she was.

"*Is* there someone you're looking for, Jo?"

She'd know he didn't just mean at the party tonight. She'd definitely had romantic interests through the years. He and Cam had vetted every one of them, fiercely protective of their Jo. If Cam was the brother he'd never had, Jo was certainly the sister.

"I'm not looking." She smoothed the sleek cap of hair that had grown to hang just above her shoulders. "I'm too busy trying to get you and Cam settled. There'll be plenty of time later to figure out my own situation."

"I'm not settling down any time soon."

"That's not how Sofie tells it." Her laugh told him how his face must look. "Would it really be so bad to marry a supermodel?"

"Look, Sof and I have been friends forever. She's great. She's just not my type."

"I thought your type was willing and breathing."

"This is me you're talking about, not Cam."

"Cam has been a one-woman man for some time now." Jo looked over his shoulder, a tight smile tugging at her lips and dulling her eyes to pewter. "And that one woman is on his arm right now."

Walsh glanced to the doorway, where Cam and Kerris were

laughing with his mother. What a picture Kerris made in her yellow dress. A lemon iced confection that would melt in his mouth. Sweet and tart.

A white orchid nestled behind her ear, contrasting against the rumpled elegance of the dark hair pulled up and away from her face. A beaded bodice topped the strapless dress, and a nipped waist flared to an A-line skirt floating just below her knees.

His stomach roller-coastered. All the blood in his body migrated south and pushed against the zipper of his tailored slacks. He fought the urge to retreat up the stairs to his room like some teenager suffering from his first crush.

It was bad enough he'd had to watch Cam and Kerris together all summer. Now he had those stolen moments in that hospital room to torture him. Kerris's butter-soft skin, her sweet vanilla scent, the silky weight of her hair. Damn, the feel of her leg under his hand and the firm curve of her breast…

"Walsh, you're hurting my hand."

"What?" Walsh wrenched his gaze back to Jo, surprised to find her hand squeezed between his. "Shit. Sorry."

"Walsh, you know Cam is serious about Kerris, right?" Jo used her don't-play-a-player voice on him. "He's going to propose again."

"What's that got to do with me?" Walsh's eyes itched to look away, but Jo pinned him to the wall with those orbs.

"Nothing." Jo threw the word at him low and hard like a ground ball he couldn't catch before she threw the next one. "It's nothing to do with you. Don't forget that."

"What are you two arguing about?" Cam asked. He and Kerris had crossed the room without their noticing.

"We're not arguing." Jo cleared her frown, offering a quick smile designed to reassure Cam and Kerris. "I'm just reminding Walsh of a few home truths."

"Unnecessarily." Walsh poured his displeasure into that one word and compressed his lips into a straight line around it.

"You look beautiful, Jo." Kerris offered his cousin a sweet smile.

"So do you." Jo softened her expression for Kerris. "Everyone can't wear that color, but it looks just right on you."

"Thanks." Walsh saw Kerris touch the lemon chiffon skirt and glance around at a cluster of well-dressed women.

"And those shoes are incredible." Jo pointed to Kerris's small feet.

Kerris smiled, looking down at the shoes, too. Kitten heeled, with delicate gold straps and topped with a crystal orchid, they might have been the most adorable things Walsh had ever seen on anyone's feet. And thanks to his mother, he knew shoes. "Hey, looks like it's time for dinner." Cam snagged Kerris's hand and leaned down to brush her cheek with a kiss that lingered a moment, staking a subtle claim before leading her away.

* * *

Walsh flashed a smile he'd been cultivating in expensive schools and exclusive parties since he was twelve years old, hoping no one was the wiser. As long as he avoided Jo and Cam at the other end of the long table laughing with Kerris, he probably wouldn't be found out. One of the Walsh Foundation's largest donors had questions about the orphanage expansion under consideration, but Walsh struggled to focus. Sofie's wandering hands weren't making it easy.

"Excuse me just one moment," he said to the silver-haired donor, turning in Sofie's direction. "Sof, we're friends, right?"

"At the very least, Walsh." Her eyes, set at a low boil, traced his features.

"And we've known each other a long time, right?" He lacquered his smile to a high shine for those watching them.

"Yeah, what are you getting at?" Sofie allowed a rare frown to pleat her perfectly smooth forehead.

"Well, given our history, I'd hate to embarrass you, but if you don't remove your hand from my *very* upper thigh, I will."

She flashed him a chagrined smile, shifting her slim hand under the table to his knee, where she squeezed for good measure.

"A girl's gotta try." No shame. "One day, Walsh, you'll be ready and I'll be right there waiting."

"Don't hold your breath." He made sure not to smile so she'd know he meant it. "There's a line of guys waiting for you, Sof. Don't wait on me."

"You're the one I want."

"It's not gonna happen."

"We're still young." She patted the knee she'd just squeezed. "You have wild oats to sow."

"We're friends. Leave it there."

"Walsh," his mother said from the head of the table a few feet north of him and Sofie. "Will you open the dancing with me?"

Walsh lobbed a silent yes-get-me-out-of-this expression to his mother. She returned with a mama-always-knows smile. Walsh walked the few feet down the table to extend his hand to his mother. She certainly didn't look fifty, whatever that was supposed to look like. They stepped to the center of the floor cleared for dancing.

"No Sam Whitby tonight?" Walsh asked.

"No Sam Whitby, period." She twisted her carefully painted mouth into a resigned smile. "He's just a friend who got the wrong idea. Thanks for working the crowd, by the way."

"I have no idea what you mean." He kept his face perfectly straight.

"I saw you talking to Mr. Donovan. You know he's one of our biggest donors."

He swirled her with a flourish, smiling at her girlish laugh.

"I do recall."

"Hmmmm." She smiled up at him, the no-strings love and maternal pride clear for him to see. "You're such a good boy."

"Not too loud. I have a reputation to maintain."

"Like you need it with Sofie around. That girl has been chasing you since the fifth grade."

"Actually, since first grade, but she hasn't caught me yet, and she won't."

"Try telling her that."

"I *have* tried. She doesn't listen."

"Now here's a man who's been caught." Kristeene looked past Walsh's shoulder, affection softening her expression. "Cam, where have you been all night? I haven't seen you since you first got here."

"Well, you're seeing me now." He danced Kerris over closer to them. "Walsh, lemme cut in for a dance with the birthday girl."

Walsh and Kerris shared a knowing glance. Finally, Walsh nodded, handing his mother over to Cam and stepping aside to stand in front of Kerris. His palms moistened, wet with the excitement percolating in his belly. Tension marbled his shoulders.

"We *are* in the middle of a dance floor." He slipped the words between tightly held lips, reaching for her elbow to pull her into his arms. "Seems crazy to just stand here."

The heat of her body this close made him forget where he was and what he wanted to say. Her sweet vanilla scent seduced him. The muscles in his abdomen contracted, drawing the tension of the moment into his core. Her eyes were trained on the top button of the dress shirt he wore without a tie. The silence lengthened and tightened, a thread on the point of snapping. She gnawed the pillowed flesh of her bottom lip. He exhaled a short breath.

"This is ridiculous." He pressed the small of her back, forcing her to look up at him. "Let's get this out of the way. I'm sorry I kissed you at the hospital."

"Shhhh!" She conducted a quick, furtive survey of

the dancers around them. "Good gosh, could you *be* any louder?"

"I'm sorry." He swallowed an ill-timed chuckle. "I didn't think I was that loud."

"Can we just forget it happened?"

Her eyes begged him to conspire with her; to pretend his heart didn't swell up in his chest every time he was near her.

"Yeah, we can forget it."

He lied. He'd never forget. She had brushed up against his soul in that hospital room and exposed newly discovered nerves and emotions.

"And you won't…tell?" Kerris's words were only for him to hear. "You won't say anything to Cam?"

He couldn't help but tease her. She was so adorable.

"I'm sorry." He cupped one ear to hear her better. "I didn't make out that last part. You said I won't tell who?"

"Will you stop it?" She loaded her look with censure. "This is serious."

"It doesn't have to be." The brief humor drained from him like a fast tire leak. He returned his hand to her back. "I won't mention it."

"Thank you." He felt her release a breath of relief, a false, forced smile like a stain on her pretty face. "Let's talk about something else."

"Like what?" he asked, deliberately uncooperative.

"How about your trip to Kenya. How was that?"

"Hard."

She pressed on like he wasn't being an ass.

"I'm sure everyone is grieving for Iyani."

Her sweetness was chipping away at the hardness he wanted to hold on to.

"Yeah. She was something else."

"She was."

"You did so much to make the last few months of her life fun." He stroked the hand he held as they danced.

"No, you did that."

"Okay, we did that."

"We did that."

She rested her hand on his chest for a moment before pulling away. He trapped her hand under his against his chest. He wasn't ready to lose her. Wasn't ready to give up the rare moments alone.

"Now what should we talk about?" he asked into the silence that had lost the hardness and tightness of before.

"Cam said you went to New York before you came back. How was that?"

"It was work." He pulled shutters down over his face.

"What's that look?"

"What look?"

"Your face. You look…kind of mean."

"Oh, that. Work. My dad." He made a conscious effort to relax his facial muscles. "He brings out the worst in me because I have to be *like* him to deal with him."

"And how's that?"

"A narcissistic, mercenary douche bag."

"I can see that." She nodded, teasing him with a smile.

"Oh, you can? How about this?" He ran his fingers mercilessly and surreptitiously up her ribs, making her erupt in laughter. "Can you see this?"

She dipped her head to his shoulder, still fighting laughter. Several dancers turned in their direction.

"Stop, Walsh."

He refused, leaving her gasping, wriggling, and squeezing her eyes shut.

"People are looking at us."

"They can't help themselves. You're the most beautiful thing in this room."

Kerris sobered, standing still and pulling away when the music conveniently stopped.

"I'm sorry." He was only sorry because he'd made her pull away. "I shouldn't have said that."

"It's okay." She offered a papier-mâché smile, fragile and stiff. "Every girl loves a compliment."

"What was so funny?" Jo stepped into the conversation like she owned it, followed closely by Sofie.

"I was telling Kerris about my father." Walsh took half a step back from Kerris, governing his features before looking at Jo and Sofie.

"What a great man." Sofie twisted the diamond bracelet around her narrow wrist. "I've always loved Uncle Martin."

Jo snorted, exchanging a quick look with Walsh. He knew exactly what she was thinking. Sofie wouldn't score any points with him complimenting his father.

"Walsh, that man over there wanted you to come see him

after you were done…dancing." Sofie said the last word as if Kerris and Walsh had been grinding in the middle of the ballroom dance floor, her mouth twisted with distaste.

"Which man?" Walsh followed the direction of Sofie's finger. "Oh, Mr. Donovan. He's a big fish. Let me go over there and see if I can close this deal. I'll be back, ladies."

Walsh didn't allow himself one last look at Kerris. He didn't want to see the mask she'd pulled in place now that they weren't alone. He hated what she was hiding. Hated it because he had to hide it, too.

Chapter Fourteen

Walsh walked toward the silver-haired gentleman Kerris had seen him talking with during dinner, leaving her alone with Jo and Sofie. Jo had been watching Kerris like she was the last clue on the crossword puzzle you could never figure out. The tickle session on the dance floor with Walsh probably hadn't helped. Jo had eyes you couldn't hide from. Not for the first time, Kerris wondered if everything she was trying to hide, Jo could clearly see.

"That dress is lovely, Kerris." Sofie addressed the words to her French manicure. "Where'd you get it?"

"It's vintage." Kerris hated the note of uncertainty she heard in her own voice. She lifted her chin in a show of pride she didn't feel.

"Is that what they call it? So quaint." Sofie tossed a chunk of silvery-blond hair over one shoulder. "And how bold of you to wear something that…modest when all the other women are dressed…differently. I just admire you. I mean, you obviously have never been in an environment like this, and you're just conducting yourself so well."

Kerris noticed Jo widen her eyes at Sofie's insulting tone and comments. Kerris zipped her mouth into a fine line, holding back her own retort. Her palms itched to smack Sofie. She balled her fingers into the delicate fabric of her secondhand finery, crushing the material.

"Thank you." Kerris looked around the room for an escape, not sure if she was saving herself or the rude woman standing in front of her. "I think I'll go find Cam."

"He was talking outside with some of the guys smoking cigars," Jo said, sympathy apparent on her face.

Kerris didn't want sympathy or pity or whatever had her cheeks burning. She wanted out. She slipped off, stiffening her back against the urge to slump her shoulders. She had survived too much for someone like Sofie to break her, but she still felt the blows and wanted to lick the wounds in private.

She walked through the French doors, stepping down onto the dew-moistened lawn and heading for the gazebo. She slipped off her shoes, hooking the flimsy straps over her index finger. Glancing over her shoulder, she watched the clusters of glittering people chatting and laughing with one another in the makeshift ballroom. Her insides still stung from Sofie's acid-tipped talons. She'd painted Kerris as some shabbily dressed misfit.

Who was she kidding? That's *exactly* what she was.

Kerris wanted to go home, take off her Goodwill dress, curl up in her vintage kimono, and fall asleep with the scraps of her dignity and confidence. She settled onto the bench inside the gazebo, leaning back to admire the delicate latticework trimming its frame.

Kerris blew a cool breath out, air hissing across her lips until her chest hollowed out and her body drained of the tension.

"That bad, huh?" a deep voice asked from the shadows.

Kerris's head jerked toward the familiar baritone, narrowing her eyes in the dim light just beyond the steps of the gazebo.

"Walsh?" His name rested on her lips, mixed with hope and dread. "Where'd you...how did you..."

"I saw you leave and wanted to make sure you were okay."

He stepped onto the platform and into the light cast by the small lanterns suspended from the ceiling.

She blinked against the sight of him, the sharp planes of his face softened in the glow to a beautiful symmetry she could have looked at all day. Their eyes held too long before she made herself look away. Her tongue felt twice its normal size in the dried-out cave of her mouth. Delighted panic knifed through her. Her fingers played Twister in her lap.

"I'm fine." Kerris answered the question in his eyes.

"You could've fooled me."

"I thought you were closing a deal."

"Check's in the mail. Now stop trying to change the subject. You sure you're okay?"

"I just..." She hesitated, looking up at him, lowering her eyes again, weighing how much she should tell him.

"You just..." He prompted.

He sat, scooting until he could rest his back against the wall and pull his knees up, feet on the bench. She felt his eyes on her profile.

Tonight had conspired with her past to pound her confidence into a fine powder.

"I don't belong."

"Belong where?"

"Here. In there." She smoothed the silky material of her dress with a sweat-moistened hand. "With those people."

"That's ridiculous." He leaned forward a little, resting an arm on his knee. "What makes you say that?"

"Everyone is haute couture in there."

She hoped she didn't sound as miserable as she felt in that room with the glitterati. She had thought she was doing fine until Sofie reminded her of why she always hated these parties.

"I'm Goodwill. My dress is from Goodwill, Walsh."

"Let me get this straight." Walsh's mouth hitched up at the corner in the smallest of wry smiles. "After all you've endured with so many odds stacked against you, you're out here alone because of your outfit?"

"Well, when you say it like that—"

"Is belonging so important?"

"It would be hard to find anyone who 'belonged' more than you." She heard the bitterness in her own voice. Despite all she'd experienced, cynicism sat on her like an ill-fitting jacket, gaping under the arms and sagging at the shoulders. "You wouldn't understand."

"Try me. Tell me."

She rationed her breaths for a few moments, asking herself if she actually could tell someone.

"I come from nothing." A lock of hair had escaped the knot at the back of her head, and she pulled it over her shoulder, giving her something to do with restless fingers. "I mean, you know I'm an orphan."

Walsh only nodded, eyes moving from the hair resting on her shoulder back to her face.

"I wasn't like Cam. His mom was…awful. Negligent. Horrible, but at least she tried for a while. I don't know if that ended up being a blessing or a curse, but my mom left me on the porch of an orphanage like a bag of old clothes."

Kerris swallowed, searching for courage behind her closed eyelids.

"The orphanage where I was abandoned," she said, feeling the last word settle on her tongue heavily, making her pause under its weight. "That orphanage was private, like the Walsh orphanages, and when the money ran out, all the kids were sent into the foster system."

"How old were you?"

"Three. I was kind of shuffled around until I was ten. In the third home, one of the older kids there burned me with a cigarette." She stroked the sunburst-shaped scar on her wrist. "The social worker saw it, and got me out. That was when I ended up at Ms. Jessum's."

Kerris smiled and felt her insides soften like warm butter at the thought of Mama Jess.

"It was like having a mom and a real home. Mama Jess made sure I had clothes, food, and a bed to sleep in. I wasn't only a check to her," Kerris said, as certain as she'd ever been about anything. "I could tell she *loved* me. Loved me like a mother loves her little girl. It was the happiest time of my life.

"For a while," she added, lacing the two words with sudden bitterness.

"What happened?"

Kerris knew Walsh was keeping his voice calm and quiet to soothe her, but his hands gripped his knees.

"Her brother moved in. TJ." She said his name like a curse.

Kerris's words trailed into the silence of her memory. She had come home from school one day, somehow immediately sensing with her child's intuition that a dark force had entered their safe haven. The curtains had been drawn, keeping out the bright after-school sunshine, casting shadows in the front room. TJ had been there, lounging in the corner, slumped in the lumpy recliner. His predator eyes had lingered on her long hair and her baby-fat cheeks. Kerris had clutched her backpack to her flat chest, feeling the hairs lift on her arms and the back of her neck. Feeling hunted for the first time.

But not the last.

At dinner that night, Mama Jess explained that her brother would be staying with them for a while. And wouldn't it be good to have a man around the house? Kerris had pushed her peas around her plate, feeling TJ's eyes on her like a tiger watching a rabbit. Waiting patiently to strike. She lived in fear of an unknown threat she could not articulate to herself or anyone else. Unknown, but real. Then finally he'd pounced, devouring her until the only thing left was the ravaged carcass of her innocence.

She had never spoken of it before; never been tempted to pull back the heavy covers shrouding this part of her past. Cam had unburdened himself to her today. She wondered if his office hadn't called, would she have done the same? And why now? Why Walsh? She remembered her first impression of him. Dangerous, especially now with that sweet, wary, waiting concern on his handsome face.

"At first he only watched me." She braced herself for the shame she knew would engulf her once Walsh knew the whole truth. "He watched me all the time, and I knew it wasn't right. There were five girls in the house, but it was just me he watched all the time. He started…"

"Started what?" Walsh's voice was warm and still, the eerie calm before a storm breaks.

"Started coming in my room at night."

The words struggled their way up her throat, escaping in a tortured gasp.

"He was so quiet." Kerris fixed her eyes on the gazebo floor, but didn't really see it. "There was another little girl in my room, in the twin bed beside me. I wondered why she didn't wake up; why she didn't hear him. I thought maybe I imagined him, like the boogey man or a monster under my bed, but he was real. Just so quiet."

A single tear streaked down Kerris's face. She didn't try to catch it.

"Ker, you don't have to tell me—"

"He told me if I didn't let him touch me, that if I told anyone, they would take me away from Mama Jess. And I didn't want that." She went on as if Walsh had not interrupted. "Someone finally loved me, wanted me, and I couldn't risk losing that. So I didn't tell. I *wouldn't* have ever told.

"Then he…he…" The ugly truth hiccupped in her mouth. "Did he…"

"Yes."

Kerris methodically stripped the confession of the pain she would never forget. She looked at Walsh for the first time since she had started.

"Yes, he did."

The muscles in Walsh's face tightened around his horror-washed eyes.

"He said it would be our secret." Kerris shifted her numb bottom on the gazebo bench. "And I would have kept it. I just couldn't leave Mama Jess. I know it was sick, but I thought I could put up with that, with anything, if I could stay where I was loved and wanted. I couldn't leave her."

"I understand." Walsh slid into the space beside her and entwined their fingers, thumbing tears from her cheek. "Of course you didn't want to leave."

"But the next morning, I could barely…" She licked her lips, tasting the shame and pain of her past. She had to close her eyes, finishing in a rush. "I could barely walk, and Mama Jess noticed. And there was blood. I didn't know there was so much blood, but it was on my sheets. She called the doctor, and it wasn't a secret anymore. They took me away, just like he said they would. All I could think was he was right. He was right."

"Kerris." Walsh's fingers tightened on hers until she looked at him. "He wasn't right. They didn't take you away from Mama Jess because you told. They took you away because he was a monster. He had no right to touch you. What was his name?"

"What?" She blinked, dazed at the question, so specific, the tone low and deadly.

"I want his name. Tell me his name."

A wild bloodlust colored his eyes, and she realized that was for her. That righteous vengeance all over him was for her. She squeezed his hand as he had done hers, finding herself ironically the one soothing.

"He died in prison."

"Good. Saves me the trouble."

She saw the truth of it. The hand not holding hers was clenched, and his jaw hardened to a stony angle. She reached a shaky hand up to his face, passing it over his eyelids, hoping to wipe away the violence she saw there, so at odds with his gentle hold on her.

"It got better from there." She curved her lips into a smile for his sake. "I went to live with the Murphys."

"You were happy?"

"I was safe. They were good people, they just never loved me. They weren't mean. Just indifferent."

"I wish I could reach back and undo what happened to you, but I can't and you can't," Walsh said.

"No, I can't." She kept her eyes on her feet, barely visible in the darkness. She flexed her toes, curling them to hold on to the last of her courage. "And when I'm in a roomful of people like that, I just can't help thinking I shouldn't be there. There's TJ, and the foster homes, and…Walsh, those people in there come from the best families and went to the best schools. Wear the best clothes. I come from nothing. Literally nothing."

Walsh reached behind her ear, pulling out the orchid lodged there in her tousled knot of curls.

"You wear flowers in your hair a lot."

She blinked and nodded, unsure what this had to do with what she had just shared.

"Which flower is your favorite?" He stroked the velvety petals of the flower he held.

"The orchid." She didn't even have to think about it.

"What would you say an orchid needs to grow?"

"Um, soil, water, sunlight." She rattled off the list, trying to read the inscrutable expression on his face.

"Those are optimal conditions for growing, right?"

"I suppose so." She frowned, unable to wrench her gaze away from the fragile flower cuddled in his strong hand.

"What would you call an orchid that sprang up out of thin air?" He leaned forward to look into her eyes, so close she could feel his breath on her own lips. "A flower that had no soil, no roots, the worst conditions to grow in, but just sprouted out of thin air, beautiful and exotic and perfect?"

She shrugged, dazed and unable to assemble words. His impassioned description and the heat of his eyes mesmerized her.

"I'd call it a miracle." Walsh bathed the words in tenderness, sliding a finger down her neck like it was a delicate stem.

"Kerris, your childhood was a nightmare sometimes, but you managed to become this amazing woman. This smart, independent, compassionate, ambitious person who drives old ladies home and cries for little girls she barely knows. Your past haunts you, but it hasn't twisted you, it hasn't ruined you. If anything, it's made you a stronger person. That's a miracle. *You*'re the miracle, baby."

She closed her eyes at his sweet endearment, feeling it wrap around her nerve endings like a blanket. And then his arms twined around her, bindings for wounds left too long unattended.

One Sunday at the Murphys' church, Mt. Olive Baptist, the preacher talked about healing by the laying on of hands. She had scoffed at the idea, as she did so many of his ridiculous notions. But tonight she *believed*. Believed in Walsh. His hands made soothing tracks up and over her back, suffusing every pore with warmth, starting from her center and working its way to her extremities. To the tips of her toes and fingers.

She wasn't sure when the tears began, or how long she wept into his once-crisp shirt. She only knew that with each stroke of his hand on her back, another layer of pain, another layer of shame, fell away, until she was bathed in the waters of her healing, baptized in her own tears. Made new. Made whole. It was such an unfamiliar feeling that she had to search for the emptiness and dirtiness she had carried with her since TJ stole her innocence.

It wasn't there.

She raised her head, staring at him. Tears wet his cheeks, too. She trailed her fingers down the carved planes of his face, tipping her head to the side with a watery smile.

"What did you do to me?"

This man had reset the broken bones in minutes, during one conversation in a dimly lit gazebo. He smiled, reaching behind her where he had laid the orchid, replacing it in her hair.

"Feel better?"

"You could say that." An understatement.

She felt lighter, cleaner than she had since she was ten years old. While she had been nestled in the protective circle of his arms, the world had faded, a blurry reality they could hide from. Now the cooler air of the dying night raised goose flesh on her arms, and she remembered. Remembered Cam. Remembered Sofie. She needed to get away from Walsh, away from these moments that could so easily muddy the path she needed to take.

She stood, smoothing her wrinkled dress.

"We'd better get back in before Sofie sends out a search party."

"Sofie?" Walsh lowered both brows, confusion crowding out the warm tenderness she had toasted in moments before. "Why would Sofie be looking for us? If anything, Cam's the one looking."

"You're probably right about that." She turned to leave the gazebo and this strange and wonderful interlude.

"Hey." Walsh took her elbow gently, turning her back toward him. "Can I ask you something?"

She nodded without hesitation, sure that there could be no subject more awkward than the one they'd just discussed.

"Are you planning to marry Cam?"

Well…maybe there could be *one* topic as awkward.

"Um, why do you ask? I know you're his friend, but—"

"Don't do it." He squatted from his superior height until he could pierce her eyes with his. "He's not right for you, and you're not right for him. You're not meant for each other."

"Meant for each other? You mean like destiny? Fate? Soul mate kind of stuff?"

"You don't believe in that?" He didn't take his eyes off her face.

"No, I don't." She steeled herself against the sweetness left over from the moments they had shared. "I believe in making choices. Every time I've been left at the mercy of fate, or destiny, it's ended badly for me. So excuse me if I decide to take one of the most important decisions of my life into my own hands. Not wait for 'fate' to deliver some nonexistent soul mate to me."

"That's mighty cynical of you."

"Hearing my story, you don't think I should be cynical?"

"Hearing your story and knowing you're *not* cynical is what I love about you." His voice was so soft and sure. "It took faith, belief, hope—something for you to press through what you experienced to be who you are."

Kerris remembered hope. She'd hoped TJ would not come back to her room, that he would leave her alone, but he had come again and again and again, each time peeling away her illusions and pillaging her girlhood.

She tugged to free her arm, but Walsh didn't let go.

"What do you feel when Cam kisses you?" Walsh backed up his demand with the heat of his eyes.

"That's none of your bus—"

"What do you *feel*?" He tightened his fingers around her elbow and held her hostage to his intensity.

"I won't talk about this with you."

"So you can be honest with me about the most traumatic thing that ever happened to you, but you can't tell me how you feel when Cam kisses you?"

Kerris looked away from the unrelenting heat of his eyes chasing every emotion across her face.

"It's fine."

The silence of the gazebo swallowed her words almost before she'd even said them. She heard the inadequacy of it. The word "fine" lay flaccid beside the sensations she'd experienced with Walsh in that hospital room. She didn't have to look at Walsh's face to see him remembering. He dropped her elbow, his fingers curling into his palms, like he had to stop himself from touching her. From reminding her how it had been.

"That's not how it's supposed to be with the person you marry." Walsh left space around each word as if that would help her understand.

"Maybe not for you, or for other people, but that's how it is for me. I just don't think I have the capacity to be affected that way." She looked back into his face, silently daring him to call her a liar. "I've always accepted that what happened with

TJ just turned a switch off in me. Not that I won't be intimate with my husband, but…"

"That's not fair to Cam, because his switch has not been turned *off*." Walsh brushed a hand across his eyes, evicting a heavy breath from his mouth. "He deserves someone who'll love him the way he loves her, want him the way he wants her. I know for a fact Cam feels more than 'fine' when he thinks about making love to you."

Heated blood stormed Kerris's cheeks. Despite the fact that she had just shared her most closely guarded secrets with this man, his candor on this particular subject embarrassed her. And his persuasions were pointless. Her decision on whether or not to marry Cam would not hinge on their sexual chemistry. Cam wanted whatever she had to give, and she could live with what she felt for Cam.

What she had with Walsh…it was emotion and feeling and passion. All the things she couldn't trust to sustain her for the long haul. Those things could be gone as quickly as they flared to life. And he would never consider someone like her to start the dynasty everyone expected of him. She wanted forever, not a fleeting attraction.

"Let's go on in." She turned her back on him and placed one foot on the first step out of the gazebo, not bothering to address his last statement.

"So you've never talked to Cam about what happened with TJ?"

His question petrified her, left her afraid to even move or breathe with him at her back. The silence puffed up with all the evasions she could offer instead of the awkward truth.

"No. You're the first person I've talked to about it since it happened."

"Why me?" His voice was soft, but insistent, pinioning her arms and legs to the spot where she stood.

"I'm not sure."

"Do me a favor." His voice hardened and bounced off her troubled mind like pebbles against a windowpane. "Figure that out before you marry my best friend."

She looked over her shoulder, lost for a moment in his unwavering stare. She refused to acknowledge the heat that flared between them. Without another word, she crossed the lawn as quickly as she could, hoping he would not follow.

* * *

Walsh watched Kerris cross the yard, his stomach a cauldron of heating, stirring emotions. He shouldn't have followed her when he saw her slip through those French doors. He could tell himself what he told her. That he'd just been concerned, but the truth was an ugly thing he owed himself. He'd wanted to be with her alone and unguarded. Even as disgusted as he was with himself, he would have chosen these last few moments with her over every Bennett holding he stood to inherit.

He sat down on the gazebo bench, leaning his elbows on his knees and dropping his head into his hands. There was too much information to process. What she'd been through. That monster had touched her, hurt her. The primal beast inside him pulled against the restraining chain of civilized behavior. Not just because of the abuse she'd suffered, but at the thought of Kerris marrying Cam. He knew in his gut that would be disastrous for them all, but he didn't know how to stop it without ruining the most important relationships in his life.

He shook his head, twisting his lips in self-mockery. How ironic that she derided fate, soul mates, and destiny. Hadn't he held similar views? Hadn't he always assumed he'd just marry the girl he enjoyed the most in bed? Someone who'd be a good mother to his children and the arm candy he'd need to impress his exclusive social circle? Someone to whom he could remain faithful, given how his father had disrespected his mother with his blatant infidelity. That idea was so tepid beside this hurricane of feeling for Kerris.

Meeting her rocked every notion he'd held about love and marriage. How could he explain the instant recognition he'd felt for her? The confusion of feeling he'd wrestled with all summer crystallized into something so frightening he could barely breathe as it permeated his consciousness. His heart had known, and his head was just now catching up.

Kerris was his.

Despite the differences in their backgrounds—the advantages he'd grown up with and she had never known, the family he'd practically been smothered by and the gaping void in her life where familial love should have been—despite everything about them that was opposite, they fit.

The kiss they'd shared in the hospital had been more than

"fine." It had been consuming, flaming, desperate. To hear that she didn't experience a measure of that passion with Cam humbled yet confounded him. It angered him to think she would settle for less. That she would turn her back on something so rare. Fear wrapped steely fingers around his throat, constricting his breath. If she accepted Cam's proposal tonight, it would set them on a course of inevitable destruction.

"Dammit." He scrambled down the gazebo steps, racing across the lawn and into the house. "Sorry, Kerris. I can't let you do it."

Chapter Fifteen

Hey, I was wondering where you were," Cam said when Kerris returned to his side and took his hand. "Ker, this is Sebastian. He owns that new gallery on Main we saw a couple of weeks ago."

"Oh, that's a beautiful space." Kerris smiled at the man without really registering his features, still off kilter after her conversation with Walsh. "Did Cam tell you he paints? His work is amazing."

"She has to say that." Cam shrugged, modesty like a rented jacket on his shoulders. "She's my girlfriend."

"You're a lucky man." Sebastian's eyes lingered on Kerris's face. "I've actually seen some of his work. He's very gifted. I was telling him I just got back from Paris. Still the strongest artistic community in the world. Such a convergence of culture and art and expression."

Kerris nodded, her mind only half on the conversation. She wasn't in the mood for Sebastian's pompous posturing.

"Cam, I'm going to the bathroom for a minute." She leaned into his shoulder. "And then maybe we can go?"

"Yeah." Cam bent to kiss the top of her head, whispering in her ear. "We still have a lot to talk about."

Tonight there would be no escape. She knew what her answer should be, but she couldn't imagine "yes" actually coming out of her mouth; that word would burn any bridge that could ever lead to Walsh, but she would say it tonight.

She didn't have to use the bathroom, but needed a few moments to herself. She sat on the lid of the toilet seat, collecting her scattered emotions in a closed stall. She'd thought it strange that a residential bathroom would have stalls, but she realized the Walshes had built this section of the house with entertaining on a grand scale in mind, almost like a reception hall.

Kerris rehearsed the night in her head. Sofie's deliberate needling. Sharing her past with Walsh. Her argument with Walsh about marrying Cam.

What right did Walsh have to care? He wasn't offering her anything, had never hinted at a permanent relationship. A conflagration of sensations sparked between them every time they touched. It was incredible, but it wasn't enough. In the end, it could never be enough for her. And he'd never, *could* never, want anything more with her.

* * *

"Who was that girl dancing with Walsh?"

The voice reaching Kerris through the closed stall door was vaguely familiar.

"Got an extra hairpin, Ard? Which girl?"

That voice Kerris would know anywhere. Sofie.

"Short. Really pretty." Kerris could hear Ardis digging around in her purse, presumably for the hairpin. "Dark hair. She looked familiar."

"She should've looked familiar, she was just cleaning your bathroom this morning. Remember? That's Cam's girlfriend." Sofie laced her voice with the condescending pseudo-pity Kerris was coming to hate. "One of those foster college kids. At one point, I thought the poor thing had a crush on Walsh. Wouldn't that have been pathetic?"

Anger and hurt burned their way up Kerris's throat. She gripped the sides of the toilet seat, wishing Sofie's throat were in her hands.

"What about you and Walsh? You think he'll ever pop the question?" Ardis asked.

"Ouch, careful with that hairpin. It's not a weapon. To answer *your* question, I have to be patient for a little while longer. And then I'll have everything I've been waiting for."

"And what's that?"

"Oh, Walsh's ring, his name, his babies, and his fortune." Sofie's I-was-born-ready laugh slithered over Kerris's nerves. "We've known we'd be together since we were kids."

"Walsh didn't look like he knew tonight when he was dancing with that girl."

"Believe me, he knows I'm the one for him, Ard."

"Why? Because of your trust fund?"

"Honey, Walsh Bennett *is* my trust fund." Sofie's words were slickly coated and smooth. "I mean, not literally. Of course, I have my own money, but he's my future. I don't mind his little flirtations because I know where he'll end up. I've waited this long, and the wait is almost over."

"If you say so."

"I know so, and so docs hc. Walsh and I actually talked tonight about getting married. I gave him permission to sow his wild oats."

Kerris's mouth dropped open, the words pounding into her chest with the force of a wrecking ball.

"Wow, that's big of you," Ardis said, sarcasm evident in her tone.

"He can sow the oats. I'll reap the harvest. Come on. Let's get back to the party."

Kerris clamped her lips against a whimper. Tonight? Before he'd met her in the gazebo he'd talked with Sofie about getting married? Wild oats, huh? That only confirmed what Kerris had known all along. She was good enough to have as an appetizer, but only someone with Sofie's pedigree could be the main dish.

Walsh would never *marry* a girl like Kerris, and more than anything, she wanted a family. Cam was the man for her, and she loved him in her own way. She really did. So what if her heart didn't flutter when she saw him? And who cared if his kisses didn't enflame her?

As soon as she was sure the coast was clear, Kerris poked her head out, walking toward the door, steps heavy but sure.

Cam leaned against the wall, hands buried in his pockets. He straightened as soon as he saw her coming. The uncertainty in his eyes stopped her. With one word, she could wipe it away. She knew it. This was it. Now or never.

"Yes. My answer is yes."

"To what?" Cam frowned before her words completely sank in. "You mean…you're saying…are you—"

"I'll marry you." Kerris tested out a convincing smile, wondering if he had changed his mind.

He disabused her of that notion, scooping her up, his forearms under her bottom. He held her up to look down at him, letting out an exuberant whoop and twirling her around.

"You won't regret it, Ker," he said once they'd finally stopped circling, his expression clearer and lighter than she had ever seen it.

And in that moment, she really believed she had done the right thing.

* * *

"Dude, we need to talk," Walsh said, glad to finally have found Cam after scouring the room for the last ten minutes.

"Can it wait?" A wide grin plastered Cam's face. "I've got news."

"Sure, I guess it can wait, but not too long."

Walsh had to bite the bullet and get his feelings for Kerris out in the open. Better now than later, when it would only be more painful for everyone involved. And the sooner he told Cam, the sooner he could convince Kerris that they were meant for each other, that she shouldn't be so quick to dismiss the notion of soul mates because he was pretty sure that's what they were.

"Don't you want to know my news?" Cam looked like he would combust any minute.

"Shoot." Walsh's patience frayed at the delay.

"She said yes, man."

"Who said yes?" Walsh's blood slowed to a crawl through his veins. His heart punched him from inside.

"Kerris!" Cam hooked his elbow around Walsh's neck. "She's gonna marry me. The ladies have her over there oohing and aahing over the ring. I was gonna ask her tonight anyway, so I had the ring in my pocket. Can you believe that? And she didn't even wait for me to ask. Just said yes."

Walsh nodded, twisting his mouth into a board-stiff smile. The truth of Kerris lost to him forever burned a hole in his mind. It wasn't possible, but he glanced across the room and saw Kerris at the epicenter of a circle of gushing women, all admiring the diamond on her ring finger.

Chapter Sixteen

Where the hell have you been?" Jo's voice snapped at Walsh through the phone.

"Well, hello to you, too, cuz." Walsh had to laugh. Jo was more growl than bite.

"You've been AWOL for the past six weeks, ever since Cam got engaged. You missed the engagement party. You've left *Brad*, that asshole, to plan Cam's bachelor party tonight. Where have you been?"

"Whoa, one question at a time." Walsh's tone noticeably iced over under her rebuke. "You and Mom decided you wanted to get into the wedding planning business, not me. Dad's got me running point on my first acquisition. Your dad has me scoping for a new orphanage in Haiti. I haven't been sitting around with my thumb up my ass, so back off."

"Touch-y." Jo softened her voice a fraction. "Now I can't stop smiling at the image of you with your thumb up your ass. I guess you're excused, but are you on your way?"

"I'll be there, but late. Got drafted into a last-minute meeting. I'll miss most of the rehearsal dinner, but I'll get there as soon as I can."

"Okay. Sorry I lit into you. My caterer is about as smart as paint, and she almost ruined everything. Lobster ravioli, not lobster fettuccini. Geez. There are so many details. It's become such a production."

"Maybe you should've listened to Kerris when she tried to tell you what she wanted."

"What? That little ceremony at the covered bridge?" Jo gave an "oh please" smack of her lips. "Cam has always wanted to get married here in our garden. You know that. I want this to be perfect for him."

"I'm sure it will be." Walsh made sure to sound resigned and distracted. "Look, I need to get back in here for this meeting. I'll see you around nine o'clock or so."

"Good! You'll make it in time for the bachelor party."

Whoopee, Walsh thought, hanging up the phone with more force than necessary. Knowing Brad, there'd be floor to ceiling strippers and a plethora of porn. Not Walsh's speed.

Trisha, Walsh's new assistant, poked her head around the corner into his office.

"Want me to get you on an earlier flight since the Merrist meeting was canceled?"

"No, that's okay." Walsh shifted his eyes from Trisha to the projections displayed on his laptop. "I could use the extra time to catch up on a few things."

"You could make that rehearsal dinner, though, if you catch

the next flight out. There's one leaving for Raleigh-Durham in a couple of hours."

He paused in his typing long enough to flick an annoyed glance her way.

"No, really. Just leave it."

He waved her back to her desk, making sure not to appreciate her departure too much. She really was a feast for the senses. Long legs in her short skirts, heart-shaped ass, breasts full and firm, mocha skin, closely cropped burnished hair. Even aside from his no fraternization policy, he wasn't interested. He was in a funk, a malaise fast approaching depression. Approaching about as fast as tomorrow's wedding.

"Damn." He closed his eyes, pressing the bridge of his nose and running a hand across the back of his neck. "Kerris, why are you doing this?"

The question had ricocheted in his head a million times since his mother's birthday party. He hadn't even tried to corner Kerris, to get her alone and ask what the hell she thought was doing. Even after what had happened in the gazebo, the intimacy they had shared and the tears they had shed over her past, he'd known they still had a long way to go before she would admit what was apparent to him. But this?

He rushed into that ballroom determined to lay all his cards on the table with Cam, even if it destroyed their friendship. He was that certain Kerris was supposed to be his. The shock of Cam's announcement was like a blow to his solar plexus, robbing him of air for precious seconds. And then anger, violent emotion, had flooded in. He congratulated Cam, didn't speak a word to Kerris, and took the stairs up to his room two at a time. Jo followed only minutes later to check on him.

"So this is where you disappeared to," Jo said from the door she'd just opened without invitation. "You're missing the celebration."

"Yeah?" He loaded the monosyllable with enough hostility to put her off, only Jo hadn't ever acknowledged his Keep Off the Grass signs.

"Yeah, Cam was asking where you were." The challenge in Jo's eyes reminded Walsh so much of his mother, he almost got up and docilely followed her back downstairs.

"Not feeling well. I already congratulated Cam. Tell him I'll see him tomorrow."

"But, Walsh—"

"Fuck, Jo! Will you get the hell out? Just go. I can't...I just can't do this right now."

He couldn't bring himself to look up from the threading of the duvet covering his bed. He knew Jo was standing there, probably shocked and trying to figure out what was wrong with him. When he finally glanced up, she looked completely unfazed. He was afraid she already knew what was wrong and had for some time.

That moment came back to him as he deboarded his flight later that evening. He glanced at his watch. Nine o'clock. He had missed the rehearsal dinner, but would still make the bachelor party. At least he wouldn't have to see Kerris.

The disappointment, hurt, and frustration all rested on a bed of anger. Anger at Kerris for not facing what he absolutely knew was between them. Anger at Cam for settling for what Kerris offered instead of the passionate marriage he deserved. Anger at himself, most of all, for letting it all happen. For doing what he'd always done—protected Cam from things that were unpleasant. Jo did it. His mother did it. They all did it; shielded him from harsh realities to somehow make up for the crap he'd suffered during his childhood. It had never been good, but this time it might destroy him and Cam both.

And Kerris.

He dropped his bags in the foyer, overpowered by the almost obnoxious smell of flowers. He walked into the front room and was nearly assaulted by white calla lilies. Lilies?

Which flower is your favorite?

The orchid.

He suspected this wedding was his mother and Jo's creation. He had experienced firsthand their tendency to take over. If it were up to them, he'd be married with a couple of kids by now. Maybe "producing" Cam's wedding would assuage them for a little while.

The grim reality of tomorrow's farce pressed in on him. How the hell was he going to make it through tomorrow's ceremony?

Not a rhetorical question, Bennett. You can't make a fool of yourself. Don't look at her coming down the aisle. Make sure you keep your trap shut when the preacher asks if anyone has a reason these two shouldn't be wed.

Um, yeah, it should be me standing beside her, Rev.

The simpler, truer, impossible answer was that she was…his.

He knew it every time he looked at her and she looked back at him. It had taken him all summer to figure it out, and maybe now she never would.

"Sorry, the front door wasn't closed all the way."

The closest thing Walsh had ever seen to a real life pixie stood in the doorway. Her sharp little bob was dyed the color of plums, and there was something elfin about the shape of her face. He didn't know her, but she seemed familiar.

Based on the little he'd heard from Cam and Kerris, he thought this might be Kerris's roommate and business partner. And they might actually have met a couple of times when everyone was hanging out by the river, but he couldn't be sure. One way to find out.

"Meredith?"

"Yeah, and you're Walsh Bennett, right?" Her wide smile tilted her eyes.

"You're Kerris's friend."

"Yeah, and so are you." She shot him a look spiced with mischief.

Walsh's gaze narrowed at that comment.

"I guess I'm Kerris's friend, too." He kept his tone careful.

"Well, any friend of Cam's is a friend of Kerris's now, I guess." She smiled before gesturing back toward the door. "I'm a little lost. We're staying in the guesthouse tonight, but I didn't see how to get to it? When I saw the front door cracked, I thought somebody could help me."

"Who's staying in the guest house?" Walsh demanded with a quick frown. "You and Kerris?"

"Yeah, since the wedding's here at the house, your mom and Jo thought it made sense."

Not only was Kerris marrying another man in his backyard, now she was spending the eve of her wedding under his roof. Could there be any other forms of torture left before this was all over? He thought about standing at the end of the aisle as Cam's best man, Kerris walking toward him, but not *to* him. He knew that would be the worst torture. Or thinking about their wedding night. Their first child.

Actually, a lifetime of torture lay ahead of him.

"The guesthouse is out back." Every word felt like wood on his tongue. "Is Kerris already here?"

"No, she'll be coming a little later. She, um, needed some time on her own."

"She's okay, though, right?" Walsh glanced over his shoulder at the little nymph following him to the guesthouse.

"Bridal nerves," Meredith said, but Walsh recognized strain when he saw it, and it was all around her forced smile.

Walsh stopped in his tracks and turned to face Meredith, looking her straight in the eye like they'd known each other for years.

"Is she having second thoughts?" He refused to release her startled gaze.

"Did I say that? I didn't say that." Her laugh was light and false.

"Is she sure this is what she wants to do, Meredith? I don't want them making a mistake."

Meredith looked up the distance stretching between her

four eleven and his six three. Walsh saw her open her mouth and close it before anything could come out.

"Kerris loves Cam, Walsh."

Walsh drew a quick breath, disappointment taking up all the space in his chest, leaving him swollen and yet deflated. With the finality of Meredith's words, he had to face it, had to check that ruthless determination that could compel him to take, take, take and apologize later. He felt like a tiger whose prey had disintegrated into thin air.

"Of course." He slipped back into the self-assurance perfected through years of practice. "I've waited a long time for Cam to find someone, and Kerris is a remarkable girl. The guesthouse is right back here. It would've been hard for you to find on your own. I gotta get to Cam's bachelor party."

"Oh, yeah." Meredith's face seemed to relax with his change of topic. "You guys have fun, but not too much fun. The wedding is tomorrow, so take care of our boy."

Walsh set his shoulders at the perfect angle to carry the weight of the world. He'd take care of Cam, all right. Hadn't he always?

Chapter Seventeen

Walsh half stumbled through the front door, reaching out to steady himself against the wall, but it moved under his hand. He was vodka's bitch. Invariably, when things went wrong, he hit the vodka hard. Though they hadn't stocked his favorite, Kauffman—not surprising considering its hefty price tag— he'd made do with whatever swamp water they'd had at the bachelor party. He hadn't drowned any sorrows, though. They were still very much alive, just flailing and sloppy and wet around the edges.

His mind crawled back into the stuffy hotel room Brad had secured for the party. As he'd anticipated, he'd been met with a wall of exposed flesh and cheap lingerie. He got it. It was a bachelor party. He had politely declined every stripper who had approached him, ignoring Brad's goading that he was wasting perfectly good, already-paid-for ass.

He'd had almost no time alone with Cam before he had to go, to get out of there before he confessed everything in a loose-lipped, vodka-laced miasma. He couldn't do that to Cam...could he? Walsh had never seen Cam happier. It was a bone-deep happiness Walsh had taken for granted most of his life. His parents' divorce had been a war zone, but they had fought to ensure he remained a relatively well-adjusted kid. He had always sensed, though, that Cam was braced for an emotional blow, poised for flight. Was Walsh the only one who saw the steel-plated undercarriage of wariness beneath Cam's carefully cultivated nonchalance? Tonight, his eyes had been clear and his face, genuinely open. Cam looked like he'd finally found a home. And it was Kerris.

Without his permission, Walsh's feet took him to the kitchen, through the back door, and down the path to the guesthouse.

How had he gotten here? Not just at the guesthouse, but *here*? In love with his best friend's fiancée, soon-to-be wife? Here, sitting on the sidelines as the woman he'd connected so deeply with married another man? Here, fighting against his every instinct to charge into the guesthouse and compel her with kisses, coerce her with chemistry, and do everything short of abduction to stop this wedding.

He compromised with his inner warrior and settled on the bench beneath the stairs leading up to the guesthouse door. There was a ground-level garage, and the main rooms were on the second floor. He and Cam had sat on this very bench a thousand times under these very stairs, plotting, planning, laughing, confiding, dreaming.

A sound caught his attention, and he noticed Jo walking

toward him from the garden. Probably making some last-minute adjustments to the decorations out there.

"What exactly are you doing, Walsh Bennett?"

"Kinda late for you to still be up and out, isn't it, Jo?"

"I asked you a question." Hands on hips, feet apart, chin lifted high. Maybe Jo was the real warrior of the family. "What are you doing skulking around in the shadows under the guesthouse?"

"Just chilling," he mumbled, too steeped in vodka to be clever.

Jo settled on the bench beside him, laying her head on his shoulder.

"She doesn't belong to you, cuz." Jo wove thorns around the compassion in her whisper. "Don't do it."

Walsh went completely still and quiet. So Jo was as astute as he'd always believed her to be.

"I think I love her." He dropped his head back against the wall, perversely glad to say the words aloud to someone other than himself.

"No, you don't." Jo lifted her head and grabbed his chin, forcing him to meet those penetrating gray eyes. "What you feel is no different from what every other man feels when he sees Kerris. It's called a hard-on, Walsh. Not love."

"You don't know what the hell you're talking about." Walsh wrenched his chin from her tight grip, his tone low and fierce.

"Oh, okay. Don't tell me. You have a connection with her, right?"

"Yeah, I do actually."

"And I guess she's your soul mate or something, right?"

"You don't have to make it sound weird." He rubbed his eyes against the soporific effect of the alcohol.

"Have you ever seen Cam happier?" Jo leaned in to look directly into his bloodshot eyes, not waiting for him to answer. "Let's think about this. You pretty much hit the life lottery, Walsh. Looks, wealth, a great family—minus your dad, of course, who's practically certifiable. Most people would choose your life. Cam got snake eyes. Crappy childhood. Bitch of a mother. Abuse. Shuffled from home to home. No family."

"You can't make up for that, Jo." Walsh leaned forward, elbows to his knees. "I'm guilty of it, too. So is Mom. We all are. We enable, protect, and coddle him to make up for something that won't ever change—his past. And I don't think, especially in this instance, that we're doing him any favors."

"Oh, you are so noble." Sarcasm twisted Jo's pretty face. "You want what's best for Cam. It has nothing to do with the fact that you want to screw his fiancée, right?"

Walsh literally bit his tongue. What could he say? How could he convey that, as selfishly presumptuous as it sounded, he just knew that Kerris was his. That sounded like some circa caveman crap, but it was the truth that hummed through him every time he saw her. He'd tried, but couldn't change it. And the galling thing? He felt like she knew it, too, but wouldn't admit it. Why? What had so thoroughly convinced her that what she'd have with Cam was so much better?

A heavy, uneven tread on the steps over their heads startled them both, their eyes catching and holding. They heard a persistent banging on the guesthouse door before it squeaked open.

"Cam?" Meredith asked, her voice husky with sleep. "What are you doing here? Do you know what time it is?"

"I think around one o'clock." Cam paused and then said the next words in a rush. "I need to see Kerris."

"Are you drunk?"

"Not this time. She's here, right?"

"I'm here." Walsh's gut tightened at the sound of Kerris's voice. "Is everything okay, Cam? It's late."

"I know, baby." His voice dipped a little lower. "I need to speak to you alone."

"Okay. Mer, go on back to sleep."

"Just holler if you need me," Walsh heard Meredith say before the sound of her feet shuffling off reached his ears.

"I had a lap dance tonight." Cam's abrupt confession sounded sharp and clear.

"Okaaaaaay." Walsh could almost picture Kerris's delicate features crinkling with the question before she asked it. "Did it make you realize you're not ready to get married or something?"

"No!" The fierce denial disappointed Walsh. "Just the opposite. I didn't...feel anything. I mean, you know, I'm a guy. So I was aroused."

"I think we can skip certain details." Walsh heard a smile creeping back into Kerris's tired voice.

"I just didn't want us to go into tomorrow with that between us," he mumbled. "Guys were taking pictures and stuff, and I didn't want that to get back to you. For you to think I'd done something wrong. She just sat down and started grinding on me."

"Again with the details, Cam." Kerris's husky laugh made Walsh want to run up the stairs and tickle her sides like he had at the birthday party, so she'd laugh some more.

"I just want you to know I won't hurt you that way." Walsh had never heard Cam so solemn. "I've never been faithful to anybody, Kerris, but I will be to you. I promise."

"I believe you, Cam."

"I love you, Ker."

And then it was quiet. Walsh gripped the edge of the bench, cutting off the blood flow to his fingers. Cam was kissing her. And he had every fucking right, but Walsh wanted to rip his head from his shoulders.

"Time for you to go." Kerris accompanied the admonishment with a laugh. "I've heard it's bad luck to see the bride before the wedding,"

"We already had all our bad luck. Tomorrow's a fresh start for us."

"A fresh start. Yeah." Walsh could hear the smile just beneath her words. "See you in the morning."

"G'night."

It was Cam's last word before he stomped down the stairs over their heads. Hearing Kerris excited about her fresh start with Cam had sobered Walsh. He still believed she was making a mistake marrying Cam with this attraction between them, but hearing his friend's desperate grasp at the happiness that had always eluded him, and was now so close at hand, convinced Walsh that he could not be the reason it slipped away. He blinked a few times, wishing the pain would shift. It felt like a rock lodged under his heart.

He noticed for the first time that Jo had tears in her eyes. She blinked several times, but a few managed to trickle down the keen lines of her face. A realization started unfolding in his mind, at first questioning and then, as he saw her still holding back tears, it hardened into certainty.

"You're in love with Cam," Walsh whispered, awestruck that he had been so close for so long and never seen it. It was skywritten all over his cousin's face.

"That's ridiculous." Jo swiped at a tear, reining her mouth into a stiff line.

"I know what I saw, Jo, so don't try to play me off. I know you."

She was silent, rubbing her palms up and down her slim thighs, biting her lip.

"Why torture yourself planning their wedding?"

"I don't—"

"Please don't insult me," Walsh cut in. "I didn't see it before, but I do now. So why'd you do it?"

She hesitated, closing her eyes before finally speaking.

"Because he deserves to be happy. And she makes him happy."

"Did you ever tell him? There's still time to stop this."

Jo lasered her eyes on him, pointing one long finger in his face.

"I couldn't stop Cam from marrying Kerris now even if

I wanted to, which I don't. I love him, yes, but she makes him happy."

"Why, Jo? Cam loves you!"

"Like a sister, Walsh. He's not attracted to me."

"How do you know?"

"I just know." Jo twisted the ring on her thumb. "Let's leave it at that."

"No, what do you mean?"

"He doesn't see me that way. I put feelers out once or twice. The second time I did it, I wasn't subtle. He didn't speak to me for almost a month." A bitter smile settled around Jo's full mouth. "I finally went to him and apologized for doing anything to give him the wrong impression. I could see the relief on his face. It took a long time for things to get back to normal."

"But if—"

"Look, this is useless. I've accepted it and have moved on."

"That look on your face was not 'moved on,'" Walsh said, more convinced than ever this wedding was a mistake.

He thought this was a love triangle between him, Kerris, and Cam. It had taken on quadrilateral proportions, with Jo adding a new dimension to his fear that this wedding shouldn't happen. But what could he do? He wanted to charge up those stairs Cam had just left, bang on the door, scoop Kerris up, start running to New York, and make a life for the two of them where no one would bother them.

But they would be bothered.

There were too many people he cared about who'd be

left brokenhearted, disappointed, angry, and resentful. Starting with Cam and ending with his own mother.

Walsh could only hope he was wrong about how badly this could turn out. But hope couldn't make things right. The only thing that felt right was him with Kerris, and with each minute ticking toward tomorrow's wedding, Walsh knew there wasn't enough hope in the world to make that happen.

Chapter Eighteen

It's disgusting how beautiful of a bride you are, Kerris." Jo shared a small smile with Kerris in the mirror.

Kerris studied herself as a bride for the first time. The honey gold of her complexion set in ivory satin and tulle snatched her breath. Her full mouth was painted a deep berry, like ripe fruit. Her amber eyes stared back at her. She'd been called beautiful more than once in her life, but now she felt it truly for the first time. She assumed every woman did on her wedding day.

"Cam may run up the aisle to snatch you." Jo said it like a joke, but her face held no levity.

"He's kind of doing that already, isn't he?" Meredith zipped up her chocolate-colored maid-of-honor dress. "Isn't he meeting you halfway?"

"Yeah, he is." Kerris tugged at the neckline, needing something to occupy her. "I didn't have anyone to give me away. He says it reinforces that we'll have each other from now on."

Jo met Kerris's eyes in the mirror again, and this time the

other woman barely caught the tears before they drifted down her cheeks. Kerris knew Jo and Cam were nearly as close as he and Walsh. She must be as happy as a sister would be to finally see Cam settled.

"You love Cam, right, Kerris?" Jo's voice held such emotion, Kerris found herself blinking back tears, too. "You'll take care of him, won't you?"

"Yes, I'll take care of him, Jo, and yes I love him." Kerris felt this vow somehow was just as important as the ones she would exchange with her groom.

"It's time." Jo's smile was a mere pull at the corners of her mouth. "Cam's waiting for you."

"It's time?" Kerris's hand flew to the ivory snood encasing her long, dark fall of hair, the netting barely containing it all.

She had forgone a traditional veil, and was glad to at least feel good about what she was wearing from head to toe, including Iyani's bracelet. She cast one more rueful glance at the cymbidium orchid Jo had insisted wasn't in keeping with the army of lilies they'd ordered, its velvety yellow petals uselessly beautiful. She picked up the bouquet of lilies Jo had selected.

Kerris crossed the few feet of grass to Cam, who waited halfway down the garden aisle to take her to the preacher. Goose bumps broke out over her skin and a cold trickle of perspiration slid down the center of her back. It was early October, and they were experiencing a classic Second Summer. Summer and fall split custody of the weather, yielding defiant bright sunshine and cool air. It wasn't just the light breeze cooling her, though. She looked into Cam's face, so sincere and open and earnest in a way she didn't deserve. Apprehension trembled along her nerve endings like a premonition. This was permanent. This was forever. An irretrievable promise.

Her eyes snapped to the tall, silent man already waiting at the clearing, facing Meredith. She felt the weight of a hundred pairs of eyes. All eyes but Walsh's, which were trained on some point over Meredith's shoulder. Her heart contracted into a tightly muscled ball, frozen between beats. Her feet faltered, causing the tiniest of stumbles.

She looked back at Cam, hating herself for the question unfurling in his blue-gray eyes. She'd always thought of them as thundercloud eyes, not only in color, but the tumult that lay behind them. Ever since she'd accepted his ring, they had been placid and cloudless; they had settled into a peace that had been a long time coming. Her resolve returned. She, whose own parents had not seen her worth, and who had never in all her years as a child inspired one couple to adopt her, brought someone peace. Was necessary to someone's happiness. Walsh had made people happy all his life, and he had an enviable circle of friends and family, people wanting to be with him, to know him, to cater to him. The world was at his feet; he was a charmed prince oblivious to the void she and Cam had lived with their entire lives.

This is right. This is right. This is right.

The rhythm of that chant drowned out the whisper of Walsh's name, a raspy reminder of the closeness, the desire, the rightness she'd felt with him and no one else.

If he had been anyone else. If she had been anyone else.

You don't believe in soul mates?

Walsh had whispered the question in a darkened gazebo, the air thickened with the lingering intimacy of shared nightmares and cleansing tears. She wouldn't leave this choice to her soul, or to her heart, those fickle twins who leaned on the caprice of emotion.

Cam's hand had been extended mere seconds, but long enough for that question in his eyes to fully form. She answered with a sure smile and a firm clasp of fingers. Yes, she would be his only. And he would be hers. She took her cue from Walsh. He had it right. Better not to even look into the green eyes she'd never figured out how to hide from. Her path was before her and she would not stray.

* * *

Walsh settled onto the couch where he'd lost his virginity, in the living room of the guesthouse. He looked down at the cellophane bag that had been thrust into his hands. It was filled with the petals of lilies to toss at the bride and groom as they drove off to their honeymoon.

Their honeymoon.

Walsh's gut pretzeled at the thought of Cam initiating Kerris into lovemaking. He hoped she'd found time to tell him about TJ, and that Cam would be gentle and patient and sensitive and selfless and considerate. All the things Walsh would have been if that privilege had fallen to him.

He clutched the bottle of Kauffman he had found like it

was a rope dangling him over the fires of hell. Walsh knew he'd need plenty of vodka to eradicate the hundreds of images that had tortured him all day. Kerris walking up the aisle to his best friend, like a fairy tale with a tragic ending. Cam's face, lit with joy when he reached back for the ring buried in Walsh's pocket. Kerris's solemn face when she'd promised to love, honor, and obey a man, *a friend*, Walsh wasn't sure could ever be worthy of her. He knew Cam's weaknesses as intimately as his own. What if Cam hurt Kerris as he'd hurt most of the women who had passed through his life? What if he was unfaithful? Unkind?

A growl slid from Walsh's throat, low and vicious. The hurt and anger and confusion he'd held back all day penetrated the wall of self-control set rigidly in place since the sun rose on what felt like the worst day of his life.

He kicked the coffee table in front of him, relishing the pain that shot through his foot and leg. He strode over to the small kitchenette, rifling through the cabinets in search of a tumbler, a plastic cup, anything to drink from. Hell, he'd drink from his shoe if he didn't find something soon. He banged the counter with the palm of his hand before taking a long draw from the bottle, sucking it down inelegantly, rivulets of the liquor sliding into his starched collar.

"Mind sharing?"

Walsh looked over his shoulder, surprised to see Sofie.

"Not in the mood, Sof." He hoped she'd take the hint and clear out before he said something that would hurt her irreparably. "I thought you'd already left."

"I was talking with Jo." Sofie sidled up beside him to run

her long fingers down his arm. "She told me I'd probably find you here."

Thanks, cuz.

"She shouldn't have sent you." He drew another quick swig of the deceptively smooth liquor. "I'm not in the best mood."

"And why's that?" Sofie knit her brows into a beautiful puzzle, looking at him from beneath her heavily mascaraed lashes. "I mean, your best friend just married a lovely girl. They looked so happy. And that toast you gave. It was perfect."

Walsh tightened his lips, remembering the hardest part of the farce. The toast. As the maid of honor, Meredith had shared her best wishes first. Under the cover of the light applause, she'd leaned up to his ear.

"Your turn, big guy." The knowing sympathy in her eyes had jolted him. "You can do this."

"I couldn't tell who you loved the most." Sofie jerked him back to the small guesthouse that still smelled of vanilla and brown sugar. A scent that would haunt him forever. "You were so generous with your words for both of them."

He looked at Sofie, sure that she was sniffing around the truth, trying to figure out something he didn't want her to know. Something no one could ever know.

"I haven't known Kerris long, obviously." Walsh kept his tone neutral and caressed the vodka bottle. "But she makes Cam happy, so I'm happy."

"Yeah, you look real happy." Sofie drenched her words with sarcasm, gesturing to the bottle of vodka.

He walked over to sit on the couch, placing the bottle of

liquor carefully on the coffee table. Control. That was what would get him out of this conversation, with Sofie none the wiser.

"I *am* happy." He forced one of his old rakish grins. "Who doesn't love a wedding? Especially when it isn't yours?"

Sofie crossed over from the kitchenette, her rolling hips and easy stride better suited to the catwalk than the small living room above a garage.

"Weddings make me horny." Her voice was a hot rasp, and she towered over him like a Nordic queen, contemplating a subject she planned to reward handsomely.

"Yeah?" His tone didn't want to give her any ideas, but it looked like she already had them.

"Yeah." She nodded her silvered head, green eyes gleaming with building desire. "You know why?"

She didn't wait for him to ask, but lowered herself onto the couch beside him, leaning in to slip a hot-breathed whisper in his ear.

"I think of how the bride and groom are going to be fucking all night, all day for the next week." Her lips brushed his ear with her words. "I'm pretty sure Kerris was holding out on Cam. There's just something so…innocent about her, don't you think? Like she's never been touched. But Cam'll touch her tonight, won't he? All over her, inside her. Riding her. Doesn't it make you just a little bit horny, too?"

It made him sick to his stomach. He closed his eyes, his jaws wired together with tension. Sofie leaned one perky breast into his shoulder, followed closely by a pale, mile-long leg over his thigh, exposed by the short dress she wore. She grabbed his hand, dragging it under her dress and between her legs.

"Weddings make me so horny, I don't even bother to wear underwear."

She tilted her head as if she hadn't placed his hand on what should be most private. He didn't move a muscle, waiting for desire, repulsion, disgust, passion—anything.

Nothing.

He hated that Kerris had neutered him this way, that he could remain completely numb in such an intimate position with a woman whose picture half the men in America jerked off to at night. Taking his stillness as compliance, Sofie pulled herself up to straddle his lap, her fingers working at the buttons of his stiff white shirt like she could do it with her eyes closed, apparently not noticing or caring that it was the only thing *stiff* in this situation.

He didn't stop her wandering, insisting, deft hands from unzipping his trousers. Sofie was no innocent. She'd been around the block more than once. Blocks in New York, Paris, Milan, LA. Surely in all of her sexual travels, she had figured out how to arouse one physically disinterested male. He looked up into the eagerness of her clear eyes, wanting to ignore the emotion he saw there.

Guilt was a bayonet piercing his gut. This was Sofie, who'd knocked a hole the size of Manhattan in the piñata at his sixth birthday party. Sofie, who'd gone with his family to Disney World the last happy summer of his parents' ill-fated marriage. Sofie, who had cried when he took Greta Von Stratton to the prom instead of her. He knew because Sofie's maid told Sofie's mom, who told his mom, who had told him. He'd pretended not to notice the long looks she had cast over her date's shoulder at him that night. He couldn't do this to Sofie.

"Sof, get off." He gritted the words out, grasping her hips to move her off him.

"No, Walsh." She moved his hands from her hips to cup her ass. "You shouldn't be in here drinking alone. Let me make it better."

Nothing could make it better. Certainly not a quickie with his longtime friend.

"Sofie, I can't take advantage of you this way."

"It's only taking advantage if I don't know what I'm getting into." She leaned down to suckle his earlobe before sitting back up to stare at him. "My eyes are wide open."

Walsh averted his eyes from the vulnerability he saw behind all that bravado. A glimpse of yellow caught and held his attention.

Beneath the table was a single orchid. Discarded, left on the floor, trampled. And he knew that it had been Kerris's first choice, not the lily she'd carried in her bouquet. She'd discarded the choice of her heart, allowed herself to be persuaded by other forces, other factors, other priorities. Just like she'd ruthlessly trampled on the possibilities brewing between them since the first time they'd laid eyes on each other.

Anger surged in his veins, a ruthless battalion squashing the rebel tenderness he felt for Kerris. Squashing the kindness of his refusal when he looked into Sofie's eyes again. He no longer saw the girl he'd grown up with, but the supermodel siren who knew the score. He slid his hands up her thoroughbred thighs, pushing the silk of her dress even higher.

"Why the hell not?"

He possessed the mouth poised over his, ignoring the howl of his darkening soul.

Chapter Nineteen

One Year Later

Walsh opened one eye and then, carefully, the other. Either his head was having contractions, or he was really hungover. In addition to the bass drum echoing inside his mind, whatever he drank last night roiled around in his stomach. He drew a quick, stale breath, fighting back nausea. Worst of all, the night before was a huge, dark, gaping void. The last lucid memory he had was of Sofie dragging him into his bedroom as he'd complained that the party in the living room was getting out of control. He had come home from a late meeting with the Merrist VP only to find Sofie already there directing a caterer on the best placement of canapés.

They needed to have the talk.

They'd been dating for almost a year. She slept at his apartment most nights and had carved out a niche in his closet for a full quarter of her wardrobe. Walsh focused enough to see her silver-blond head lying peacefully on the pillow beside him. He knew they were coming to a fork in their relationship road when the sight of her naked body barely covered by the sheet did nothing for him, even this early, when he pretty much woke up at attention. He kicked himself for letting it go on for as long as it had. After the wedding—

He pressed his swollen eyelids back together. Despite the pounding headache, the thought of Cam married to Kerris made him long for the oblivion of his vodka. He was drinking too much. Fucking too much. Playing too hard. Working even harder. Hoping something would ease the near-constant ache surrounding his heart.

Kerris.

Could he not wake up one morning without thinking of her before even getting out of bed? He shoved the thought of her aside, focusing on the svelte form beside him. If he was pushing the envelope, Sofie was ripping it up and tossing the shreds in the air like confetti. She had never been a shy girl, but her meteoric modeling success jettisoned her into another social stratosphere. Unfortunately, as her plus one, he'd been dragged, kicking and screaming, into the spotlight with her.

He hated the attention they received wherever they went. Couldn't get used to finding photographers waiting at the entrance of Bennett Enterprises. Despised their frequent appearances on Page Six. Abhorred the stupid moniker the media had given him once they discovered his philanthropic leanings. *Do-Good.* That was maybe the worst part of all. He wanted out.

Yes, it was time for the talk.

He'd known a romantic relationship would only ruin the friendship they'd always shared, but Sofie had been available, willing, and hungry. And the woman he really wanted...

He and Sofie were both living a little wild. Every night took him further down a path he wasn't sure he wanted to travel anymore. Sure, the liquor, sex, and parties had dulled the pain, but it never went away. And in the process of trying to forget, he was losing too much of himself. He'd probably already damaged his friendship with Sofie beyond repair. He had to end things, and sadly, hurting her was unavoidable. Who knew what boneheaded move he'd make next if he didn't pull himself back into check?

"Mornin'," a husky voice drawled at his back. Walsh stiffened, shocked when a silky thigh slid between his legs from behind. "*You* are something else."

Walsh looked in slow dread over his shoulder, jumping a little when he saw the beautiful face and perfectly rumpled auburn bedhead hair. She rose up on her elbow, a grin stretching across her face.

"Um, who are you and why are you in my bed?" Walsh's voice croaked like a hungover toad's. His vocal cords must have atrophied overnight.

"Wow, you really were out of it, huh?" She gave him a naughty look and laugh. "Your girlfriend wanted to play some three-way. Ring a bell?"

"Honestly, no." Walsh snapped his teeth together over a curse. "Did we, um, did I...I don't remember anything. Maybe you could fill in the blanks?"

"First blank, it seems, is my name." She had the nerve to sound offended. "I'm Lynda."

"Nice to meet you, Lynda. I need you to get the hell outta my bed." Anger roughened Walsh's voice even more.

"You got some nerve. First you pass out before I even get any action—"

"Thank God for that." Walsh celebrated the first good news of the morning. "So we didn't have sex? Nothing personal. I just like to actually remember the women I've had sex with."

"We got pretty far, but I guess all that vodka you kept downing caught up with you." Lynda crinkled her face and rolled her eyes. "You weren't really…um…*up* for the challenge."

Walsh never thought that particular insult would make him happy, but he gulped with relief.

"Mornin', Lynda. Mornin', Walsh," Sofie rasped from the other pillow, her voice still roughened with sleep and liquor. "Walsh, baby, can you fix us some coffee? My head kills."

"Sofie, what the fuck." Walsh spoke as loudly as his pain-addled head would allow. "I get drunk and you pull me into a three-way with some chick?"

"The chick's got a name," Lynda piped up from the rear.

"I told you to get dressed and get out," Walsh said over his shoulder to the half-naked succubus behind him. "I don't even know this woman, and you coerce me into bed with her?"

"You were safe." Sofie sat up, stretching her arms over her head, letting the sheet fall to display her naked breasts. "Check the one-eyed monster. He's covered."

Walsh jerked the covers aside, confirming that he was

completely naked, wearing nothing but an apparently unused condom. Walsh released a breath he'd been caging in his chest. He climbed over Sofie, graceless and awkward, wrapping the sheet around his waist in belated modesty.

He paused by his discarded suit pants on the floor, reaching down to grab his wallet from the pocket. He extracted a hundred-dollar bill, walking back to the bed and offering it to Lynda.

"What's this for? I'm not a prostitute."

"I know." Actually he didn't know for sure, but he needed to placate her into a peaceful, drama-free departure. "I was rude, so let me cover your cab fare, Uber, whatever. It's the least I can do."

Lynda grinned, her open, outstretched palm waiting.

"When you put it that way."

She unfolded her shapely self out of the bed, slid into her jeans, and bent to retrieve her shoes from beneath the bed. He had to admit it was a nice rear view, but he wasn't even tempted. He strolled back toward his awaiting showerheads, praying their powers of rejuvenation would get him in gear. He had a flight to catch.

Aw, damn. To North Carolina.

He wouldn't be able to avoid Kerris. It was Cam's birthday, and there was a party tonight. And it just so happened to coincide with Unc's summons home. Uncle James wanted him to go to Haiti. He was ready to move forward on their plans for an orphanage there.

Walsh was eager to do some globetrotting for the foundation. He'd been benched too long finalizing the Merrist acquisition, which had stopped and stalled so many times over the last year he'd lost count. He had been to Kenya only one other time since Iyani's funeral. He'd actually taken Cam with him. That was a compromise that allowed him to see Cam without having to see Kerris. As a courtesy, he'd invited Kerris along and held his breath until Cam told him she'd refused. Was she avoiding him, too?

Dammit, Kerris, why didn't you listen to me?

His front door slammed. Lynda was gone. Sofie had drifted back off to sleep, and he was headed for a much-needed shower. Walsh stepped under currents of life-giving liquid force coming from every direction.

Seeing Kerris was more dangerous than anything he had done over the last year. He dropped his forehead to the tile wall of the shower, swallowing against the pain of her living with Cam as his wife.

"Nice butt." A pair of pale, slim arms slid around his chest. Fingers twisted and pulled at his nipples.

Behind him, Sofie wore only a mischievous grin. Even naked and sliding to her knees in front of him—nothing.

"Sofie, get up." He tugged her arm as gently as he could, pulling her to her feet.

She fell back to her knees, reaching for him again, that wicked, who's-a-bad-girl gleam still in her eyes.

"I said get up." His voice was sharp, like the water pinging against the shower wall. He closed his eyes against the hurt he'd caused on her face. "I mean, not this morning, Sof. I'm still upset about finding..."

"Lynda," she supplied helpfully, standing up to reach for her shampoo and lathering her long hair. "We didn't actually have a threesome, so chill."

He hated this intimacy with her. The fact that they were having a conversation in his shower. That her shampoo sat proudly beside his body wash as if it belonged there. Her underwear nestled by his boxers in the top drawer. Her shoes sat under his bed. And he had no one to blame but himself.

"Sof, we need to talk."

"Okay, so talk."

"No, not that kind of talk. A real, grown-up talk."

"Can we talk on the plane?" She rinsed the shampoo from her hair, blocking one of his showerheads. "Are we on the Bennett plane?"

"No. Dad has it in Hong Kong." Walsh tried to keep his tone even. He really did. "I don't remember inviting you to go with me to North Carolina."

"Walsh, we're together." Her hands slowed their lathering. "I don't need an invitation, do I? And Trish can get me on the flight easily enough."

"I want to go alone." He stepped out of the shower, as much to get away from her as to get dressed.

"I bet you do," she said, low enough for the water to almost drown her out.

"What'd you say?" He reached for a fluffy towel and glanced back at her, still in the shower.

"I can understand you wanting to go alone." Sofie amended what Walsh knew he had heard. "I just have a little break before I have to be in Paris, so I thought we could spend it together. Besides, I haven't seen your family in ages. Not since the wedding."

He dried off and got dressed, barely paying attention to what he put on or tossed into the personalized Louis Vuitton luggage his mother had given him a few Christmases ago. Not seeing his mother had been the hardest part of staying away from Rivermont. Guilt settled hot and heavy in his chest.

This was the first year since his parents' divorce that he'd spent so little time with her. Even though his father had insisted on custody when he was growing up, wanting him to have a New York private school education, Walsh saw his mother several times each month, and spent every summer with her, traipsing all over the world to Walsh Foundation camps and orphanages.

"I love your Pegase." Sofie entered the bedroom and eyed his roll-on. She slipped on a silk robe from his closet.

"I'm taking that with me," Walsh lied, extending a hand for the black silk robe he rarely wore.

"Oh, I…I've never seen you wear it, so I thought it was okay." She handed it to him and slipped on one of his T-shirts instead, inhaling. "You always smell so good, babe."

"Thanks." Every word reminded him how deep her feelings went, and how much this breakup would hurt her. They had been friends and he had screwed it up with sex.

"Look, Sof, I need to go, but we really have to talk when I get back."

"Well, I was gonna drive you to the airport." Sofie scrambled to slip on the designer jeans she'd worn last night. "Lemme just find my keys. I know they're somewhere around here."

"Don't bother." He slapped his watch on. "Pierce is taking me."

"Who's Pierce?" She paused in her search for the keys.

"My dad's driver."

"Oh, well, I um, guess I'll see you when I get back from Paris." She deflated like last week's party balloon. "If you don't mind, I'm gonna hang here for a little bit then."

He did mind. He wanted her to go to her own overpriced apartment and vacate his when he wasn't here, but these were the small intimacies he'd allowed over the last year. He couldn't snatch them all back because he'd had an epiphany waking up with a strange woman in his bed.

"Whatever." What was he? A thirteen-year-old girl now? "I'll wait for Pierce in the lobby."

"Wait." Sofie grabbed his wrist. "I don't even get a good-bye kiss?"

By all rights, he should be pouncing on Sofie at every opportunity. Five eleven. Body most women could achieve only through surgical enhancement. Blond hair down to here, and legs up to there. He leaned down and kissed her, knowing this might be the last time.

"Mmmmmm." She pressed her perfectly perky breasts into his chest. "I wish we had more time so I could send you off properly."

What could he say to that?

"I'll see you when you get back from Paris, Sof."

"K, I love you."

He saw see the vulnerability in her eyes. He couldn't fake it this morning. He nodded once, brushing past her, hurrying to the door. As much as he didn't want her, she still deserved better than this.

She was in love with a real asshole.

Chapter Twenty

The dreams are getting worse, Cam." Kerris poured fabric softener into the washing machine, pointing to the basket behind Cam on the dryer. "Could you pass that to me?"

"I told you I've got it under control, babe." He passed her the basket, a stiff smile on his face and a frown on his forehead.

"Sweetie, you were screaming last night." She reached for his hand. "And crying."

"I wasn't crying." Cam jerked his hand away like she was a hot stove.

"Okay, maybe you weren't crying." Kerris turned away to open the dryer, giving him the privacy he needed to compose himself. "But you were definitely upset."

"Did I..." Cam leaned his hip against the washing machine, training his eyes on his scuffed boots. "Did I say anything?"

"I couldn't make it out." Kerris frowned, reaching again to hold his hand. He let her. "Maybe you should talk to someone."

"Pffft. What, like a therapist?" Exasperation twisted Cam's handsome face. "I'm not some circus freak."

"I didn't say you were. Just talk to someone. If not a therapist, or me, maybe Jo."

"Or Walsh."

His name fell like a tree into the washroom.

"Oh, I didn't think about Walsh since he hasn't been around much."

Her voice was even, right? She sounded normal?

"He's coming to the party tonight."

Kerris forced her face into submission, not allowing it to show surprise or concern.

"You didn't tell me Walsh was coming."

Kerris leaned into the dryer, retrieving warm towels and giving her face time to recover from the shock that she'd be seeing Walsh for the first time after so long.

"That's not a problem, is it?"

Did Cam watch her closer? Was she paranoid?

"No, of course not. I hope I have enough food."

Cam laughed, grabbing her from behind and pulling her out of the dryer.

"Walsh is a big guy, but he doesn't eat *that* much."

"No, of course not." She tried to laugh, too, and must have come close enough. "I thought maybe he wouldn't be coming alone?"

Cam hoisted her onto the dryer, making her squeal. He nudged her denim-clad thighs open to stand between them, leaning in to nuzzle her neck.

"Only him, I think." Cam freed the buttons of her blouse, slipping in to caress her breast with a possessive hand. Kerris leaned into his palm, begging her body to respond the way it had with Walsh. Guilt and shame clenched her muscles tight, ruining any chance of arousal.

It wasn't that she didn't enjoy sex with her husband. It was fine. Better than she'd ever hoped after what had happened with TJ. And on good days, she could set her guilt aside long enough to enjoy the closeness between her and Cam. If she'd never experienced the lava rush of liquid fire that invaded her body at the mere brush of Walsh's mouth, it would have been…fine. She wouldn't have known it could be like that. That compulsive wanting, needing, longing, that connection of soul through a thin layer of skin.

Sitting on the dryer, she closed her eyes against the remembered sensations, shamed that her body was melting from the inside, not because of Cam's touch, but from the memory of Walsh's kiss. She knew that would be an unconscionable betrayal, to make love to her husband with the fire stoked by her memory of another man. She pushed Cam away, gentling the rejection with a smile before sliding down from the dryer.

"Baby, not now." She gave him a quick kiss on his perfect mouth. "I have a million things to do for the party tonight."

"Sorry, babe." Cam kissed her neck, drawing the skin into his mouth, sucking hard.

Kerris pulled back, her hand flying to her neck.

"What are you doing? Did you just give me a hickey?"

"Probably." He watched her, mouth smug and eyes satisfied.

"I've marked you, babe. Everyone will know you're mine."

"This isn't high school." She stepped past him and down the hall to the bathroom, inspecting the already-forming bruise on her neck. "How embarrassing."

"Why? We're married. People know we fuck."

"Language, Cam." She rolled her eyes at his crudity. "You have the worst potty mouth."

"Potty mouth?" He barked his amusement, leaning over her shoulder and catching her eyes in the mirror. "When we have kids you can get on me for cussing."

Kerris's irritation dissolved when he mentioned children. She'd made her choice. She was Cam's "only." She belonged to someone, and he belonged to her. And one day, they would have a family. It was her greatest desire. They both wanted to start a little tribe of people they'd do better by than their parents had done by them. She was carving out the life she'd always wanted.

She walked through the cottage door a few hours later, juggling grocery bags and reaching for keys. Hearing steps behind her, she glanced over her shoulder.

"Jo, you're just in time. Could you grab this bag before it falls?"

"Sure thing." Jo smiled, grabbing the tottering recyclable bag. "Is all this food for tonight?"

"Yeah. Of all things, Cam wanted Mexican for his birthday. So I'm making tamales, quesadillas, enchiladas, and my soon-to-be-famous guac."

"Sounds delish."

Kerris noticed Jo had let her dark hair grow out some, the angles of the bob softening and settling on her shoulders. She followed Kerris through to the kitchen, admiration clear in her silvery gray eyes.

"Kerris, you have really transformed this place."

"Thank you."

Kerris ran pleased eyes over the warm tones of the kitchen. The granite countertops, stainless steel appliances, and colorful backsplash seamlessly integrated modernity into the cottage's old-fashioned charm.

She and Meredith had pillaged every peddler's market, antique shop, and high-end thrift store in the greater Triangle area and beyond. They'd had the best time redecorating the lovely cottage, updating it without destroying its character.

Kristeene had given her and Cam the cottage as a wedding present, making it the first home she had ever owned. That's what she loved most.

Kerris put the groceries away, leaving out the things she needed to start Cam's birthday dinner.

"Your aunt Kris couldn't have given us a better wedding gift."

Jo's face clouded, her smile slipping. She lowered her lashes, running her fingernail along the newly installed granite countertop.

"Is everything okay, Jo?"

Kerris's heartbeat seemed to pause along with her hand, which was poised over a jar of chiles. She'd grown up waiting for something bad to happen. Maybe she had overactive Spidey senses, but Jo's expression made them tingle.

"I'm a little worried about Aunt Kris." Jo's fingers drummed an anxious cadence on the counter.

"Is she sick or something?" Kerris's heart resumed its regular beat. She opened the chiles, keeping her face as deliberately blank as Jo's had become.

"She's probably tired. I'll make sure she gets some rest. The fall is such a busy season for her, gearing up for all her holiday projects."

"You'd let us know if there was anything wrong, though, right?"

"Sure." Jo looked back at her, the usually clear eyes opaqued with something Kerris couldn't quite identify. "I think, more than anything, she wants to see Walsh. I could kick his ass for staying away so much this year."

Kerris turned to the sink, washing her hands before she started cooking. She acknowledged Jo's remark with only a grunt.

"I know Uncle Martin has him learning the ropes, but damn." Jo leaned a slim hip against the sink, and Kerris felt the weight of the searching look Jo settled on her profile. "If I didn't know better, I'd think he was avoiding Rivermont."

"I'm sure he's just busy." Scrubbing the corn required all of Kerris's attention. "Okay, I'll need cilantro from my herb garden. Excuse me while I run out and grab some."

"No, I'll get going." Kerris still felt Jo's close regard. "I was hoping to see the birthday boy before the party tonight, but we'll catch up later."

Kerris grimaced at the thought of a roomful of people she

barely knew and with whom she would have little in common. They would all spill out into the backyard to the picnic tables and benches she'd borrowed from the rec center. She'd already strung lights through the trees. People could play horseshoes, Xbox, poker—whatever they wanted. Cam hadn't wanted much, just to be surrounded by his friends. That was the least she could do. It would be a pleasure.

She tried to remind herself what a pleasure it was a few hours later when her peaceful cottage had been invaded by Cam's sophomoric friends, mostly male. There were a few women mixed in other than Kerris, Meredith, and Jo, but not many. The testosterone in the air was thick enough to choke a lady. Kerris replenished the beers in the coolers outside, offering a grim smile to a Neanderthal or two along the way.

She dashed back inside to whip up another batch of guacamole. They'd run out twice. She'd asked Cam to grab a couple of tomatoes from the garden for her when he got the chance, but he'd probably gotten caught up in the festivities. She should go get them herself, or snag Meredith when she surfaced from under a pile of men. Her friend loved being a single bee in this male-dominated honeycomb.

Two ripe tomatoes plopped down on the counter beside her. She barely took her eyes off the cilantro she was dicing.

"Thanks, baby." She glanced over her shoulder, almost cutting a finger when she faced Walsh instead of Cam.

Walsh grinned with his arms outstretched. She stumbled toward him, experiencing a shiver and a shock when he pulled her close. The scent that was so distinctly his insinuated itself into her nostrils. The knot of tension she'd been carrying in her stomach ever since she'd heard he was coming liquefied, pureeing her insides until she could barely stand.

"You're welcome…baby." She felt his wide grin in the curve joining her neck and shoulder. "Meredith asked me to bring these in to you."

"I didn't know you were here."

She pulled back, needing some distance to stand the ground she'd gained in the last year. They had not spoken to each other since that night at the gazebo. Hadn't exchanged even a glance since the toast he'd offered at the wedding reception. She'd dreaded this moment for the last year, while perversely looking forward to seeing him again. Now she didn't know what to say. Pretending with him never came easy, and certainly not now. Not after so long. Not when he was here, siphoning all the air from the room.

* * *

The skin on Walsh's face tightened, his smile becoming harder to hold. There was still something just beneath her honeyed skin that he could never ignore. All the defenses he'd built up in the last year and had hoped would hold against her appeal gave way. The familiar scent of vanilla and brown sugar reached his nostrils and made his mouth water.

"Yeah, I've been busy." He adopted a casual tone. No need for her to know he wanted to crush her against him and never let go. "It was impossible to get home."

The quick glance she threw up at him, her fingers pausing in their chopping, told him she might know he was lying. He couldn't care. They had become experts at lying to each other, and consequently to those they loved. He wasn't sure he could stop now, or ever. The truth could destroy them.

"I was disappointed you couldn't come with Cam to Kenya," he said.

"Disappointed?" Confusion pleated her forehead. The chopping stopped altogether. "I thought…"

Her voice trailed off and her frown deepened for a second before clearing. She bit her lip and crossed over to grab an avocado from the windowsill over the sink.

"You thought what?"

"Nothing." She said it too quickly to convince him, offering her own tight smile. "I thought I might be able to get away, but there was too much going on. I couldn't leave Mer."

Something wasn't right.

"Cam and I have never gone that long without seeing each other." Walsh still searched her closed expression for what he was missing. "I was glad he could come. He'd never seen our Kenyan operation. You'd have loved it, too."

"I'm sure I would have," she said, her smile now honest and wistful. "Maybe next time."

"Well, did you at least like the gift I sent?" He was eager to hear what she'd thought of it. He'd seen it and known she would love it.

"Gift?"

"The gift I sent back with Cam?"

The feeling that something wasn't right persisted, squeezing around the muscles of his chest like a giant rubber band.

"Oh, the…the gift." Kerris crossed to the refrigerator, staring at the food packing each shelf. "I loved it, of course."

Silence filled every corner of the small kitchen. Even the refrigerator seemed to hum more quietly as the truth sank in for both of them. Cam had not told her she was invited to Kenya. Cam had not given her the gift Walsh sent. Walsh knew they were reaching the same conclusion.

Cam knew something.

Or suspected.

They had been above board in all of their interactions. Cam would have nothing to point to. Maybe just a sixth sense. It was too much to consider, the possibility that the person they had done so much to protect might end up hurt and disillusioned anyway.

"It was a dashiki."

Walsh's voice was hushed, not with secrets, but with regret. The African dress had been breathtaking and unique, and had immediately reminded him of her. It was probably too extravagant a gift, but Cam seemed fine with it at the time.

"I'm sure it was beautiful." Kerris still faced the refrigerator, one hand braced against the door, head hung toward the floor.

"I thought so." He needed to change the subject. The kitchen was too crowded with unspoken impossibilities. "So how's the vintage business treating you and Meredith?"

They spent a few minutes discussing the ups and downs of starting such a unique venture. She regaled him with a few of her funnier stories about their first year in business, easing the tension, but the truth stayed in the room with them like a chaperone. Cam might not be oblivious to the bond they shared; he might have even lied to keep them apart.

"Here ya go." Kerris passed him an onion. "Make yourself useful if you're gonna invade my kitchen. Speaking of good use, what's this ridiculous nickname you've earned yourself?"

He sliced into an onion, shoulders shaking with suppressed laughter.

"I had nothing to do with that, and if I could get rid of it, believe me I would."

"Do-Good, huh? I don't know what to believe. The nickname, or the rumors I'm hearing that you are definitely being very bad."

He sobered and stopped chopping, seeing the ounce of censure in her eyes, underscored by at least a liter of concern.

"What have you heard?"

"Oh, what everyone else has heard." She wiped a nonexistent spot from her spotless countertop. "That you and Sofie have been living the wild life. Is it true?"

"Yes."

He didn't hesitate, wanting to confess his debauchery to her like a penitent altar boy. Wanting to tell her about all the alcohol and the sex. Even about the threesome he'd escaped by the skin of his teeth. Knowing she'd understand, that one forbearing look from her would scrub his soul clean.

"Why?" She studied him with cautious eyes.

"Don't ask me that." He looked away, soaping the smell of

onions from his hands, unable to free his voice of grimness. "Let's just say I needed to work a few things out of my system and leave it at that."

"I was worried." Her words were a sigh and a confession.

"Don't waste your time worrying about me."

"But it's out of your system?"

"I don't think…it…will ever be out of my system, but I'm better." He captured the braid hanging between her shoulder blades, studying the dark, fire-studded length of it skimming down to her waist, the ends brushing against the leather of her belt. "Your hair's grown. I like it."

She closed her eyes and pushed back against his fist shackling her braid. He could feel the heat of her flesh hidden beneath the clothes. His hand splayed against her back, trapping the braid for a second before grasping it again, wishing he never had to let go.

"What are you two up to?"

Kerris's eyes jerked open, and Walsh set her hair free. She stepped away from the sink, crossing over to Cam in the kitchen doorway to link her hand with one of his. In the other he palmed two small tomatoes.

"Oh, the tomatoes." She took them both, her smile forced. She tipped up to press a kiss to Cam's cheek. "Thank you."

"I see Walsh got here first." Cam's jaw relaxed under her lips.

Walsh stopped himself from flinching at Kerris's deliberate affection, the necessary cruelty of her kiss. He got the message. He knew she'd never do anything to hurt Cam. Never cheat on him. Neither would he, but he looked at her trying not to glance in his direction. He knew it wasn't as easy as she made it seem. He wanted it to be easy—for her and for Cam, which was why he would cut his trip short.

"'Fraid I gotta head back to New York in the morning." Walsh dried his still-damp hands on a nearby dishtowel. "I thought I'd be able to stay until Tuesday, but I'm leaving right after tomorrow's board meeting. A project I've been working on."

"Damn, Walsh." Disappointment clearly marked Cam's even features. "I was hoping we could hang out a little. We haven't since Kenya."

He meant it. Walsh could see that Cam really meant it. He was genuinely sorry they wouldn't get to spend more time together. Cam was fighting for their friendship and fighting for his marriage, both equally important. Their eyes locked across the room, and Walsh hated the open secret that lay between them. He needed Cam in his life as the brother he'd never had. And never seeing Kerris again, even in innocent snatches, would be a lifelong suffocation. He would fight, too, as best he could.

"I know." Walsh focused all his attention on Cam. "I promise we'll catch up when things slow down."

"You've been busy with your supermodel girlfriend." Cam's good-natured taunting hit a sore spot, but Walsh locked his smile in place. "When are you gonna make an honest woman out of Sofie, by the way?"

"Honest woman?" Cam knew him better than anyone. Surely he was joking. "What do you mean?"

"You know. An honest woman. Here comes the bride, all dressed in white. It'll be the wedding of the year."

"What the hell." Walsh let out a short bark of laughter. "Cam, you know I'd never marry Sofie. I know everyone else is deluded, but you know me better than that."

"I tried to tell 'em." Cam aimed his legendary smirk at Kerris. "I told Kerris last summer you'd never marry Sofie, but she, Jo, and everyone else thought you would."

"That's ridiculous." Walsh caught a glimpse of Kerris's stricken face before she turned away and started wiping out the sink, her movements quick and jerky.

Had she thought...?

"Hey, Cam!" Jo yelled from the next room. "We're up. You playing poker, or what?"

"Gotta go whup some ass." Cam rubbed his hands together. "Don't leave without saying good-bye, Walsh. I know what an antisocial bastard you've been lately, so I wouldn't put it past you."

The quiet in the kitchen was broken only by the clanging of dishes as Kerris loaded the dishwasher with less than her typical grace.

"Did you think I was going to marry Sofie?" Walsh tried to keep his tone calm, despite the horrific suspicion blossoming in his mind.

"What? I'm sorry, what'd you say?"

He walked up behind her to cover her hands, halting the methodical loading.

"I asked if you thought I was going to marry Sofie."

"Yeah, everyone did." She looked down at his large hand eclipsing hers. "Does."

"Did you think I was going to marry Sofie the night you got engaged?" His voice roughened like a Brillo pad. "Did you, Kerris?"

Her lips slammed shut, a flimsy gate guarding her emotions. She finally looked up at him.

"Yes."

He stepped back, jerking his hands from hers.

"Was that why you accepted Cam? Because you thought I was going to marry Sofie?"

"I wanted a family, a commitment. Roots." Her words came out in a rush, but she could have said them slowly and they still would make no sense. "Those have always been the most important things to me. I thought…I thought you were going to marry Sofie, and Cam was perfect for me. It was the right choice."

"You honestly believe that? Or are you trying to convince us both because you made a mistake?"

"I didn't make a mistake." Her eyes drifted to the floor. "It was the only choice for me."

"The only—" He sealed his mouth against the words fighting to escape. "You've ruined my friendship with Cam. Made everything so damned complicated—"

"Things are not complicated." She had the nerve to glare at him. "It's very simple. I'm married to Cam, and you're his best friend. Simple."

"Is it simple that I can't stop thinking about you? About the kiss in that hospital room?" He took one step, eating up the small space separating them until he knew she could hear his whisper. "About how you taste? How you feel? Is that *simple*, Kerris?"

"Stop it." She spat the words, looking over his shoulder at the open door.

"Is it simple that I'm in love with you?" He couldn't hold it back, even with the guilt eating him. To be this close to her again after so long was rapture and torture. "'Cause it feels pretty complicated to me."

"Don't say that." Her voice was soft, but fierce. "Don't ever say that again."

"What? The part about me being in love with you?" He narrowed his eyes to frustrated slits. "Should I also not mention that I think you feel the same way about me?"

"You're wrong." She lifted her chin and lowered her brows. "You're a good friend. That's all."

"We'll just ignore this thing between us for the rest of our lives, huh?"

"Marriage is sacred to me." One tear escaped her unblinking eyes. It looked so lonely on her face, Walsh was glad when she swiped it away. "Having children, a family, it's all I've ever wanted."

"We could have had that *together*."

Walsh grabbed her shoulders, being careful of her even in this pressure-cooker moment. The feel of her under his hands was almost too much. He wanted her mouth. He wanted to lick every inch of exposed skin and uncover the rest.

"It's too late." She twisted away from his hungry hands. "I love Cam. You have to believe that."

"You won't make me believe you feel for Cam what you feel with me."

"I can't control what you believe. I can only control myself, and I choose to go forward. You should do the same. Forget all of this."

"Well, you really didn't leave us much choice. Do you know why I stayed away all year?"

She wouldn't look up even when he waited for her to answer.

"I couldn't stand seeing you together, so I stayed away."

"Don't do that."

She reached toward him before dropping her hand to her side. *Wise.* If she touched him, he might combust. He might spread her out on that spotless counter and possess her completely, Cam and the rest of the world be damned.

"Walsh, your mother, Jo, your uncle James and…Cam missed you so much."

"What do you expect me to do? Hang around and watch you and Cam sharing your life together? Watch you have his children? How did you see this playing out?"

"I didn't think in those terms." She drew a deep breath, tremors agitating her small frame. "I didn't think you felt that way about me."

"You're lying." He couldn't let her get away with it. Not now. "You knew there was something between us from the beginning. You ignored it, and then when it flared up in the hospital, you denied it. I was stupid enough to go along with that. It's just as much my fault as yours. I honestly didn't think you'd go through with marrying him, not with that between us."

"There's nothing between us."

"Stop lying to me." He kept his voice low, conscious of the others just down the hall, but his words reverberated through the room like a gong.

"I thought you were marrying Sofie." By now her voice was flat and final. "I didn't see you settling down with someone like me—marriage, commitment, kids. I thought you would ultimately choose her."

"Could you have asked me?" His shoulders slumped under the futility of this discussion. "Could you have checked before you took the irreversible step of marrying my best friend?"

"As long as you know it *is* irreversible." He'd never seen her soft face so stony.

"What do you think I want? An affair? You think I want you to cheat on the man who's been like a brother to me?"

"No. I'm just saying we can't ever talk about this again," she said, her tone low and resolved. "It won't do us any good. We need to…get past it."

"Get past it?" He looked at her like she had grown another head. "If you feel even a fraction of what I feel for you—"

"I don't. Whatever you think you feel or I feel, or whatever, will pass. I'm married."

"Oh, you don't have to remind me of that." The words dissolved on his tongue like a bitter pill. "Just don't expect me to stand around and watch it."

"What do you mean?"

He closed his eyes, exhaling deeply. This was so hard, but he had to do it.

"I don't want to see you, Kerris." It was a lie, but it was the truth, too. "And for a while, I don't think I should see Cam, either. I'll come home when absolutely necessary, but other than that…"

"You're the best friend Cam has." Her voice was wet with tears. "Please don't do that."

"I'm sorry. I just can't do this. Not to Cam. Not to us. It's too much."

Walsh left the kitchen without allowing himself one more look at her. He went down the hall to where Cam was playing cards, gesturing for him to step out onto the privacy of the front porch.

"I'll let you get back to the game in a sec." Walsh shoved his hands deeper into his pockets. "My dad is riding me hard on this acquisition, and I don't know when I'll be home again."

"All right." Walsh could feel Cam searching his face, but he couldn't meet his best friend's eyes. "Sure it's just work?"

"What d'you mean?" Walsh raised one brow to underscore how very sure he was that it was work.

"I mean, I don't know. It seems like you haven't been around all year. Just doesn't feel right."

"Unavoidable." Walsh shrugged for good measure.

"Well, you may be an uncle soon. You'll at least have to come home for that."

"Kerris is pregnant already?" Walsh's gut wrenched at the thought, his eyes burning.

"Not yet, but we've thrown her pills out." Cam smiled sheepishly. "You know how bad she's always wanted kids."

"Yeah." Insides withering, Walsh tried to assemble a smile from the scraps he had left. "I do know that."

"I'll keep you posted."

"You do that." Walsh looked into his friend's face for what felt like the last time.

He knew it wasn't; he hoped that somehow he'd be able to exorcise Kerris from his system and reinsert himself back into Cam's life someday soon. Right now, he couldn't envision a time when the sight of her didn't make his pulse pound and his heart constrict. He wanted to be the one holding her at night and waking up with her in the morning. To be the one laughing with her and taking care of her, spoiling her the way she deserved. He wanted to be the father of her children, and that would never be. The finality of that burned like acid through the blood racing toward his heart.

"I won't be around much for a while." Walsh reached for his wallet. "But if you need me, if you need anything, call me. And if you can't get a hold of me for some reason, I have an assistant now, Trisha McAvery. Her number's on the back of my card."

Cam accepted the proffered card, but his eyes never strayed from Walsh's face.

"You sure everything's okay?"

For a moment, Walsh wanted to spill it all, starting with that first night when he'd seen a tiny angel helping an elderly woman in the parking lot. How his heart had been halfway lost then.

To tell him about the kiss in the hospital, and how he'd never known a kiss could be so sweet and hot and perfect until he'd kissed Kerris that day. About their encounter at the gazebo, and how she had taken a portion of his soul hostage that night when she bared her scars, and he wasn't sure he would ever get it back. He wished he could tell Cam everything, but the time to do that had passed. Nothing would be gained by it now, and it was up to him to do whatever it took to rid his mind and heart of Kerris, at least to the point he could bear to be around them again.

"Everything's fine."

Walsh made his way down the steps with dragging feet, unsure when he'd be able to return.

* * *

"Promise we'll see you again soon." Kristeene Bennett walked Walsh out to where Jo waited in the car, on the phone.

"Mom, I told you Dad's got me working on this acquisition." Walsh set his luggage on the ground, linking his arm through his mother's.

"You don't fool me." She peered up at him, a small, knowing smile playing around her mouth. "Like you're not enjoying every minute of your work with Bennett."

Walsh couldn't suppress the grin that split his face. She did know him after all.

"It's fantastic." He laughed, too, shaking his head. "This company really would be much better off under the Bennett umbrella, Mom, and persuading them to our way of seeing things has been incredibly challenging."

"Just don't forget you're not only your father's son. You're also your mother's."

"Hey, I'm an equal opportunity son." He held up his hands in defense. "Unc is sending me to Haiti in a couple of months to scope out a potential orphanage. With all the corruption there, we may be better off just building our own, putting our people in place, and starting from scratch. Won't know until I get there."

"That's my boy," she said, obviously pleased that he wasn't neglecting his philanthropic responsibilities. A small frown pulled her brows together. "I don't like what I've been hearing, Walsh. I've always liked Sofie, but if she's influencing you to do these things I've heard about in the papers...well, I just don't know about that girl. Although she's Ernest's daughter, and he and your father have been arranging your marriage since kindergarten, I—"

"Stop right there." Walsh couldn't help but groan, his patience so thin on this subject. "If one more person implies that I'm marrying Sofie, I won't be responsible for my actions."

"Well, what are you doing with her?"

"Mom, I honestly don't know." He sighed, running a hand over the back of his neck, trying to ease the tension that had gathered there. "I never should have gotten involved with her."

"Then why did you?"

Walsh looked at the house behind them, looked up at the sky, even at his shoes. Everywhere but into those omniscient eyes.

"It was a mistake, one I wish I could take back. I hate myself for it."

"Hating yourself never gets you anywhere." She reached up, pushing a maverick lock of hair back off his forehead. "All you can do is make it right, ask for forgiveness, and move forward. Stringing her along only makes it worse, son."

"I know. I don't want to do that, but I don't want to hurt her. She's a great girl. Just not the one for me."

"Well, you have to let her know that. As kindly as you can. And you'll know the one when you find her." His mother ran her hand down the side of his face. "Cam did."

Walsh stiffened, the smile congealing on his face. He turned away, picking up his luggage and stowing it in the back of the luxurious midnight blue Land Rover.

"Is this Jo's new Rover?"

He hoped to set his mother on a different course. She was too much of a bloodhound not to sniff out the fissure in his friendship with the man she saw as her second son.

"No, it's actually mine." Her smug smile cajoled him to smile back. "I told Jo if she loves it so much, she needs to get her own. She drives it more than I do. Cam loves it more than both of us combined."

"That's Cam. He loves a good car."

"Walsh." She put her hand on his arm to stop him before he climbed into the passenger seat. "It'll all work out."

"I don't know what you mean." He looked no higher than the patch of ground between them.

"I do know you." Voice quiet, she lifted his chin and forced him to look into her eyes. "You and Cam are like brothers. Nothing's worth ruining that, son."

He froze, horrified that his mother might know about his traitorous heart. Might think, after what his father had put her through, that he would violate anyone's marriage vows.

"What makes you think I'm ruining anything?" He swallowed shame and guilt. "I'm not."

"I know you're not. You're loyal and honest. In that way, you're your mother's son. Don't forget it."

Before he had time to respond, Jo leaned over, pushing the passenger-side door open and bumping Walsh's hip.

"Get in. It won't be my fault if you miss your flight."

"Okay, Mom," Walsh said, glad to escape her piercing stare, but reluctant to leave her again since he wasn't sure when he'd be back.

He reached for her, surprised at how fragile she felt in his arms. He leaned back, noting how her beautiful face had narrowed. There were lines around her eyes and mouth he hadn't noticed before.

"You've lost weight. You taking care of yourself?"

"No." Jo leaned forward from the driver's seat. "She's been losing weight and is tired all the time. I've been trying to convince her to see her doctor, but she won't."

"I'm fine." Kristeene leaned down until she could see into the car. She quelled whatever Jo would have said with a warning glare.

"Mom, please go see your doctor." Walsh felt bad for not noticing the signs before. He'd have to dig with Jo later for more intel. "For me. Please."

"All right, all right." Kristeene patted his shoulder, reaching up to kiss his cheek. "For you, baby. I'll make an appointment this week."

Pulling out of the driveway, Walsh couldn't shake the feeling that things were shifting inevitably on every front of his life. He wanted to make Jo stop the car and turn back around so he could run to his mother, huddle in the safety he'd always found in her as a little boy. She'd always known just what to say, just what to do to make it better. Watching her stately figure getting smaller and smaller in the rearview mirror, he was afraid that this time, even a mother's love couldn't hold back the dark tide he sensed coming.

Chapter Twenty-One

T hank God that's over." Walsh sliced into his filet mignon. Delmonico's made a mean steak.

"Your first acquisition." Martin Bennett raised his glass. "Congratulations. Merrist is now a Bennett holding."

"You knew it would be," Walsh said around the tender, rare meat nearly falling apart in his mouth.

"I know you're my son." Martin flashed his pirate's smile. "Despite all that charity your mother has infected you with, my genes are still under there somewhere."

Walsh snorted, flicking a grudgingly admiring glance across the elegantly set table. The man had a killer instinct, he had to give him that.

"I was hoping to avoid the threat of a hostile takeover," Walsh said, watching his father sip his merlot. "But you were right. They didn't want to tangle with us."

"You'd done a masterful job winning them over already," Martin said, the rare compliment freezing Walsh's hand on its way to deliver another mouthwatering bite of steak. "They just had to be reminded that if it came down to playing dirty, they wouldn't fare well."

"It worked." Walsh shook the shock of his father's approval off and took his next bite. "I'm just glad we got it all sewn up before I leave tomorrow."

"Where are you going again?"

"Haiti, Dad. You know that."

"Oh, yeah, Haiti. St. Tropez? No. Paris? No? Dubai? No. Destination Haiti."

"Don't try to talk me out of it." Walsh set his fork down, giving his father a warning look. "I've busted my ass for the last year getting this Merrist deal done. I'm entitled to some time off."

"Time off?" Martin cocked his head, pretending to consider this alien concept. "I remember time off. I took some once. I found it overrated."

"Well, I'm taking some. And I'm doing with it exactly as I choose."

"And you always choose orphans in the most godforsaken places."

Walsh let his father's chiding roll right off his back.

"Haiti's not 'godforsaken,' and don't complain until I ask you to come along."

"How does your mother feel about this trip to Haiti?" Martin didn't look up from his steak.

"Mom?" Walsh frowned, still disconcerted when his father asked him about his mother after years of stoic silence. "She thinks it's great."

They continued eating for a few moments, each occupied with their own thoughts.

"And she's doing well?" Martin finally asked.

"Who?" Walsh sipped his cabernet sauvignon, trying to pick up the thread of the conversation.

"Your mother, Walsh. For God's sake, keep up."

"She's okay. I haven't been back much lately."

"I noticed. Nothing's ever kept you from Rivermont in the past. Something you avoiding down there?"

"Avoiding?" Walsh's voice was sharp enough to slice through his succulent steak. "I've been working hard on Merrist, Dad. There's nothing to avoid in Rivermont, but now that you mention it, I'm actually concerned about Mom."

"Why? Something wrong?" Martin went still and glanced up from his plate.

"She's lost some weight. Tired. Not feeling her best."

And Jo hadn't given up any information on the ride to the airport, though he'd sensed she'd wanted to.

"What'd the doctor say?"

"She hasn't been to see her doctor," Walsh said, his mouth an exasperated line. "Jo and I have been trying to get her to go."

His father threw his napkin over his plate and drummed his fingers on the linen-covered table.

"That woman never took care of herself."

"Maybe you should have," Walsh said, as shocked to hear the words aloud as his father obviously was.

"What did you say?"

Walsh forged ahead, never one to back down from a

challenge like the one he saw in his father's eyes. "I said maybe you should have taken care of her."

"You don't know what you're talking about. You don't know the whole story. You never did."

"Why did you marry her, Dad?" Walsh asked the question he'd held all these years. "Was she your meal ticket?"

Something violent flared unmistakably in his father's eyes, firing a warning shot across the table.

"I loved your mother." The words barely passed through his father's clenched teeth. "Don't ever forget that. Don't ever question it. It's actually none of your damned business."

"You're right."

Walsh softened his tone, prepared to abandon the topic, even though he wanted to dig deeper and excavate answers to the questions that had plagued his mind since he was thirteen years old.

Martin's phone vibrated on the table, drawing his attention and a subsequent scowl.

"I have to take this. Call Pierce and ask him to bring the car around so we can get back to the office."

He sounded like he actually regretted having to cut the conversation short.

Chapter Twenty-Two

After a long day at the shop, Kerris went into their home office and grabbed her sketchpad. She always seemed to have the energy to create, no matter how tired she was. Her fingers were tracing a pattern of intricate scrollwork on a necklace when the aroma of her favorite Earl Grey tea wafted in. Cam bowed at the waist, offering the delicate cup and saucer.

"Jo wanted to stop through and hang out. Is that okay?"

"Sure, of course." Kerris accepted the tea and Cam's kiss on her hair.

Jo was a regular at the cottage, always popping in. She and Cam often talked even after Kerris went to bed. Kerris couldn't resent the closeness they'd shared for so long.

"Good, since she's bringing Tony's pizza with her." A pleased grin split his face.

"So you get out of cooking again. No credit, mister."

"Do I need credit?" He slid his arms around her and brushed her lips with a tender kiss. "You're mine, right, Kerris? Only mine?"

She pulled back with a frown. She had never broached the Kenya trip or the gift Walsh had sent that Cam never delivered, even though she knew she should. That was a can of worms she didn't want to get anywhere near.

"Why do you always ask that? Have I done anything to make you doubt me?"

"No, of course not." Cam tightened his grip around her waist. "I just...I don't know what I'd do without you now."

"You won't ever have to figure that out, baby." She wished she could chase away the lingering shadows in his beautiful eyes.

"Promise me," he said with swift urgency, pressing her closer still.

"I promise." She didn't even blink, making sure he saw the resolve in her unwavering stare.

He seemed to slump a little, satisfied at what he saw in her face. He dropped a quick kiss on her forehead, making his way over to his desk and opening his laptop.

"I can get a few things done on this design for our new client before the pizza gets here." Cam turned on the small lamp Kerris had found for his desk.

"Me, too." She returned her attention to the pad in front of her.

They both tuned inward, Kerris humming softly under her breath, and Cam slipping in his earphones and bobbing his head to a Tupac classic. He raised his head when the doorbell rang, slipping the buds from his ears and striding to the living room to let Jo in with their pizza. Their laughter drifted back, making Kerris smile. She continued sketching a few more minutes before gathering her tea to head inside. Their laughter tapered off when Jo answered the strident ring of her cell phone.

"Hi, Aunt Kris." The residue of their laughter still colored Jo's voice. "Slow down. I can't understand you. What's wrong with Walsh?"

Kerris couldn't will herself to move. Every fiber strained toward Jo's conversation with Kristeene Bennett.

"But how? Okay, okay. We're on our way." Jo jangled her keys and Kerris heard the door open again.

"What is it?" Kerris heard Cam ask the question, his anxiety clear.

"It's Walsh," Jo said, her tone clipped and strained, tears lubricating the words that cleaved Kerris's heart. "He's been kidnapped."

The crash was probably small, but every shard of the teacup seemed to hit the ground, making Kerris jump. She looked down at the shattered cup at her feet, unsure of when it had slipped from her numb fingers. Her knees buckled, leaving her in a heap on the floor in the midst of the broken pieces. Her heart rattled against her chest. Fear wrapped around her, making every breath short and painful.

Cam walked in, his eyes roving the devastation of Kerris's face.

"You okay, Ker?"

She picked up a few pieces of shattered porcelain, laying them in her palm.

"Be careful." He rushed to the corner for the dustpan she often used to sweep in the office. "You heard?"

"Yeah, I heard," she said, lips barely moving. "What do we know?"

"Only that he was taken in Haiti. We're heading over to Ms. Kris's now," he said, his voice breaking. "I know you're tired. You don't have to come. I can update you later."

Kerris shot a sharp look at her husband. She rose, slowly wiping the last drops of spilled tea from her hands, running her palms down her denim skirt.

"I'm coming, too."

Her flinted tone left no room for challenge. If Cam thought he could keep her away from the Bennett house, she would have to disappoint him.

"Come on then." He ran a finger down the side of her face, wiping away the tear she didn't realize had streaked its way down her cheek.

* * *

Kristeene Bennett was pacing when they walked in, clenching her fists against the flatness of her stomach. She ran a trembling hand to smooth her hair in its already-perfect chignon. She sat down on the leather-covered stool at the kitchen counter.

Kerris trailed Jo and Cam into the kitchen, her face frozen into a mask that hid her thoughts.

"What have we heard?" Jo faced Kristeene, their profiles like two sides of the same coin.

"It's not good." Kristeene walked over to the refrigerator. "Water, lemonade, anything?"

Kerris realized the small rituals of hospitality occupied Kristeene, grounded her in some reality other than this nightmare.

No one was playing along, though. Everyone refused refreshment. Kristeene sighed, turning to prepare jasmine orange tea for herself.

"He was kidnapped yesterday, we think." She steeped her bag in the steamy water. "Locals who knew he was American, and they've requested a ransom. Martin should be here soon to tell us what he knows. He called from the air."

"How are you holding up, Aunt Kris?" Jo kept her eyes on Kristeene's thinner-than-usual face. "Don't lie to me."

"I'm fine." Kristeene diced up the words, narrowing her eyes at Jo. "Don't fuss. It's Walsh we need to worry about now."

"But Aunt Kris—"

"I said stop it." Kristeene hurled the words through the air like a knife. "I'm sorry, Jo. Just…we'll talk about…other things later. I'm worried about Walsh and won't rest until he's home."

"Neither will I," a deep male voice commented from the kitchen doorway.

The man looked so much like Walsh, Kerris almost rubbed her eyes. This had to be Martin Bennett, and he was so much a picture of what Walsh would be in twenty years, Kerris wanted to lift her hand to trace his features, reaching through time to touch Walsh.

"Martin." Kristeene swallowed visibly. She walked over to her ex-husband, stopping just short of actual contact. "What do we know? Was the embassy any help?"

"No help at all." Martin's lips thinned with his disgust. "They have no clue where Walsh is, but I'm working on it."

"Just pay them the ransom, Martin." Kristeene grabbed his sleeve. "Whatever they're asking, just give it to them as soon as you can. Get Walsh back."

"I have no intention of paying any damn ransom." He looked fearlessly into the horror Kerris saw in Kristeene's eyes. "And I am *not* relying on an inept government, Haiti's or ours, to get my son back. You can believe that."

"Martin, this isn't one of your hostile takeovers." Kristeene didn't back down from the man towering over her. If anything, she seemed to rise an inch or so. "This is our son. Don't play the hero. I want him back home, alive. Not in a box."

"You don't think I want him alive, Kris? That's exactly why I refuse to leave my son's safety to bumbling locals."

"Well, what then?" With her hands on her hips, Kristeene's eyes dueled with Martin's. "And this better be good."

"I have some military connections," Martin said, his voice low but confident. "I'll get my son back, and make sure those presumptuous bastards who took him pay the highest price."

"Martin, don't—"

"Don't 'Martin' me. They need to be taught a lesson, and I'm more than happy to do the honors. My contacts are analyzing the information we've received."

"What information?" Jo stepped into the fray for the first time since her uncle arrived.

Martin Bennett looked hesitant, but still hoarded all of the room's oxygen and energy for himself. Just like Walsh did without even trying.

Martin reached into his suit pocket, laying a grainy photo

down on the marble countertop. Kristeene, Jo, Cam, and Kerris moved as one toward the picture, gasping aloud at the grisly sight. Walsh's passport, his expensive Tag Heuer watch, and the bracelet Iyani made for him lay in a pile scattered on the scarred wood of a table. In the center lay a bloodied finger.

"No!" Kristeene turned her face into Martin's chest, clutching the lapels of his impeccable suit. "Oh, God, Martin. No!"

"Kris." Martin rhythmically rubbed comfort into the tense muscles of Kristeene's narrow back. "He's not dead."

"His *finger*, Martin. They've cut off his finger. Oh, God, they'll kill him. Just pay the damn ransom."

"It's exactly because of this that I'm not giving in to their ransom."

Kerris watched Martin put enough distance between him and his ex-wife to look into her face so she could read the confidence in his.

"We can't trust them to do what they say they will, Kris. We just can't."

Jo was weeping softly into Cam's shoulder while he stood completely still, his eyes averted from the ghastly sight of the photo. Kerris leaned in closer, peering at the gruesome picture again, forcing the bile back down her throat long enough to concentrate all of her attention on the disembodied finger.

"That's not his finger," Kerris said, so softly no one acknowledged her comment for a moment.

When her words finally penetrated the chaos surrounding them, Martin Bennett looked at Kerris, sitting at the counter still as a corpse.

"What did you say?" Martin eyed the leather and wood bracelet, exactly like Walsh's, wrapped around Kerris's fragile wrist. "Who are you?"

To my son.

Though he left the words unspoken, Kerris heard them, even if no one else did.

"I...I'm Cam's wife. And Walsh's friend." She tugged on the bracelet that had garnered his full attention. "I said that's not Walsh's finger."

"Of course it is, Kerris." Jo's voice was weary and thick with tears. "You know that's his stuff."

"Yes, it's his stuff." Kerris nodded and then shook her head, equally adamant. "But that's not his finger."

She glanced at Martin Bennett's hand still stroking Kristeene's back in an ancient rhythm of consolation.

"*Those* are Walsh's fingers."

Martin looked over Kristeene's shoulder at his hands, holding them out for inspection. Walsh had his hands, his fingers, and the finger in the photo was too dark, too short, too stubby.

"She's right." Martin's stern mouth hitched, his only concession since he'd walked in the room. "They placed someone else's finger with Walsh's things."

Kristeene turned back toward the photo, studying it more closely before closing her eyes, tears streaking down her sunken cheeks.

"Not his finger," Kristeene mumbled through trembling lips.

"They're playing games, Kris." Martin grabbed her chin and forced her to meet his eyes. To look into his eyes. "Nobody mind-fucks me. Certainly not these pieces of shit. Forget the government. They can't even balance a budget, much less fly under the radar long enough to find my son. We'll work through my contacts."

"Just bring him home." Kristeene leaned forward until her forehead flopped against Martin's broad chest.

Kerris watched, fascinated and bewildered by Martin's tenderness. His hand stroked the soft hair constrained at Kristeene's neck. These two people, whom everyone considered combatants, genuinely cared deeply about each other. The potential for battle crackled between them at every turn, yes, but the intimacy they had fallen back into was like a favorite garment lost at the back of your closet, once rediscovered still fitting, still beloved. Comfortable. Right.

Kerris could almost see Martin galvanize himself, squeezing his ex-wife's hand before scanning the faces turned to him with varying degrees of expectation and despondency. His eyes settled, inexplicably, on Kerris, seated at the counter, resting her hand on the photo of Walsh's effects, like it was a conductor to his soul, sending her strength and resolve and hope to him.

"I'll bring him back," he said to the room, but looking directly into Kerris's eyes, every inch the buccaneer, ready to impose the violence of his will on all who opposed him.

Kerris took heart and almost felt a pang of sympathy for Walsh's captors.

Almost.

Chapter Twenty-Three

*M*_{ange!"}

The gruff voice was followed by a cracked bowl of beans and rice sliding across the floor to Walsh. He gulped back the nausea he had fought for the last two days. He assumed it had been two days. They'd taken his watch and there were no windows in this rank hole. It wasn't the rats and roaches he could hear scurrying around him that caused his stomach to turn and his skin to crawl. They'd shot Paul, the missionary from the orphanage the foundation had considered funding. It was the stench of Paul's corpse beside him that sickened him. In addition to the rot of early-stage decomposition, his body had expelled its final waste, and it puddled around him. The poor man had been in the wrong place at the wrong time.

With the wrong man.

Walsh blinked back useless tears, still reeling from the incomprehensible events that had landed him here. He would not give the thug bastards the satisfaction of one tear. Not one. The emotion almost leaking from his eyes was not from fear of what they'd do to him, though he did feel fear. He kept seeing Camille and Josiah, Paul's wife and young son, in the pictures he had so proudly shown Walsh. Surely by now Camille knew her husband had been kidnapped. What she didn't know, couldn't know, was that it was Walsh's fault.

He had pieced it together in his mind. It was no secret he was from a wealthy family. In addition to his being on a fact-finding mission to identify where they could pour large sums of money, his profile had been pretty high over the last few months. Hell, the kidnappers might even know about his "supermodel" girlfriend and their extravagant lifestyle back in the States. His captors had probably been watching him almost since the beginning, and when he and Paul had struck out to scope land in the mountains for possible expansion, they had made their move, ambushing their car and snatching them both.

Walsh banged the wall behind him with a weakly clasped fist. He had awakened in this darkened, infested pit to find Paul already sitting up beside him against the wall. Both of them had nursed wounds on the backs of their heads.

"These men are mercenaries," Paul had whispered, his eyes holding Walsh's in the dim light. "But they aren't fools. Your family is one of the most wealthy, prominent families in America. They won't kill you. They just want money. We'll get out of this."

The door had burst open, revealing two of the three men

who'd snatched them in broad daylight. Their tirade of French went over Walsh's head, but Paul understood every word.

The tallest pointed to Paul, his voice echoing off the narrow walls.

"Tenir à vos pieds!"

Paul had stood slowly, casting an uncertain glance back at Walsh before unfolding to his full height.

"Faire demi-tour!" Their captor gestured for Paul to face Walsh, his back toward the three men with guns. Paul turned to face him, and Walsh saw a deathly resignation on his face. He spoke in a rush.

"Take care of my fam—"

Paul didn't get to finish, but Walsh knew Camille and Josiah were in his final thoughts when the tallest captor pulled the trigger.

"No!" Walsh heard himself scream as if from a distance, the horror and senselessness of Paul's death stealing his breath.

Paul collapsed, falling forward, eyes stretched open in a death stare, a crater blown into the back of his scalp. Walsh surged to his feet, heedless of the danger, lunging toward the tall man looking at Paul's lifeless form dispassionately. The man raised the barrel of his gun, catching Walsh under the chin. He used the butt of the gun to hit Walsh in the face, slamming his head to the side and leaving a thin trail of blood under his eye.

"Sit down," he said in heavily accented English, his eyes flat and expressionless, as if killing a man didn't even scrape the surface of his soul.

Walsh stumbled back, tripping over Paul's body. He fell

against the wall, sliding down its length into a crouch, resting his head back, wincing when the already-painful wound hit the wall.

"You have seen I am not afraid to kill." The man gestured with his gun toward Paul. "This is not an idle threat. I know your family will pay to get you back. I am not asking for much. One million American dollars. They will pay. You will go free. It is a simple transaction, as long as you cooperate."

Walsh hadn't said a word, only watched, wishing he could make out the man's features. They'd all worn bags over their heads before, and even then, the man's dark face had been hard to see in the dimly lit room.

"Mange!" the man repeated now when Walsh made no move toward the bowl of rice. He couldn't eat with Paul's body there beside him. Complete darkness shrouded the room, but nothing could obscure the image emblazoned in his mind's eye. The image keeping him sane. Keeping him hopeful.

Kerris.

He hoarded every image he'd collected in the short time they'd known each other. As he awaited his fate in that darkened cage, he held on to the hope that he would see her one more time. He hated to think his last words to her would be those he'd spoken in her kitchen. Words of anger, frustration, and resentment.

The scratching of unseen rodents tortured his ears, and the shadows tore at his sanity, but Walsh clung to the depth of the feelings he had for her. Though she'd never be his, she had ignited and illuminated something inside that he knew would make him better. It ennobled him, elevated him, expanded him. He lost the fight against oblivion, succumbing to undernourished exhaustion, clinging to the promise of things to come.

* * *

Walsh pried his eyes open. He glanced at the bowls of untouched rice lining the wall. They kept coming with depressing regularity even though he hadn't eaten even one. Three new bowls meant another day had passed. He must be up to five days in this crevice of hell.

The sound of raised voices, a bastardy of French, Creole, and broken English, roused him. He forced himself to his feet, unsure of what to prepare for. Death. Freedom. At that moment he welcomed either with equal enthusiasm. Two men dressed in camouflage with grease-painted faces, wielding automatic weapons, rushed in.

"Walsh Bennett?" one of them demanded, his eyes rapidly assessing the small, dank space, seemingly unsurprised to see Paul's body at Walsh's feet.

"Yes." Walsh's voice was a wisp of smoke.

"Your father sent us," the other man said. "Come on."

Walsh glanced at Paul's long-still form and guilt welled up inside. Paul would still be alive if it weren't for him. They'd taken his life to prove a point, to gain a psychological edge. Now Camille was a widow and Josiah, fatherless.

"We have to bring him with us," Walsh managed to say, nodding toward Paul.

The men exchanged a quick look of disbelief before swiveling that look to Walsh. He planted his feet and hardened his expression. This was the least he could do.

"He has a wife and son." With a look Walsh dared them to challenge him, straightening his back despite the ache. "We're taking him home."

Chapter Twenty-Four

Walsh was home.

Kerris had managed to avoid seeing him since he'd returned from Haiti a few days ago, but Cam and Jo wanted to throw a "we're glad your ass didn't die" party at the cottage. As much as she had hoped for Walsh's rescue, she did not want to see him. She couldn't trust herself not to throw her arms around his neck and rain kisses all over his face. Just to feel him, solid and alive. He could never be hers, and she could never be his, but to think of him dead or harmed was more than she could bear.

She wouldn't see him alone tonight. She might be able to control herself, but she couldn't fight them both, and in her heart she knew his defenses would be like hers—low and weak. They had so much to celebrate, but she had a bad feeling about tonight. As hard as she tried, it wasn't a feeling she could shake.

* * *

A few hours later, the party was in full swing. All the old gang was there, and many people Kerris didn't recognize. She really wasn't sure how they'd ended up hosting the party, but Jo had been insistent that it would not be at Kristeene's house.

"I want Walsh's friends to see that he's okay," Jo had told Cam and Kerris a few days ago. "But I don't want all those people at Aunt Kris's house. She's been through a lot and doesn't need any more stress. She needs to rest."

Kerris laid out more of the wings they'd picked up, arranging little pots of ranch and blue cheese dressing within dipping distance. She paused, remembering Jo voicing similar concerns right before Cam's birthday party. She made a note to ask her if Kristeene Bennett was in good health. She shuddered to think how Cam would take it if anything were wrong with Kristeene. And Walsh—he'd be devastated. On the heels of the kidnapping, she wasn't sure how much more her little family could take.

Family.

She really did think of Jo and Kristeene and even Uncle James as family now. She swallowed the guilty lump in her throat, thinking of Walsh's self-imposed exile from his family for the last year. Even though the circumstances that had brought him home were horrific, at least they would get some time with him.

She made sure nothing needed to be replenished. Everyone seemed to be eating and having a great time. The hostess in her let out a sigh of relief. The woman in her braced for the first sight of Walsh. She needed a few moments to bolster her defenses.

"You okay?" Meredith snatched a wing and a stalk of celery to munch.

Kerris avoided her best friend's sharp-eyed glance.

"Yeah, I'm good."

"You look great."

Meredith gestured to the bright green tunic Kerris wore, falling about mid-thigh over her black leggings. She'd finished it off with black knee-high boots. Peacock feather earrings peeped out from the dark tendrils of hair she'd left falling around her shoulders and down to her waist.

"Thanks." Kerris plucked at the feather earrings dangling by her neck.

"When's Walsh getting here?"

"Um, I don't know." Kerris scoured the room for anything that needed doing, cursing her own efficiency. Everything was perfect. "Soon, I guess."

"And what about Sofie?"

"Who?" Kerris struggled to focus on the conversation.

"Uh…his girlfriend, Sofie?" Meredith's wide eyes and raised brows asked Kerris if she was losing it.

"Oh, yeah. Sofie was on an assignment in Dubai. She's on her way back." Kerris scooped her hair up off her neck and fanned. "Is it hot in here? Maybe I should adjust the temperature."

"Feels fine to me. Besides, you don't want to miss Walsh's arrival."

Kerris wondered what Meredith saw with those eagle eyes.

"Yeah, wouldn't want to miss that." Kerris glanced around the room, wanting the night to be over already.

"Well, speak of the devil and he shall appear." Meredith nodded toward the cottage entrance.

Walsh stood in the small foyer, flanked by Cam and Jo. The simple jeans and navy blue sweater he wore didn't fool anyone. The wealth hid in the details of his expensive watch and Italian shoes. The power lay in the force of his personality and the way he commanded a room just by entering. He shared an easy grin with the people who immediately surrounded him. The party noise reached a joyful crescendo, swelling up and around Kerris, giving her cover to study Walsh with covert concern. Did anyone else notice how his smile strained at the corners? The dark circles under his eyes made them seem greener, though not as bright. Whatever horrors he'd experienced in Haiti had dulled the somber, beautiful eyes that eventually, inevitably, met hers across the room.

It was only an instant. The look that passed between them was like a flare in the pitch of night. Bright. Hot. Sudden and then gone. Her skin heated as if Walsh had kissed her. As if he had caressed her. As if he had possessed her. And maybe he had with one look. Kerris glanced around, searching each face, certain someone had witnessed the moment. So intimate out in the open. All the things she couldn't say and shouldn't feel rose up in her chest, suffocating her from the inside.

"I'll be right back," Kerris said without looking at Meredith, afraid her friend would see all her secrets.

"Where are you going?" Meredith's eyes seemed to peel away layers of skin and see all the way to the bone.

"Just to the office to grab my phone." Kerris pointed to the stack of old albums lining the living room shelves. "If it's up to Cam, we'll listen to his records all night."

"You're going now?" Meredith raised one perfectly plucked brow.

Kerris turned and tossed her words back, feeling the weight of Meredith's probing eyes between her shoulder blades. "Unless you want to hear Marvin Gaye and the Doors all night. We won't even make it to the seventies. I'll be back."

Kerris steadily plodded through the crowded room and toward the screened-in porch. She walked into the office, pulled a cleansing breath into her restricted lungs, and hoped no one had noticed her abrupt departure. She had always considered herself strong, but tonight she was as vulnerable as a tower of toothpicks. One wrong move and everything would tumble.

She leaned against the closed French doors. This was her oasis. Vanilla-scented candles dotted the windowsills and tables, some even scattered on the floor, illuminating the dimly lit room with soft light. She could let her guard down in here for a few minutes.

"And these boots are killing me."

She slipped off the high-heeled boots and even her socks, relishing the cool hardwood under her feet. She pulled out her pad and charcoal pencils, settling into the darkened corner of the window seat. Using the little light reaching her, she sketched the pictures she'd been carrying around in her head, needing something to distract her from that moment. From that man. She heard the French doors open and close, but didn't move or make a sound. From her secluded nook, she watched Walsh walk in and prop himself against the wall, flopping his head back. The sigh he released sounded like he had held it all the way from Haiti and waited for this moment to let it out.

"That bad, huh?" she asked, wondering if he'd recognize his own words from the night in the gazebo.

Walsh opened his eyes, and even though she knew he hadn't known she was here, he wasn't surprised. Whatever force always seemed to draw them together was still at work. Wouldn't leave them alone, even tonight. Especially not tonight.

"Hi." He didn't bother with the smile he'd given everyone else.

"You're the guest of honor." Kerris laid her pad down, sitting up from her lounging position. "Shouldn't you be out there?"

"I needed a minute." He crossed one ankle over the other, looking at the floor instead of at her. "It's a lot."

"Was the party too much too soon?"

"Nah. It's good to see everyone, but it'll take me some time to get back in the swing."

Walsh pushed off the wall and took a few steps in her direction, close enough for her to smell the scent that was his alone, but not close enough to touch. The flickering candles vaguely lit the thinner planes of his face. She winced at the cut below his eye and the angry bruise laying bluish black against his left cheekbone.

She was a danger to herself. That needy, wanting thing

inside her longed to burrow into him and hold on tight. One wrong word, one wrong move could ruin everything. She had to be careful. They could talk about the weather. About global warming. About peace in the Middle East. They could talk about everything except what bubbled under the surface of every word and every look that passed between them.

"It's certainly good to have you home." She tucked away the emotions that would overtake her face if she let them.

"It's good to be home."

He lifted his brows and quirked his mouth as if to mock the inanities varnishing their conversation.

"Are we really going to do this, Kerris? I almost died. Someone *did* die. It was…life-changing. And you want small talk?"

"No, Walsh." Her fingers were a fleshy, twisted mess knotted against her stomach. "Of course not. I just don't know what to say. I'm glad you're okay. I wasn't…Jo said you hadn't wanted to talk to anyone about it. So I didn't want to pry."

"Pry." The one word was measured and careful, but his eyes were reckless. Telling her everything he should not say. Drilling into her heart. "I'd talk to *you*."

She shouldn't. With the sparks crackling between them, she shouldn't. She should wish him well, walk through the French doors back into the party, and find her husband. To stay, to talk, to be the one Walsh confided in, was a recipe for catastrophe. She knew it, but she scooted over anyway, making room for him beside her on the window seat.

He poured out every detail he could recall, along the way fighting back emotion when he spoke of Paul and the family

he'd left behind, Camille and Josiah. Walsh told Kerris he'd
seen Camille before they left Haiti, her eyes bleak and abandoned as she held on to Josiah. She had quietly thanked him
for his empty condolences. He'd already had Trish make sure
all of her financial needs would be more than met, and he had
every intention of doing anything he could for as long as she
needed his help.

"I feel awful for her." Kerris blinked several times, unable to
hide the sheen of tears his words pricked behind her eyelids. "I
can't imagine losing someone you love that way."

Kerris couldn't imagine losing Walsh.

Though the words didn't leave her mouth, her watery eyes
said them. Every fiber of her body screamed them. And she
knew Walsh saw them written on her face. Their eyes caught
and held until his jaw clenched and her nails cut into her
palms. Kerris closed her eyes over the tears sliding down her
cheeks. Walsh cupped her face in both hands, rubbing his
thumbs over her tears. She leaned deeper into the roughness
of his palm. She raised her hand, touching the bruise under
his eyes. She watched her touch affect him. Saw him close
his eyes and shudder when she ran her fingers gently across
the cut on his face. She traced the prominence of his cheekbones and brushed shaking fingers across the firm beauty of
his mouth.

"Kerris."

His breath on her fingers and her name on his lips made her
tremble. She saw it too late. Saw his will to resist topple and fall
around them. Before she could say another word, he pulled her

thumb into his mouth. Past the knuckle and up to the base of her hand. He feathered kisses across her palm and suckled the pulse that pounded in her wrist, laving the raised daisy-shaped scar with his tongue. He dropped her hand only to reach around to her nape and bring her forehead to rest against his own. He fisted his hand in the luxury of hair spilling across her shoulders and down her back. They were silent, both with eyes closed and every cell, every fiber, fixed on the other.

"If anything had happened to you…" She didn't finish the thought, starting another. "I was so scared. We didn't know if…if…All I could think about was how we argued the last time we saw each other."

"I know." He barely moved his lips, but she tasted his minty breath feathering across her mouth. "The thought of seeing you one more time was the only thing that kept me sane. I know this is…nothing, but it saved my life. It was my lifeline when I wasn't sure I'd make it."

Kerris bit her lip until it hurt. This was not *nothing*. It was a betrayal. It was more intimate than anything she had ever shared with anyone, and it shamed her to acknowledge it. Cam had been inside of her, had been her only lover in life. And this was deeper, closer than that? She reached for Walsh's hand, entwining their fingers for a stolen moment before pulling away, guilt ripping through her.

Her husband was down the hall. She *did* love Cam. This was…she didn't know *what* this was. Didn't have language to articulate this desperation, this recognition she had never asked for nor been able to escape. Her emotional lexicography was limited, stumped by the depth of her response to Walsh from the moment they'd met.

"I should go." She glanced up, pulling back. "Good-bye, Walsh."

She leaned in to drop a chaste kiss on his cheek, with every intention of walking through those French doors. But he turned his head, brushing his lips across hers, and they both went still. The sweet, hot memory of the one kiss they had shared paled beside the reality of his lips against hers. With a groan, Kerris pulled the curve of his bottom lip into her mouth, the taste of him a forbidden pleasure she promised herself she would never know again.

His large hands wrapped around her jaw and the delicate bones at the back of her head, thumbs pressing against her chin until her mouth dropped open. He hovered there for seconds, savoring her breath flowing in his mouth in sharp pants before leaning forward. He sucked her bottom lip as she had done his, the kiss an illicit covenant between them. She groaned, pulling his top lip between hers. His tongue plunged in, frantically exploring the roof of her mouth, running over her teeth, bathing the lining of her cheek. It was mere seconds, but the outside world seemed to freeze, allowing them this slice outside of time.

The bright overhead light flaring the room into unnatural brightness shocked them both. Kerris pulled back abruptly, but not soon enough.

"Get your damn hands off my wife, Bennett!"

* * *

Cam crossed the room in a few steps, manacling Kerris's wrist and roughly jerking her behind him. Walsh heard her moan.

"You're hurting her," Walsh said, keeping his tone even.

He could still hear laughter down the hall from the few guests who remained. He wanted to spare Kerris the scene their raised voices would cause.

"Ease up, Cam. It's not what you think."

"Oh, that's good to know because I *thought* I saw your tongue down my wife's throat."

Grit and anger littered Cam's voice. He looked only at Walsh, not even glancing at Kerris. Cam's fury encompassed the three of them, squeezing the air from Walsh's lungs until he wasn't even breathing.

"It was a kiss, Cam." Walsh's calm tone belied the quickened beat of his heart. "It meant nothing."

"Nothing!" The word torpedoed from Cam's mouth. "It's been 'nothing' since the day you met her, hasn't it, Bennett? You wanted my girl that first night and ever since, right? You think I didn't see it? That *everyone* hasn't seen you making a fool of yourself over her?"

There was nothing Walsh could say. It was true. That first night he had been bowled over. Enraptured. Practically oblivious to everyone at that scholars' ceremony except the slender woman Cam still held in a painful grip.

"Nothing to say?" Cam sneered, eyes slitted by anger. "All your life, everything's been handed to you on a silver platter, and I get this one thing. This one thing you want more than anything else and can't have."

"And you made sure you capitalized on that fact. Didn't you?" Walsh unclenched his fists at his side, forcing his breathing to slow. "How's it feel to have guilted your wife into marrying you? You knew how I felt, so you rushed to get her to the altar because you were afraid I'd do something about it."

"Maybe I did," Cam said. Walsh saw Kerris's sharp glance at her husband. "She was mine, Bennett. The only thing I ever had of my own, and you thought you could have her like you have everything else."

"That's not true, Cam." Walsh shook his head slowly. "I knew she was yours. I was attracted to her. That's all."

"Liar!" Cam dropped Kerris's wrist to lunge toward the man who had been like a brother to him.

Kerris quickly slipped between them, taking the brunt of Cam's weight, which knocked her back against Walsh and sandwiched her between them.

"Cam, Walsh still has a concussion." She held him back with her hand on his chest. "Tonight was…wrong, but it was just a kiss. We were talking about the kidnapping, how close Walsh came to dying, and just got…emotional. Nothing more happened and nothing ever will."

Nothing ever will.

The words reverberated through Walsh like a benediction. Though true, it rocked him to the core. Of course she would choose Cam. Her life was here with him. It was the only choice, but it snuffed out an unspoken, impossible hope that had hidden in his heart. That one day, somehow, she would be his. But no. She would do what was right. That was what he loved about her. That line of integrity that ran through her as surely as the river cut through the earth. A force, compelling and pure.

"So here's where the guest of honor disappeared to." Jo strolled through the door, a margarita in her hand, a smile on her face. She took in the tense triangle of Kerris, Cam, and Walsh. The smile froze on her face and then melted. "What's going on?"

"What's going on is that your cousin can't keep his hands to himself." Cam pressed against Kerris's hand, still on his chest, straining toward Walsh again.

"What have you done?" Jo spat at Kerris, her eyes snapping her fury.

"I'm…I'm sorry." Kerris ran the one hand she had free through her hair. "We didn't mean—"

"You didn't mean what, Ker?" Cam looked at her like algae growing on the river. "You slipped and fell into Walsh's arms?"

"No. Cam, just listen to me."

"I'm done listening. I'll deal with you later."

"Don't you hurt her." Walsh's jaw tightened until it ached.

"She's *my* wife, Walsh." Cam pulled Kerris from between them, moving her back behind him. "You don't seem to get that. You're one arrogant, entitled bastard, aren't you?"

"Maybe I am." Walsh stared at Kerris's distraught face over Cam's shoulder.

"You should go, Walsh." Her eyes begged him not to make this any worse.

"I know." But Walsh couldn't look away even now, clearly

seeing the pain and the regret in her eyes. Feeling all of those things, too. "I'm sorry, Kerris. This was my fault."

"Yeah, it was." Anger distorted Cam's handsome face. Disappointment dulled his eyes.

"Let's go." Jo tugged on Walsh's wrist.

"You heard her," Cam said. "Go. And don't come back. We're done, Bennett. Don't come sniffing around my wife. I don't ever wanna see you again."

The pain of a lost brother, of the enmity that tangled like barbed wire between him and the best friend he'd ever had, sliced over the still-throbbing wound of his futile, thwarted love for Kerris. His heart was being ripped from his chest. He rushed over to the door, now desperate to get away.

"I'm going." He wouldn't allow himself even one more glance at Kerris. "I'm sorry. I didn't mean…If you ever need anything—"

"We won't." Cam's eyes were like diamond chips against his tanned skin. "Clear the hell outta here, Bennett."

Walsh and Jo walked through the door leading outside to the backyard instead of back into the party. Walsh refused to respond to Jo's questions and accusations on the way home. He withdrew, holding the taste of Kerris on his lips as long as he could, certain he'd never be that close again.

Chapter Twenty-Five

You fucking whore," Cam snarled, standing over Kerris, who sat completely still on the edge of their bed.

Kerris winced, biting her lip to keep from crying. She knew Cam could be vicious when angered, but she also knew he would not physically harm her. He leaned in, bringing them practically nose to nose. She braced herself.

"Is this how you show me you're my only, Ker?" Cam's blue-gray eyes sparked with rage.

"Cam, if you'd just listen—"

"My best friend. Have you fucked him?"

"Cam, no." Shame weighed heavily, drooping her head until her chin rested on her chest. "It was just a kiss. It shouldn't have happened."

"No, it shouldn't have." Cam tossed the words back at her head like boulders. He paced back and forth.

"It won't happen again," she rushed to say. "We were both emotional talking about Haiti—"

"And why would he talk to you when he's refused to talk to anybody else, even his own mother?" Cam came to a halt to stand in front of her, a tightly held column of wrath.

For the same reason she had talked to him about TJ after years of painful silence. For whatever reason, Walsh had held the key to unlock those painful memories, to heal her wounded soul. And she knew she'd held the key to his. Walsh had been a salve to her hurt, and she had been a salve to his. She couldn't say that to her husband.

She sat in numb silence, waiting for him to spew more venom. She saw his great hurt, the soul-deep laceration she had inflicted tonight. She saw the hard-won, rarely offered trust that Cam had been so stingy with all his life, laying in tatters around them. And she felt low and dirty and unworthy. She deserved his rage.

"You betrayed me." Cam resumed his pacing in the wake of her guilty silence. "With my best friend. He was like a brother to me, and you've killed that."

"I'm sorry."

"You're sorry?" Seething anger bubbled up in the eyes running over her face. "Sorry that you cost me my best friend?" he whispered in her ear, sucking on the tender lobe before continuing.

"Are you sorry you deceived me?" He trailed furious kisses down the downy curve of her neck.

"I didn't deceive you." Kerris shuddered as Cam wove a cocoon of raging intimacy around them. "I made a mistake.

It was thoughtless. I wish I could take it back, but it won't happen again."

"You're damned right it won't happen again." Cam pulled the edge of her tunic back and tongued her collarbone. "You're mine, Kerris."

"Yes, I am." Kerris was quick to agree. Eager to remind him of it. "Cam, please don't forget that. I am *your* wife. I chose you. I love you. We still have our family to build and our future together."

"Oh, there's no doubt we'll have a future together, angel." He laughed against the exposed skin of her neck. "I'll never let you go, Kerris. You know that, right?"

"I don't want to go." She pulled back to look into the shadowed beauty of his face, still mottled with temper. "I want to stay with you."

"Prove it."

"How…what—"

"Take off your clothes." His staccato words cut into the quiet of their bedroom, pelting her nerves.

"Cam, don't do this." She clutched the collar he had already pulled away. "Please don't do this in anger."

"I'm not angry anymore, Kerris." His swiped his expression free of the fury she knew still boiled under his skin. "I've just discovered that seeing another man kissing my wife turns me on."

Kerris gulped, willing to do anything to heal the hurt she saw behind his rage, but afraid he could do irreparable damage to their marriage, more even than what she had done. Sex had never been easy for her. Her twisted history with TJ had made it hard and complicated and scary, but she had overcome the pain of it, had given herself freely to her husband and could find some pleasure in the act.

Cam had always been gentle and considerate. She had told him the story of TJ on their wedding night. He had seen them as two broken spirits coming together to heal each other, finding each other and helping each other. He'd always been tender with her, but there was no tenderness in him now. He folded his arms across the lean muscles of his chest, waiting for her to strip. Wanting to reestablish himself as her husband in the most fundamental way a man could.

Kerris pursed her lips, blinking back tears of shame and hurt, knowing she would not refuse. She tugged at the hem of her tunic, pulling it over her head, exposing her simple black bra. She pulled off the leggings, feeling the greedy slide of his eyes over her nearly naked body. She reached up to the front clasp of the bra, ready to take the next step in this sexual battle of wills where Cam held every advantage. His fingers covered hers, a viperous grin on his too-handsome face.

"I'll take it from here."

He opened the clasp and pushed her back against the coolness of their freshly washed sheets. Kerris closed her eyes, tears streaking her face, making a slow slide into the corners of her mouth and washing away the bittersweet traces of Walsh's kiss.

* * *

"I can't let you run this time, Walsh," Jo said while Walsh tossed clothes into his suitcase with short, tight motions.

"Yeah, try and stop me." He moved forward, ignoring the yawning hole in his chest, refusing to allow the aching emptiness to slow him down. "I gotta get out of Rivermont."

"Walsh, what were you thinking?" Jo, not for the first time since they'd left the cottage, looked at him like he was the class dunce.

"I wasn't exactly thinking."

"Of course you were, only not with your head but with your dick." Anger smelted Jo's gray eyes to hot silver. She leaned forward to poke him in the chest when he strode by.

"Is that what you think?" He stopped, forcing himself to face her.

"That you've lusted after Kerris since day one? I know you have, and now Cam knows it, too."

"Cam has known how I feel about Kerris for a long time." Walsh shook his head, hindsight bringing everything into clear focus. "That's why he rushed her to get married. The night they announced their engagement I was about to tell him how I felt. I should have. I knew this would happen."

"Knew what? That you'd cheat with Kerris? Damn, Walsh, has it gone any further than a kiss?"

"No, it hasn't." He faced his dresser, stretching his arms across its width and gripping the edges. "Kerris would never let it go further than that. She wouldn't have even let it go that far tonight if the circumstances hadn't been so extreme. We were talking, and it just got too intimate. Too close."

"Why would you talk to her about what happened in Haiti when you wouldn't even talk to me or Aunt Kris?" The hardened shell around Jo's voice didn't hide her hurt and confusion.

"I wish I could explain to you what I feel for that woman." He dropped his head to the dresser, wanting to bang his head over and over in punishment for his careless stupidity tonight. "She feels like my other half, Jo."

"You don't believe in that shit."

"I didn't." Walsh raised his head and moved back toward his closet to drag out a duffel bag. "But I do now."

"What's so special about her?"

"She is…" Walsh lost words, coming to a halt in the middle of the room, a shirt dangling from his fingers. "She's pure. There's no subterfuge, no faking. And she's kind, to a fault. She's sensitive to other people's feelings. And to be all of that, to be such a good person, after how her life began, is a miracle."

"Oh, my God, you really do love her." Astonishment swept away the anger on Jo's face.

"Like you didn't know that the night before their wedding," Walsh said through the cage of his gritted teeth. "You ignored it and wanted to make sure we didn't hurt Cam's feelings. Like you always do."

"You broke Cam's heart tonight."

"I know that." Walsh gave free rein to the guilt he'd been suppressing ever since Cam turned on that bright light. "His face…what do you think he's doing to her?"

"I think he's probably screwing her brains out."

"What?" Walsh turned to face her, a frown snatching his brows together.

"Oh, yeah." Jo nodded her certainty. "If I know Cam, and I probably know him even better than you do, he's gonna want to make sure she remembers who her husband is. He's a very sexual man. You know that."

"Stop it."

The image of Cam in bed with Kerris after what she and Walsh had shared for those few moments tonight was a screw slowly being twisted into the surface of his mind by an unrelenting screwdriver.

"I can't...I need...I need you to check on her tomorrow, Jo. Make sure he hasn't hurt her."

"Cam would never hurt a woman. And Kerris is probably willing to do whatever it takes to get back in his good graces."

"Fuck!"

Walsh squeezed the bridge of his nose, wanting more than anything to rush back to the cottage and drag her out of there. He started back toward his closet with new urgency.

"I gotta get out of Rivermont before I do something even worse. You thought tonight was stupid. Just trap me here a few days with those images in my head, and you'll see stupid."

"Walsh, that's what I'm trying to tell you." Jo drew a deep breath, placing a restraining hand on his arm; he was still flinging clothes into his suitcase. "I can't let you run this time."

"I have to." Walsh shook Jo's hand off.

"You need to talk to your mother." Her tone was wall-flat and insistent.

Walsh glanced over his shoulder to stare at his cousin.

"Of course I'll talk to Mom before I leave."

"No, go talk to her right now." Jo swallowed hard, and the tears didn't slide down her face, but they stood in her eyes. "She has something to tell you."

"What do you mean—" Walsh cut the sentence short at the pained emotion on his cousin's pretty face. "What's wrong with Mom?"

"She's in her bedroom." Walsh had never heard Jo's voice so completely devoid of shine. Dull. Matte. Reflecting nothing, not even the turmoil he knew was teeming inside. "Go ask her for yourself."

Walsh prowled down the hall toward his mother's suite of rooms, rapping on the door.

She smiled when she saw Walsh at the door, patting the bed beside her, motioning for him to come sit. She placed the book she was reading pages down.

"Walsh, come in. How was the party?"

Walsh didn't sit, refusing to go through the polite motions.

"Jo says you have something to tell me."

Her smile dissolved. She folded her lips into a taut line, dropping her eyes to the book she had just discarded, running her finger down its spine.

"Did she now?" She blinked several times, not once lifting her eyes to meet Walsh's.

"Mom, stop stalling. What is it?"

She swallowed, closing her eyes briefly before opening them to stare unflinchingly at Walsh.

"I have cancer, and it's bad."

The cartilage around Walsh's knees softened. His heart hiccupped, snatching his breath. All the air left the room. He felt himself suffocating under the force of another unavoidable blow. But nothing could compare to this. There was nothing he could have done to brace himself for the searing pain even the possibility of losing his fearless mother brought.

He dropped to the bed where she waited, her face stoic. Walsh couldn't formulate words to ask the questions he needed answered. A game of Scrabble had been tossed in the air, and every letter of every word was scattered on the floor. No words. Only an earth-shifting silence that left him disoriented and lost.

"It's stomach cancer." She plucked at the downy comforter covering her knees, fingers restless, eyes steady as she told him all she'd been hiding.

"I've been feeling tired for a while, but I'm always busy. So I didn't think too much of it. I'd lost my appetite, but I've never been a big eater. Then I started losing weight. And a few weeks ago, I started bleeding."

"How do we fight it?"

"It's stage four. We're getting a late start."

"What's the next step?"

"Well, they want to get in there and see how bad it is. How much it's spread."

"How soon can we do that?"

"I wanted to tell you first, but you'd just gotten home."

"When did you find out?" Now he couldn't stop asking questions, firing them at her in an unrelenting succession.

"I knew for sure the day you flew out to Haiti."

"You let me go to Haiti knowing this? We've lost weeks."

Walsh blinked back the burn of tears even the word "Haiti" brought to his eyes. Shitty emotion that he could barely swallow back, fight back, hold back. But he would for now.

"Walsh, I couldn't very well tell you on the phone while you waited for your flight. And then, the kidnapping. It's just been…a lot."

"Jo knew this." Anger threaded through the needle of his words. "Jo has known for weeks and she kept it from me?"

Walsh walked over to the door and toward the hall. "Jo, get in here."

Jo was already in the hall, seated on the floor against the wall with her knees up. She met the desperation in Walsh's eyes with tears pooling in hers. Uncle James's wife had died when Jo was so small that Kristeene had been as much her mother as Walsh's. He knew she felt her insides caving under the weight of this fight because he felt it, too. But what he needed now was the fierce strength she had seen in his mother, the strength she had planted in Jo.

"Get up. Come in here."

"Walsh, I can't." Her voice was a shadow of its usual self. "What if…"

"What if what, Jo?" He squatted in front of his cousin, grasping her hands in his. "What if she dies? Right now, based on what I'm hearing, the odds aren't really in our favor. But we'll do everything we can and hope for the best. You ready?"

"No."

"Me neither. Come on."

"What are you going to do?" She gripped the hand he used to pull her to her feet.

"The only thing I *can* do. Stay."

Chapter Twenty-Six

Kerris waited for the elevator doors to open, fidgeting with the bangle she wore, touching her river stone. She had finally started making a few pieces with the rocks she'd gathered from the river the last two years. Cam had complimented her on it this morning before they left for work.

He'd been disconcertingly sweet and gentle after that first night. He had not hurt her, not physically, but he had smudged her soul. She and Cam had not spoken of it again. She remembered the sex they'd had. She couldn't call it lovemaking. When he'd found his release, it was as if he'd emptied a stream of dark emotion into her body, and had also emptied his heart. She had lain there for long moments, afraid to even move. Finally he had wiped her cheeks free of leftover tears.

"I'm sorry," he whispered into her ear, pulling the long dark hair over her naked shoulder and smoothing it down her back. "Did I hurt you?"

She'd shaken her head, but could find no words. He was like a madman she watched warily, afraid his emotional pendulum would swing back into a rage from the eerie calm. She'd held herself stiffly as he lifted her in his arms, walking to the bathroom. He'd put them both in the shower, leaning his back against the tiles, watching her, his eyes slowly clearing of the ominous clouds. She had stood under the warm stream of water, arms limply at her sides, awaiting his next move.

"It was just a kiss, right?" Cam had asked softly, reaching for the shampoo and massaging a dollop into her hair. "It didn't mean anything, right?"

"It was just a kiss." Kerris had nodded her head under his hands. She had wondered if he noticed that she couldn't lie; couldn't bring herself to say it hadn't meant anything.

"Let's forget about it." In his voice she'd heard a warning and a yearning. A warning that it could never happen again, and a yearning that it never had. He'd stroked the wet hair back from her face. "Let's wash it away and watch it go down the drain."

They'd both bent their heads, watching the suds swirl out of sight. She'd known it was childish and even dysfunctional, how he wanted to handle it. To pretend it hadn't happened, but she didn't know another way to go forward, so she watched the soap disappear through the drain. She knew the selective amnesia didn't extend to Walsh. She recognized that she wasn't to mention his name, and she certainly couldn't have any contact with him.

Thus the system they'd worked out to see Kristeene. Kerris walked out of the elevator toward Kristeene's hospital room. Jo had broken the news to them. Kristeene's illness, while heart-breaking, had actually brought Cam and Kerris closer. Cam was grappling with the thought of losing the woman who had been more of a mother to him than his own, and it left him vulnerable and needy. He'd turned to Kerris, and she'd been there for him.

She could only hope someone was there for Walsh, too.

It had been six weeks since the surgery to remove as much of the cancer as possible. Kristeene's physician, Dr. Ravenscroft, had told them how badly the cancer had metastasized, its malignant tentacles stretching into the surrounding organs. Stomach cancer was one of the hardest to catch, and once as advanced as Kristeene's, was hard to defeat. After surgery, chemotherapy, and even some radiation, Kerris could see in Kristeene's eyes that she was tired of fighting. Her heart ached at the thought of that lady warrior vanquished by this merciless disease.

Kristeene had wasted away, declining so rapidly Kerris could barely believe the wraithlike figure sitting up in bed when she visited was the same fierce lady who had grilled her before awarding her the scholarship a few years ago.

Kerris, so absorbed by her own thoughts, didn't look up until it was too late. She slammed into a beautifully scented woman leaving Kristeene's room. The woman's papers spilled onto the floor at their feet. They both dropped to their haunches, scrambling to gather everything.

"I'm so sorry," Kerris said, steadily picking up papers.

"It's okay." The other woman smiled and tilted her head, studying Kerris's face. "Kerris, right?"

"Oh, yeah." Kerris studied the woman's closely cropped auburn waves, smooth brown skin, and killer body. "And you're?"

"Sorry. Trish McAvery. I'm Walsh's assistant. He has a picture of you and your husband on his phone."

"Oh, you're working here, right?"

"Yeah, we're using space in the foundation's office while his mother is sick." Trish rose to her full height. "But Walsh can work from just about anywhere. Most of his meetings are by video and he flies out at least once a week."

"He's not here, is he?"

Kerris primed herself to flee. She couldn't chance seeing him, or being seen with him. She and Cam usually visited during the day when Jo assured them Walsh was at the office.

"No, he left about an hour ago. He forgot these papers and had a meeting he couldn't be late for, so he sent me back for them."

"Are you staying in Rivermont while Walsh is working from here so much?"

"Yeah, I've relocated for the time being." Trish grimaced her distaste.

"I guess it's quite an adjustment, huh?" Kerris smiled at Trish's face. "I mean, I guess Rivermont is really different from New York City."

"Now *that* is an understatement." Trish shifted from one Manolo Blahnik–shod foot to the other, still straightening the disheveled papers. "The shopping alone."

"I've never been to New York, but I can imagine."

Trish eyed Kerris's bright orange vintage pea coat, wide-legged dark wash jeans, and wedge-heeled boots.

"You seem to be managing just fine. That bracelet is sick. You didn't get that from around here, did you?"

"I actually made it myself." Kerris couldn't stop the proud grin taking over her face.

"It's unique." Trish stroked the stone at the center. "I've got a friend in the Fashion District who would kill for pieces like that. You have any more?"

"You really like it?"

"I think it's fantastic. I'm going back to New York for the holidays tomorrow. Let me take that to show my friend. I bet she'd sell your stuff in her shop in SoHo."

"SoHo?" Kerris's jaw dropped from shock before she slammed it shut. "But this…this isn't even that good."

"You telling me your other stuff is even better?"

"I think so." Kerris slipped off the bangle, offering it to Trisha. "Take it."

"Cool." Trish shared a quick smile, reaching for her phone. "Let's exchange numbers, and I can call you when I hear something back."

Trish slipped the phone back into her purse.

"I'm leaving tonight. I almost hate to go with Mrs. Bennett the way she is."

"How *is* she?" Kerris nodded her head toward Kristeene's open door with a concerned frown.

"Not good. She and Walsh met with Dr. Ravenscroft this morning. There's nothing more they can do."

"What do you mean?" Kerris refused to believe what she was hearing, afraid to consider how it would ravage the two men she cared about the most.

"They caught this too late, and just can't get to it fast enough. It's aggressive and has spread to her liver, kidneys, back, lymph nodes. It's literally eating her alive. All they can do now is help her manage the pain."

"No." Kerris felt the sharp sting of tears behind her eyelids. "How did Walsh take it?"

"He went to work." Trish twisted her lips with something approaching contempt. "He's more like his father than I thought."

"Don't misjudge him." Kerris narrowed her eyes at Trish's tone. "He went to work because he had to. If he stops, he'll fall apart. She needs him strong, so he'll be strong. He's not like his father. Work doesn't have him. Money doesn't have him. Power doesn't have Walsh. Walsh has Walsh."

"Oh." Trish raised her brows a curious inch. "You seem to know him very well."

"He's my husband's best friend," Kerris said before changing the subject. "I assume Walsh'll be here for Christmas then."

"Yeah, she wants to be home for Christmas, and Walsh is going to focus on her completely. He's given me time off till the new year. They don't know if she'll…"

Kerris was glad Trisha allowed her words to trail off. She wasn't ready to hear that the doctors weren't sure Kristeene would make it that long.

"You think it's okay if I go in to see her?" Kerris wasn't sure she was prepared to see Kristeene, but knew she needed to.

"I'm sure she'd enjoy the company. Well, Walsh'll be waiting for these papers. I better go."

Kerris hovered at the door to Kristeene's hospital room. She fought back a wave of panic, thinking of Iyani. Sweet Iyani who had fought so valiantly, and lost. And now it appeared that Kristeene's surrender was, though delayed, a foregone conclusion. Death would hover over the holidays.

She pushed the door open inch by inch.

"Can I come in?"

"Kerris," Kristeene whispered around a weak smile. "So glad you came by."

"Cam'll come on his lunch break." Kerris sat in the hard-backed chair beside Kristeene's bed.

"Walsh just left not too long ago." Kristeene pressed her lips together and frowned. "So they still aren't speaking?"

"What?" Kerris played dumb. She hadn't realized it was that obvious Walsh and Cam were avoiding each other. "I don't know what you mean."

Kristeene gave Kerris a long look before extending a thin arm, the bones of her hand prominent from weight loss. Kerris accepted her hand, squeezing it and pulling it to her head, bowing over it like a royal subject to this queenly woman whose compassion had changed her life.

"Kerris, has anyone told you what the doctor said this morning?"

Kerris stiffened, not expecting this direct tack, unprepared to fake or hem or haw. She nodded slowly, raising her head to find Kristeene's knowing eyes on her face.

"The time for lies, hiding, and faking is over." Kristeene lifted Kerris's chin with one finger, forcing her to meet the eyes of a sage. "You love my son. Both of them, actually."

Kerris closed her eyes, hoping the thin layer of protection her eyelids provided would block out the knowledge and, she was certain, the judgment she'd see in Kristeene's eyes.

"Look at me," Kristeene commanded with gentle force, tilting Kerris's chin another centimeter. "I'm not judging you."

"How can you not?" Kerris managed a tearful whisper, swallowing the tide of shame and guilt she couldn't subdue under Kristeene's weary, steady stare.

"Kerris, I wish I had known how you felt about Walsh before you married Cam." Kristeene ran her fingers across the coolness of the sheets on her hospital bed.

"I didn't see Walsh coming. Could never have predicted anyone would make me feel…" Kerris left the words unspoken, but the truth still blared into the silence. "I care about Cam and thought we were perfect for each other. We had so much in common. We made sense. Meeting Walsh made me question everything I'd believed about myself and about my feelings. About what I was capable of feeling."

Kerris paused, swallowing past the shame clogging her throat before she continued.

"Then I saw Walsh with Sofie, and I knew she was the kind of woman for him. That he'd never marry a nobody like me. They made sense as much as Cam and I did. I believed that." Kerris chewed at the corner of her bottom lip. "Has Walsh ever talked to you about me?"

"No, we've never talked about this." Kristeene gave a quick shake of her silk-covered head. "At least not directly."

"You seemed so certain. How did you know?"

"Do you really want me to tell you?"

"You said yourself the time for hiding is over."

"Yes, I believe it is." Kristeene released a heavy sigh. "I'm afraid it's very clear when the two of you are together that there is something between you."

"Is it that obvious?" Kerris moaned and dropped her head into both hands.

"Kerris, the way my son looks at you is like—" Kristeene started, briefly hesitating. "It's like a starved man. It's like he can't bring himself to look at anything else in the room."

Kerris felt her face heating and her hands shaking. She could not believe she was having this conversation with Walsh's mother.

"I had a man look at me that way once." Kristeene's wistful smile was reminiscent of the young beauty she had obviously been.

"Who was it?"

"It was my husband." Kristeene sat up straighter in her bed, leaning into her story. "I was in New York with my family. My father was there for a restaurateur's convention, and I met Martin at a hot dog stand on the street."

"I can't imagine Mr. Bennett eating a hot dog." Kerris's lips twitched at the image of Walsh's impeccably tailored, unyielding father eating from a street vendor.

"Oh, there's a lot you probably can't imagine about my

husband." Kristeene laughed, wincing a little. "We spent every moment we could together in that week I was there."

"What happened?"

"It was like the love you read about in books. Epic. Instant. Perfect."

Kristeene fixed her eyes ahead, but she was obviously seeing a scene years past.

"He had no idea who I was, who my family was. He was so ambitious and driven and self-contained. That ambition frightened me. I was afraid he wouldn't want me for myself, but for all that came with me. I lied to him and told him I was on my own in New York for the first time. At the end of the week, we couldn't imagine life without each other. A week, and it was so deep and like I had known him all my life."

Kerris bit the inside of her jaw until she tasted blood. She knew what that felt like, but she couldn't even nod her head in acknowledgment. It would be too telling, and Kristeene already knew too much.

"We eloped." A defiant grin lit Kristeene's much thinner, but still beautiful face. "And then the trouble started. He was livid when he found out I was one of *those* Walshes. Said everyone would think he'd married me for my money, and that everything he achieved people would assume had been given to him because of my family. It all backfired. He worked so hard to prove it wasn't true that we kind of lost each other. And I only made it worse by suggesting that he'd be able to spend more time with his family if he'd just go work for my father."

"Oh." Having met Martin Bennett, Kerris could imagine how well that had gone over.

"Yes, oh." Kristeene's smile held more regret than humor. "I was so young. I didn't know how to handle a man like Martin. He needs to conquer, to win, to come out on top. He needs the pursuit. And I wanted to take that away from him because everything he pursued took him away from me."

Kristeene blinked several times, obviously staving off tears.

"Eventually, we just lived separate lives." Kristeene reached up to stroke her lustrous hair out of habit, her hand falling listlessly to her side when she encountered the silk scarf hugging her naked scalp.

"I had to raise Walsh. And Martin had to build Bennett Enterprises. He had so much to prove, and none of it had anything to do with us." Kristeene shook her head and looked up at the ceiling. "Oh, he fooled himself that he was doing it for us, but I didn't need any of it. I would have loved that man if he had decided he wanted to sell hot dogs on the street."

Kerris laughed a little, afraid to draw too much attention to herself in case Kristeene stopped. They had grown close, but Kerris suspected Kristeene had never talked about any of this with anyone. It was a precious insight into the tumultuous relationship that had shaped so much about Walsh.

"He was unfaithful, you know." Bitterness swept away the last traces of Kristeene's humor. "With his secretary. What a cliché. And I knew he regretted it. I even understood how it happened. He and I had drifted so far apart, but I never stopped loving him. For him to do that…"

Kerris frowned, dismayed at how upset this discussion was making Kristeene.

"You need to get some rest." Kerris moved to stand and leave so Kristeene could rest.

"No, just let me." Kristeene broke off to press the button that released morphine into her system. "I'll get loopy soon, so we don't have long. Sit down."

Kerris settled back into the seat, shifting under the renewed intensity of Kristeene's eyes.

"You know Walsh is a lot like his father." Kristeene's eyes left Kerris nowhere to hide. "I did my best to temper it, but that boy has his father's DNA as sure as he has mine. I always thought he escaped that single-mindedness, that ability to focus so completely on something he wants. And then I saw him with you."

"Please don't say that." Kerris looked at her hands clutching the sterile bed sheets, unable to meet Kristeene's eyes.

"I didn't really let myself see what it truly was until your wedding day," Kristeene continued as if Kerris hadn't spoken. "He fooled everyone else, but I could see how miserable he was. And then it was too late."

Kristeene's words settled around them like snowflakes, melting into their skin with the iciness of truth, quickly absorbed.

"Walsh is also like me, though," Kristeene said. "He always wants to do what's right. He would never violate anyone's wedding vows."

Kerris shifted in the hard plastic seat, thinking of the kiss Cam had witnessed. They had both lost sight of what was right for a moment, and it had changed everything. The first tear startled her, with a mind of its own, slithering down her cheek, waiting for others to follow.

"Tell me," Kristeene said, her soft voice inviting Kerris's confidence. "Tell me why my boys can't even be in the same room."

And Kerris did. She told her the whole beautiful, gory tale, not leaving out even the most shaming parts. And she told her about that last kiss with Walsh, how it had torn through her preconceived notions of fidelity and love and good and bad, dismantling everything she had always believed about herself.

"And now Cam's acting like nothing happened." Kerris plucked at the sheets on Kristeene's bed. "Like Walsh doesn't even exist. I don't know what to do."

"Can you do this, Kerris?"

"Do what?"

"Can you stay married to Cam feeling what you do for Walsh?"

"Oh, God, I'd never leave Cam." Shock widened Kerris's eyes. "I could never do that to him. After all he's been through? But I don't know how to make it right."

"First of all, figure out your course, and stay true to it." Kristeene's eyes flickered shut, snapping back open before the drug-induced darkness completely crowded out the clarity of her mind. "A girl like you can't live with guilt. You have to feel like you've stayed true. You're like the river."

"I don't know what you mean." Kerris thought the morphine must be kicking in and Kristeene was babbling.

"The river is clean and pure and strong." Kristeene's eyes popped open in one last moment of clarity. "And it's a force of nature. Literally. It cuts through rocks. And once the course was set for that river, there's no changing it. It stays the course. You understand?"

Kerris thought she understood, though she didn't feel clean or pure or strong. Certainly she didn't feel like a force, but she did plan to stay the course. She couldn't live with any other option.

"And, Kerris, you know I'm going home tomorrow." Kristeene's words began to slur as she fought off the lure of sleep.

"Yes, ma'am."

"It's for good," Kristeene whispered, making sure Kerris understood she what she meant.

"Yes, ma'am."

"I want you to make me a promise." Kristeene still slurred, but carefully straightened out each syllable. "Promise that when I'm gone, you'll do everything you can to make it right between my boys."

"I think I'm the last one who could make it right."

"And I think you're the *only* one who can," Kristeene said, her voice pretty firm for someone about to slip into morphine oblivion. "Promise me you'll try."

Kerris looked at this woman who'd given her more than a scholarship. She'd opened doors to another world, to a world where Kerris was positioned to do all of the things she wanted to do. She thought of all the orphans Kristeene Bennett had lived her whole life serving. And now she was just a mother asking for the best Kerris could do for her sons. One natural and one surrogate, but both of her heart.

"I promise."

Chapter Twenty-Seven

Happy New Year!" Walsh chorused along with his mother, Unc, and Jo, all laughing and kissing each other.

They gathered in his mother's suite, all wearing silly party hats and drinking champagne. She had defied the odds. Dr. Ravenscroft hadn't been optimistic that she would make it to the new year, but Christmas had come and gone, and she was still here. Weak and asleep more often than not, but here.

"It's late, Mom." Walsh frowned at the lines of fatigue around his mother's eyes and mouth. "We should all get to sleep."

"The night's still young." Jo pulled off her hat and shook her hair free around her shoulders. "I'm going to a party."

"Cam's New Year's party?" Uncle James sipped his champagne. "He mentioned it yesterday when he came by."

Jo and Walsh locked eyes. If it had been hard for Walsh and Cam to avoid each other at the hospital, it was nearly impossible here at the house. It was a large house, but still. Walsh had gone for a run yesterday, needing an outlet for the massive stress

he'd been under for the last few months and to run off some of
Mrs. Quinton's amazing home-cooked meals. He'd returned,
toeing off his running shoes as soon as he entered the foyer.
He'd sniffed the air, watching Jo come down the stairs.

"You couldn't wait to get me out of the house, could you?"
Walsh had asked.

"What…I don't know what you mean." Jo had avoided
his eyes.

"At least you still have trouble lying to me. You don't have to
sneak around for Cam and Kerris to see Mom."

"How'd you know they were here?"

"I smell her."

"You *smell* her?" Jo had clearly not expected that response.
"Do you hear yourself? Do you know how ridic—"

"Vanilla." He bent down to grab his shoes and turn toward
the stairs. "She wears a vanilla and brown sugar scent."

"Walsh, you have to get her out of your system." Jo caught his
arm. He had one foot on the first step. "What about Sofie?"

"I should never have gone down that road with Sof. At least
now she knows. I ended it a few weeks ago."

"But if you can't have Kerris, then Sofie—"

"I've lost Kerris and you offer me Sofie as a consolation
prize? They're practically a different species."

"You haven't lost Kerris. You never had her."

Walsh thought of Kerris's breath in his mouth, her fingers
stroking his neck urgently. He remembered the satiny roof of
her mouth and the sensual dance of their tongues together. And
he remembered their desperate communion as she'd pressed

her forehead against his, confessing her fear for his life. He'd known that their hearts were connected by a silken thread he might not ever be able to sever.

Never had her? If only Jo knew.

"Yeah, it's Cam's party," Jo said now, collecting the glasses they'd used to toast in the new year. "I'm rolling out."

Neither Kristeene nor Unc asked if Walsh was going. He and his Uncle James had never had one conversation about Kerris, but his uncle would have to be comatose not to recognize the bitter shift in his friendship with Cam.

"Be safe." Unc bent to kiss the top of his daughter's head. "Call if you need a ride home. I don't want you drinking and driving."

"I'll be fine, Dad." Jo smiled against his chest. "Love you. Happy New Year."

Unc smiled down at Jo indulgently, his face changing when he glanced past her to where Kristeene lay half asleep already. Walsh saw his uncle's features tighten. She would take a part of him with her. Hell, she'd take a little of them all.

Jo and Uncle James made their way out of the suite and down the hall, calling their final good nights to Kristeene. Walsh went to gather the cup and saucer by his mother's bed. He straightened, preparing to go when her hand reached out to him, keeping him there.

"Stay." She licked dry lips and closed her eyes briefly before opening them again to look at him with a lifetime of intensity poured into that inch of time.

"Okay." Walsh replaced the china on her bedside table and

crawled up beside her as he had done so many times before, curving his arm around her shoulder. "You want company?"

"No, I want you." Her smile, a paradox of sadness and contentment, squeezed Walsh's heart. "I'm proud of you, son."

"I don't know if I deserve that." Walsh pulled the down comforter higher up around her shoulders. "But thanks."

"I want you to be happy." His mother's eyes rested on Walsh's face. "*Are* you happy?"

Walsh hesitated, not sure how much she knew about the situation with Cam and Kerris. He opted for answering her question with a seemingly unrelated question, a tactic that wouldn't usually work. Maybe with his mother under the influence of morphine, he could get away with it.

"Do you believe in soul mates?" He reached for her hand.

She glanced up at him, her eyes still not letting him get away with anything.

"You know, your father likes to think you come from a long line of warriors," she began, seemingly avoiding a direct answer as deftly as he had done. "That may be true, but you also come from a long line of romantics."

He raised both brows, silently encouraging her to shed some light on the subject.

"Did I ever tell you about your great-great-great-great, oh hell, I can't remember how many greats, but Great-Grandma Maddie?"

"Didn't we use her recipes to start the first Walsh restaurant?"

"Her mother's recipes actually," Kristeene said. "Great-

Grandma Maddie was an octoroon. Do you know what that is?"

Walsh combed his brain for the definition of the word, but didn't think the answer he retrieved made any sense.

"Isn't an octoroon someone who is an eighth Black?" He glanced down at his hands. He might be tan most of the year, but he was definitely white.

"That's right." His mother smirked, obviously enjoying his confusion. "She probably looked almost as white as you or me, but an eighth is all it took for her to be a slave."

"Great-Grandma Maddie was a slave?" Walsh couldn't wrap his head around it, and wasn't sure how that painful history connected with what his family had become.

"She was the master's mistress, Walsh." She tightened her lips around the ugly words. "Their children looked as white as we do."

"So—my great-great-great-great-grandfather was a slave owner?" The thought left a bitter taste in his mouth.

"I'm afraid so. This is the South. Trace our families back far enough, and you're bound to find a few of those. But the story I want to tell you isn't about them. Not about what happened with her and the master. It's about what happened with her and Asher."

"Asher?" Walsh was now completely lost. "Who was Asher?"

A wistful smile broke through the line pain had pulled her mouth into.

"Asher was her second chance. He was her soul mate. He knew the first time he saw her that she was the one."

"Where'd he see her?" Walsh asked, surprised that he was just now hearing this story.

"Lay back." Kristeene motioned for him to stretch out beside her tired, narrowed body. "I'll tell you all about it. Now *this* is a real love story."

* * *

The next morning, Walsh greeted Carmen, the older woman Unc had brought in to help with cleaning a few times a week. She was taking down the Christmas decorations, humming as she worked with great efficiency. Walsh glanced up the stairs toward his mother's room. With her end so obviously near, Walsh felt like he was treading water: not moving forward, not moving back, and barely keeping his head above water. Waiting to swim, afraid he would sink.

Restless, Walsh occupied his hands with the mechanics of making his mother's favorite jasmine orange tea. The familiar aroma wafted through the kitchen, bringing back memories from his childhood. He couldn't remember a time when she hadn't loved her tea. Breakfast every morning in their New York City brownstone. A cup on her nightstand at night, a good book propped on her knees. His father in bed beside her, wrinkling his nose in feigned distaste.

Was he twisting history when he remembered his parents as a happy couple? In love, exchanging lingering glances over the breakfast table? Of course, he remembered the enmity at the end, the war zone their home became after his father's infidelity. Never had he admired his mother more than when she'd traveled the ugly road of divorce with so much grace.

He closed his eyes briefly, gripping the marble counter. The reality of her pending death set in arthritically, inflaming and stiffening his emotions. The calming notes of the tea mixed with the stench of fear emanating from inside him. He clamped his lips against his tamped-down terror, turning them down at the corners to foreshadow his sorrow.

Fix your face.

He could hear his mother's imperative even now, calling to him from distant memories.

Don't pout. You're a young man, and young men do not pout. Especially not Walsh men.

Technically, he was a Bennett, but he had known what she meant.

He arranged his mother's tray, even adding a white rose he plucked from the huge arrangement in the foyer. The sight of his father walking up the driveway almost made Walsh drop the tray, tea, rose, and all. Walsh set the tray down and strode toward the door, hoping to get it open before the doorbell rang. Just in case his mother was sleeping upstairs.

Wash couldn't help but note how much alike they were physically. It was like looking into a mirror, years down the road. Would he hold himself so stiffly? Would his gait remain as confident and sure, more like a prowl? It was the deeper-than-skin similarities that frightened him. The unfettered, selfish ambition of Martin Bennett. The ruthless disregard for anyone standing in the path of what he desired.

"Dad."

"Walsh." His father answered him with a level stare across the threshold.

"What are you doing here?" Walsh was afraid he already knew.

"I'm here...I'm here to see your mother." Martin came as close to stuttering as Walsh had ever heard. "You should've called me."

"You asked me to keep you apprised of her condition." Walsh wasn't sure what his father expected other than a call notifying him she had passed. His parents hadn't had an amicable relationship after their bitter divorce. "And you were in Hong Kong."

"Claire got a hold of me." Martin flexed a muscle in his lean jaw. "Your uncle James called."

"Uncle James?" A frown knotted Walsh's forehead. "Really? Dad, am I missing something?"

"No, I just want to...I want to see your mother before—" Martin smashed the sentence before he finished.

Walsh had never seen his father any less than perfectly composed. Arrogantly striding through the luxuriously appointed offices of Bennett Enterprises with a line of employees/minions trailing behind him, yes. Commanding a boardroom full of executives like they were royal subjects, yes. Charming a thousand people at a business convention, yes.

Discomposed? Never.

"Where's your uncle James?" Martin cut into Walsh's bewildered thoughts.

"In his study." Walsh nodded toward Uncle James's lair. "Look, I was on my way up to take Mom some tea. If you come up, come quietly just in case she's asleep."

His father watched him for an extra moment before turning on his heel toward Unc's study. Walsh climbed the stairs, still turning it all over in his head, once again balancing the tray. At the top of the stairs he drew in a deep breath, bracing himself for the sight of his mother, so different than how he had always known her. Vibrant. Glowing. Unassailable.

Walsh nudged the door open centimeters at a time with his shoulder. The sight of the small figure huddled beneath the down comforter dragged out all the ugly emotions he'd been wrestling. Depthless fear and pain clawed their way up through his belly like from the bottom of a dark well, up through his constricted air passages, asphyxiating him.

The bright paisley scarf tied around her head peeped out from beneath the bed covers. His eyes roamed the still-beautiful face. The strong bones jutted proudly from beneath the skin pulled so tautly over them. He knew beneath the covers she was almost skeletal, but somehow, even in a fitful sleep, even ravaged by this voracious cancer eating the very life from her, she still managed to radiate strength.

He noticed her bare feet peeking out from beneath the comforter and remembered her cashmere slippers. He could at least slip those on her feet. Placing the tray down beside the bed, he slipped into a closet the size of most people's bedrooms and looked around for the slippers. For a moment he just absorbed the lavishness of the wardrobe. Pants, shoes, dresses, suits, hats, scarves, jewelry—all of the very highest quality. She loved to give, but she loved to have, too. And without any sense of guilt. How could someone who gave so much feel guilty for what she had?

He resumed his search for the slippers. Movement and a whisper out in the bedroom distracted him from his self-appointed task. He started toward the door, which was ajar.

"Martin," he heard his mother rasp drowsily.

She had called for her long-dead mother, father, cousins, close friends. She was in and out of her head at this point, with windows of lucid thought, like what they'd shared last night, growing smaller and smaller every day.

"I'm here, baby," Walsh heard his father respond, immobilizing Walsh with the intimacy of his words.

His father must have entered the room while Walsh was looking for the slippers. Should he interrupt? Shoo his dad out so his mother could rest?

"I knew you'd come." She sounded more alert than Walsh had heard her in days. "I knew it."

"Of course I'm here." Martin's voice was stripped of the steel and stone Walsh was used to hearing. It was so soft Walsh barely recognized it. "I'll stay, if you want. If you'll let me."

"Oh, Martin. I've always wanted you to stay."

"No, that's not true, Kris, but I'm glad you want me here now. I wasn't sure."

"Yes, you were." Her laugh was dimmed, but throaty. "You've always been sure of me, haven't you?"

"Not always. I thought we'd…" His words trailed off, but his mother seemed to know the rest.

"So did I, Martin." Her voice vibrated with tears. "We were both so stubborn. Both so…"

Kristeene's unfinished sentence lay there in a silence growing between his parents, thickening with an emotion Walsh couldn't place. He had not heard civil words exchanged between them since he was thirteen years old, but this conversation sounded intimate, punctuated with longing and…love?

Walsh stared at the door of the huge closet, separating him from his parents, and felt that he'd somehow stepped into a Narnian wardrobe, the other side populated with satyrs and witches and other impossibilities, no less fantastical than the notion that his parents still loved each other. He took one silent step toward the door, ready to reveal himself before things became more awkward.

"I'm sorry, Kris," his father said in a rush, as if afraid the words would retract like acid reflux if he didn't get them out. "I'm sorry about Laura. It was stupid. I was lonely. We were fighting all the time. There's so many excuses I could make, that I *did* make, but it just boils down to me fucking everything up. Fucking my whole life up. You *were* my life, Kris. You know that."

"I thought I knew that," his mother replied so softly Walsh found himself leaning forward to catch the words. "That's why…"

Walsh could hear her struggling to get the words out, though whether it was the cancer, making every bodily function more and more laborious, or whether it was this emotion he hadn't known still existed between them that was choking her speech, Walsh wasn't sure.

"That's why it was such a betrayal," she finally managed to say. "I knew you loved me. To throw it all away like that. At the time, I didn't think we could ever go back. I didn't think you could be the man I married, the man I fell in love with, and do that to us. I felt like I was married to a stranger."

"I know, Kris." Walsh was astounded to hear tears soaking his father's words. "I wasn't sure what I was capable of anymore, either, if I could do that to you. I think I've been lost ever since."

"Martin, you aren't lost."

"I don't know how to get back, Kris. I always thought… eventually that we would be together again. How could we not be together? And the years just…"

"I know." His mother's words shook. "Everything got so twisted around. And now it's the end."

"No, we can fight this," Martin cut in, his voice gaining strength. "And then we'll—"

"We'll what? We'll be together?" She softened the sharp edges around her words. "Martin, I am *dying*."

"No," he cut her off, underlining the word with denial.

"Yes," she insisted, her voice still firm but gentling. "I'm dying and we don't get that second chance I thought we'd have, but know this. I never, not ever, no matter what we said in court, no matter how we fought, *never* stopped loving you. That was the biggest battle of all. Fighting myself not to come back to you. I couldn't do that. Not after Laura. I know some women get past those things, but I was too possessive."

"I would have responded the same way." The regret in his father's voice chafed Walsh's ears. "I've hated myself, and I think I hated you, Kris, for not forgiving me. For not getting past it so we could be together again."

"Martin, we don't have long." Pain reduced his mother's words to a hiss. "I...I, there's a bottle of pills on the nightstand. I need to take my medication, but after I take it, I'll be no good. Back asleep or out of my head. I need you to make me a promise."

"No, not now, baby. Let me get the pills." Walsh heard his father moving, rising to get the medicine. "We can talk later."

Walsh stepped to the crack in the door, watching to make sure his mother didn't need anything other than the pills. Kristeene had grabbed his father's wrist with surprising strength, staying his fist, which was clutching the bottle of pills.

"No, I don't know if I'll...I don't know if there will be time, Martin." The finality of that pronouncement sat like lead in the room, weighing the air with pending grief.

Martin moaned, lowering himself to the bed, the mattress dipping under his weight. He crawled up beside her and behind her, spoon fashion.

"No, Kris. Don't go. I'm so lost, Kris. Don't go."

"Listen to me." She turned with great effort to face him, her headscarf slipping to reveal the front of the smooth scalp beneath. "Just listen, sweetheart."

The endearment sliced Walsh down the middle, reinforcing that secret truth that had lain beneath his parents' years-long enmity. They had loved each other all these years, been separated all these years, seemed to hate each other all these years, and she had thought of him as "sweetheart." Walsh tasted the bitter irony that he could have known a family, healthy and whole, instead of the broken dysfunction of being shuffled between two snarling combatants, who loved each other deeply all along.

"Just listen," she said again. "It's Walsh."

Walsh stifled a whoosh of breath, shocked to hear his own name introduced into this moment. He felt like a character written in as an afterthought, or an understudy being called unexpectedly to the stage.

"What about him?" His father's voice became wary.

"You are his father, Martin," she said, her voice choppy with pain. "Not his trainer. He's your son. Not just some heir or successor. He needs you."

"Sometimes I think he hates me," Martin finally said after a long silence.

Walsh squeezed his eyes shut, twisting the delicate cashmere slippers between his fingers. His father was right. There had been times when he'd looked at his father, ruling his sprawling business kingdom, so self-satisfied, so arrogant, and he'd hated him. Hated how he'd hurt his mother. Hated that his father had always been more concerned with grooming him than raising him. And that hate warred with an insoluble love that refused to be diluted by his father's careless disregard, unreasonable expectations, and exacting standards.

He'd always thought of him as a cold man surrounded by barriers, impenetrable even by a young boy's desperate need for affection. But when Walsh peered through the crack into that fantastical land where his parents still loved each other, it was not the face of a cold man he saw. It was a man tortured, anguished with regret and horrified by what his mistakes had cost him.

"No, Martin." Kristeene shook her head slowly, sadly. "Just the opposite. He loves you so much and wants to please you. Don't you *see* that? You and me, it's too late for us, but—"

"Don't say that, Kris."

"I don't have time left for us, Martin, but you and Walsh. You've still got time to make that right."

"I don't…I don't know how." His father sounded vulnerable for the first time in Walsh's memory.

"Yes, you do." She reached a bony hand up to caress the back of his neck. "Think about it. He needs you to get this right. Promise me."

"I promise, Kris," he said, not sounding sure, his voice thickening. "But don't leave me."

Walsh saw her reach up and kiss his father, chastely at first, a mere brush across his lips. But then long-denied passion seemed to swell between them, making them oblivious of Kristeene's shining, bald pate, ravaged body, and lips chapped with illness. There was no self-consciousness, no consideration for the cancer or the years of malevolence stretching behind them. Only a long-checked hunger that seemed to consume them. They kissed like it was the first time, like it was the last time. His mother held his father's head still, kissing him as if she'd take the taste of him on her lips into eternity. As if he were the wine at her last supper, a final indulgence to be savored and swished in her mouth like liquid luxury. An interloper, Walsh averted his eyes from the deep kisses and urgent, desperate caresses.

"Kris," he heard his father say, his voice drained of passion, urgent. "Don't leave me. Don't go."

Walsh glanced up, tears setting his throat on fire at the sight of his father holding his mother's limp body in his arms. Tears ran unchecked down the lean, handsome face, so like his own.

"Don't go. Don't leave me. Don't go. Don't leave me. So lost, Kris. So lost." Martin wailed, clutching her tighter, pushing the scarf back completely from her head to look unflinchingly on the proud, ruined beauty of the body that remained behind. "Don't go. Don't leave me. Don't go. Don't leave me."

Walsh must have heard his father's anguished litany a hundred times before he finally dragged himself to huddle against the wardrobe wall, sitting down among his mother's shoes, wearing his father's face, streaked by his own silent tears.

Chapter Twenty-Eight

How would she make it through this day?

Kerris planted herself in a corner of the Walshes' elegant living room, watching an old camp counselor monopolize Cam across the room. Kerris felt so alone, though dozens of people surrounded her, chattering about what a lovely service it had been, and Kristeene's remarkable legacy, and how much she would be missed. She genuinely mourned Kristeene personally, but she knew the weight she felt was for Cam and Walsh. Both despondent. Both grasping for an anchor as they negotiated the unfamiliar waters of unfathomable sorrow. Especially Walsh.

She would keep her distance. She couldn't trust herself with him, especially not today, when all she wanted to do was drag him over the grassy hill to the gazebo, where she'd felt healed in his arms once upon a time and wanted to do the same for him.

She stood too quickly and the room twirled. She reached blindly for her chair. Feeling nauseous and short of breath, she walked out into the foyer on rubbery legs. Jo was speaking in low tones with Mrs. Quinton about food for the reception. Jo looked at Kerris, raising her brows like a queen considering a peasant, silently inquiring why she would have strayed from the herd of mourners grazing on heavy hors d'oeuvres in the living room.

"Can I help you, Kerris?" Over Mrs. Quinton's shoulder, Jo's eyes remained chilly.

The easy affection that had existed between Jo and her was gone, maybe forever. Jo saw her as the bone of contention between Walsh and Cam, the one who had broken up their tightly knit triumvirate. Since the night of Walsh's party, the warmth she'd become used to from Jo had been replaced with coolness, overlaid with a light coat of polite disdain.

"I'm just feeling a little light-headed." Kerris swallowed the water gathering in her mouth and twisted her wedding band. "I don't want to pull Cam away, though. Is there somewhere I might lie down for a little bit?"

"Sure. Go up these stairs and into the first room on your right. It was Aunt Kristeene's sitting room." She looked Kerris up and down, her tone and eyes frozen. "No one ever goes in there."

Jo resumed her conversation without further comment, a dismissal. Kerris mumbled a hasty thanks, brushing past Jo to climb the stairs, clinging to the rail. She slipped into the room, glad the setting sun provided some light through the partially drawn curtains. She flicked on the lamp by a recliner that reminded her of Kristeene, a delicate frame encased in tough but supple leather. She settled in, glad of the darkened room and the soft cushions enfolding her weary body.

*　*　*

Walsh nodded for what felt like the thousandth time when someone expressed their condolences, shared memories of his mother, or assured him that he should "take all the time he needed" to grieve. Everyone understood.

Bullshit.

He felt for the flask-shaped elixir in his interior suit jacket pocket.

"'Scuse me," he said to the chairwoman of one of his mother's committees. "I need to check on something."

He had to get out of there before he really lost it. Not tears. Those still eluded him. He was more concerned about the senseless rage lying supine beneath his grief, waiting patiently to strike the nearest unsuspecting bystander. He was so ready for them to just leave. He headed up the stairs for the one place he was sure to be alone.

He knew the closed door to his mother's sitting room would be unlocked. When he walked in, the lamp was on, which was odd. His nostrils flared at the subtle scent of vanilla reaching across the room to him. He saw the small figure slumped in his mother's recliner and stood still as a mountain.

Shutting the door behind him, he padded across the thick pile carpet until he was towering over Kerris, relishing the small liberty of looking at her without inhibition or judgment.

Her loosened hair spilled over one shoulder. He caressed the smooth face with his eyes, paying special attention to that lush mouth and the impossibly long eyelashes painting stripes on the high cheekbones. Good God, the woman was beautiful.

Kerris could be his solace. A moment in her arms wouldn't take away this bone-gnawing grief, but she could soothe him like no one else. He knew it. The years-long loyalty to Cam wrestled with the scorching desire to hold her, have her, keep her. On a day like today, when it seemed he'd lost everything that mattered, she was the one thing he wanted for himself. But his mother would have been ashamed. Cam would be broken. Kerris, with her unwavering sense of right, would be ruined. He had to accept it. He couldn't have her. When the food had been eaten and the mourners had all gone home, she would leave with her husband. Walsh knew it, but he couldn't walk away from this one moment with her. So he watched and waited for her to wake.

* * *

Kerris sensed someone standing over her and cracked her eyes just enough to make out Walsh's tall frame, hovering over her. She slowly opened her eyes, bracing herself for the vulnerability of this grieving giant. She stared back at him for a heartbeat before leaning forward, returning the recliner to the upright position. She pushed her tumble of hair back with fingers she willed not to tremble.

"Walsh." Her whisper took back up where they always left

off; as if it hadn't been months since they'd faced each other, held each other. "What are you doing up here?"

"Escaping." Something most people would have taken for a smile curved Walsh's lips. Kerris knew better.

She wasn't sure what she could say that wouldn't get them into trouble. If she opened the door to the despair she saw behind his eyes, she wouldn't be able to resist holding him, comforting him, and she couldn't be the one to do that.

"I should go."

She stood to her feet. He grasped her wrist, a gentle tether. The brief contact paralyzed her. And his eyes—burning with grief and need.

"Stay. Please. Just a minute."

She knew there was a comfort he found in her that he could find nowhere else; with no one else. She didn't understand it, but she knew it. She reached for his hand, tangling their fingers.

"Are you okay?" She probed beneath his rigidly controlled expression.

"No."

"You will be," she said, her words soft like cotton.

Walsh stared over her shoulder at the recliner she'd just vacated. She tugged gently on his hand. Pulling his glance back to meet hers.

"I feel so lost." His voice cracked down the middle, but didn't break. "I don't...I don't know if I can...if I can...I can't cry. I was at the funeral in a church full of people crying, and I couldn't cry. Why can't I cry? I kept thinking I had to get through the eulogy without crying. Just don't cry. And now, I can't. I can't..."

Without thought, she bent her elbows, laying her forearms and palms against his back, drawing him close enough to feel his heart slamming into hers. He bent to the curve joining her neck and shoulder, pushing her hair back and resting his head there. She felt him sigh, and then breathe in deeply, as if filling his lungs with fresh air. She could feel him blinking against her skin, still fighting the approach of the tears he thought he'd longed for, but was afraid to give in to. She began to sway just a little. She'd seen mothers rock their children to comfort them, though she'd never experienced it herself. The motion seemed to loosen the grief lodged inside of him. Something had slipped and set it free, leaking it in rivulets across her shoulder and inside her dress, down her back, leaving a warm, wet trail of heartache.

Chapter Twenty-Nine

W alsh marked the time by her heartbeats against his chest. He knew he should let Kerris go. He *had* to let her go, but couldn't make himself do it. His body, so weighted with loss and inexpressible grief for the last few days, selfishly burrowed into this bastion of comfort, refusing to relinquish it. She stirred, starting to pull away. His arms clenched around her small frame before he told them they could. He pressed her head to his chest, breathing her in.

"Wait. Just a little longer."

He looked down at her tear-streaked face, running his thumb along her cheek, following a wet path to her chin. He licked the salty wetness on his fingers. Her tears hit his tongue like a sorrowed liquor, heady and numbing. He clutched her closer to steady himself, not sure he could stand on his own without her as scaffolding.

Don't go. Don't leave me. Don't go. Don't leave me. So lost. So lost.

His father's howling dirge haunted him, whistling through his deserted soul like an icy wind. The walls he'd erected since the day he'd met Kerris crumbled. Walls constructed of morals and right and convention gave way, collapsing beneath the heaviness of pain and loss. And the words he'd sworn he'd never say stormed past his well-meaning lips.

"Kerris, come with me."

She stiffened, pulling away as far as the vise of his arms would allow.

"Walsh, I can't—"

"Just a week. Find a way to come to me for a few days. I can't do this without you. It's too much. This hurts—"

"Walsh, I know, but we can't—"

"We can go somewhere no one knows us."

He tightened his fingers around her arms.

"There *isn't* somewhere no one knows you."

She pulled away altogether, putting at least a few inches between them.

"Hong Kong." He stepped back into her orbit, but forced himself not to grab her. "My dad has a house in Hong Kong."

"Walsh, no." Sadness and regret darkened her eyes, but her mouth straightened into a firm, determined line. "I know you're hurting, but no."

"You'd have your own room." He pulled her close again, meshing his fingers with hers, his voice a persuasion. "I'm not asking you to sleep with me. You know I'm not. I just need you. I just—"

"Walsh, I'm pregnant."

Her whisper sliced him open with the delicate strength of a scalpel. Flayed him like a frog stretched out for dissection. Her skin burned under his fingers. He stepped away, singed.

"You're—"

"Pregnant, yes." Kerris's hands settled at her midriff. She angled her head, trying to look into the eyes he'd lowered to the ground. "So you see, I really can't."

She recaptured his fingers, raising her other hand to cup his jaw like she was afraid it might break. Nudging his chin until he was forced to look at her.

"I'm happy, Walsh. You know this is what I've always wanted. This is what it was all about. A family of my own. I want this."

"Yeah. I know. I guess Cam's over the moon."

The words piled up in his mouth like ashes.

"He doesn't even know yet. I haven't had the chance to tell him." She shook her head, dropping her hand to guard her stomach. "I found out the morning your mother passed away, and it just didn't feel right."

It still didn't feel right to Walsh. Kerris carrying another man's child felt like sunshine at midnight. Like snow on the Fourth of July. Upside down. Everything was so wrong. Kerris should be married to *him*. Carrying *his* child. His mother should be here, not buried and silent forever. He and Cam should be close, the best of friends still.

But nothing was right.

"Right." He squeezed his hand around her fingers, so slight but strong.

The silence between them thickened with lost possibility.

Walsh stroked her hair back from her face, savoring what felt like their last moments. There had never been any going back, not since Kerris's wedding day. This new life, this baby Kerris had longed for, widened the gulf between them until it was more impassable than it had ever been.

Walsh watched tears streak down from under eyelids she'd pressed together, standing still for a moment more and letting the loss rush over him. Loss not just for his mother, but for the possibility that had been so close. If Kerris had listened to him the night of his mother's party, she might have been pregnant with his child. He beat the thought back, knowing it was futile. He looked down at her and wondered if she ever thought about it. They both started when the door swung open without warning.

"Kerris, Cam is—" Jo cut the words off, dropping the room temperature with one frosty look. "Cam's looking for you. Your husband. Remember him?"

"Jo." Walsh peppered his voice with warning, glancing at Kerris with quick concern. She looked back at Jo without guile or guilt.

"I don't have anything to hide, Jo." Kerris sniffed and walked toward the door with sure steps.

"Really? Then why do I seem to always catch you off in some dark corner with my cousin? Cam's best friend until *you* showed up."

"Stop it, Jo." Walsh stepped toward the door, not looking at Kerris again. "Not today."

"You took the words." Jo's eyes on Kerris went subzero. "If

the two of you can manage to stay apart at least for today, that would honor Aunt Kristeene's memory."

"Don't you dare tell me what would honor my mother's memory." Walsh's words thundered into the tranquillity of the room. He slammed his fist into his open palm. "Talking with a friend, taking comfort from a friend, is not dishonoring anything, Jo. Now shut the hell up about things you don't understand."

He rushed past her into the hall, hating to leave Kerris, but needing to get away from the accusation in his cousin's eyes. Needing to get away from the promise growing inside of Kerris. He stormed down the stairs, almost barreling into Cam. They faced each other like wary, wounded animals, only a few steps apart.

"You doing okay?" Cam asked, finally breaking the silence.

"Hell no."

"Me neither." Cam blinked away tears.

"You wanna get drunk?" Walsh proffered the vodka-filled flask from his pocket.

"Yeah, like you can't believe, but I'll pass." The breath swished from Cam's chest in a rush. "I was looking for…"

Cam trailed off, obviously not wanting to drop the grenade of Kerris's name into the middle of their temporary détente.

"For Kerris?" Walsh kept his tone bland and his eyes steady when he looked back at Cam. "I just passed her and Jo in Mom's sitting room. You could check there."

"Okay." Cam frowned, glancing up the stairs and then back to Walsh.

Walsh brushed past him and walked toward Uncle James's study, hoping to get a much-needed swallow or two of liquid courage in privacy and away from all the consoling eyes.

Hand on the door, he caught a glimpse of a broad back rushing toward the front door in the foyer.

"Martin," he called, but his father didn't slow or turn.

Walsh followed, moving more quickly than he had all day. He stopped on the porch landing.

"Dad!"

His father stopped where he stood, but he didn't turn around. Walsh rushed down the steps, stepping into his path.

"Dad, I—"

"Walsh, could we talk another time?" His father looked down at his shiny Italian shoes.

"Well, I—Okay." Walsh felt about twelve years old. "I just thought…well, we hadn't gotten to talk since Mom…"

He cut the words off when he saw his father wince. Pain tweaked his lean features. He looked at Walsh with the most naked pain anyone had ever tried to hide.

"Another time?" His father's red-rimmed eyes revealed that he was not as unfeeling as his tone would lead one to believe. "I'm headed to New York, and then back to Hong Kong."

"Already?" Walsh couldn't believe his remaining parent was abandoning him now of all times. "You can't postpone the trip?"

"Why would I want to?" Martin's words started rebuilding a wall between them. "I cut the trip short to…I cut the trip short, and I need to finish what I went there to do."

If Walsh hadn't heard his father's howling grief himself, he'd assume he was being cold and callous, as usual. But Walsh noted the lines etched around his father's mouth and eyes. Saw his father's hands tremble. Walsh suspected nothing but pride and sheer will kept Martin's back straight and his posture rigid. He was fighting absolute collapse, a meltdown of Chernobyl proportions.

"I'll see you when you get back to New York, Dad."

His father nodded, opening his mouth to speak and slamming it back shut. Walsh could almost see him stringing together the words before he tried again.

"What you said in your mother's eulogy was perfect." His father's voice husked with suppressed tears. "She was always so proud of you. She loved you so much."

Walsh offered a dumb nod. He didn't know what to do with this version of his father. As much as Martin tried to pull the impassive mask in place to cover his grief, it kept slipping. Walsh glanced away from the pain so evident on his father's face, digging his hands into the pockets of his wool trousers against the unrelenting cold. A flash of red caught his eye.

Kerris, coming down the steps, wore a scarlet coat over the black dress he'd seen her in earlier. Walsh couldn't help but think of that first night when she'd worn a scarlet dress, an orchid nestled behind her ear. They occupied a different world now. A dystopia where his mother, his rock, had died. Where the one woman he wanted had married his best friend and carried their child.

Cam walked Kerris toward the car, his hand at the curve of

her back. Walsh hadn't seen him look so broken since he'd first met him. Walsh realized Cam truly processed this loss like a son, left behind. Finding out about the baby would help him through this. A new life. A fresh start.

A part of Walsh, the part that couldn't stop loving Cam like a brother, rejoiced for him. For *them*. But his heart—that selfish muscle pumping unrelenting blood to the rest of his body, skipped a beat when his eyes found Kerris. She looked back for a second longer than she should have before dragging her eyes away and looking straight ahead.

She wrapped around his heart like knotted string he couldn't work loose. She was pregnant. She was Cam's. And as hot and as deep as this feeling went, it was just that. A feeling from which nothing good could ever come.

Their future was ahead of them and so was his. He couldn't undo what had been done, but there was still time to make other things right. He turned to his father.

"Dad, want some company?"

Martin turned, hand poised over the door handle to his rented Mercedes.

"Company?" His father snapped his brows together at this foreign concept. "What do you mean?"

"I could go with you to Hong Kong." Walsh wondered if his father realized what it took for him to speak those words, to make that offer.

Martin's features contracted then relaxed, and Walsh knew that though they were silent, they both heard the same thing. Kristeene's plea to make things right between them. Those moments were seared into Walsh's heart, and he'd never forget that his mother's last words, her final thoughts, had been of him reconciling with this man. With his father.

"I'd like that." Martin's mouth curved into something terribly close to a smile.

"I'll just be a few minutes." Only out of habit did Walsh keep the eagerness from his voice. "I'll grab a few things and we can leave for New York right now."

"I'll wait here." His father slid into the car and turned on the heat.

This trip couldn't have been more perfectly timed. Besides getting some long overdue time with his father, Walsh needed something to pour himself into. After Cam and Kerris's wedding, he'd abandoned himself to a debauched lifestyle. Developed destructive habits. Nicked and torn at his moral fiber until right and wrong had amalgamated into some alloy made only of his basest desires. He wanted to be better than that. For his mother. For Jo. Even for Kerris and Cam.

But most of all for himself.

He would leave Cam and Kerris to their future. And as much as it hurt today, right now, he'd find his own.

SPECIAL BONUS SCENE

Keep reading for a never-before-released chapter from Cam's POV

Bonus Chapter

Cam slipped into Ms. Kris's hospital room. He'd meant to come on his lunch break, but things had gotten hectic at the office. Now it was after five o'clock, and he probably wouldn't have much time before Walsh showed up. He stopped just inside, shocked at how small and drawn she looked against the sterile white hospital sheets. Pain wrapped around his heart like a stubborn vine, squeezing out what little peace he'd had.

He remembered what life had been like before he'd met this incredible woman. The memory of that life haunted him, sometimes dogging him into his sleep, nightmare and memory inextricably woven.

Cam noticed for the first time the simple Christmas decorations someone, probably Jo, had put up. A small tree on the bedside table. A few white lights suspended over Ms. Kris's hospital bed. A large poinsettia in the corner. The festive touches couldn't dispel the sense of inevitability hovering in the room like an unwanted visitor.

Cam sat down and pulled out his sketchpad. He hated to see her this way—her light dimmed and, based on the news Kerris had broken to him about hospice, soon to be extinguished. He settled himself at the foot of her bed, careful not to disturb her. He propped the sketchpad on his knees, filling the blank page with the picture his mind's eye stored of her at her most glorious. Her dark hair spilled around her shoulders and the lovely skin stretched with taut vitality over the regal bones of her face. Her wide mouth spread into an infectious grin. She stirred, stilling his charcoal pencil and drawing his attention.

"Hi, beautiful." He tossed the pad to the floor and crawled up to her end of the bed, lying down on top of the covers in her outstretched arms.

He closed his eyes, burrowing his nose into her neck, searching for her smell. Beneath the stench of illness, antiseptic and approaching death, it was still there. He inhaled, content to be held right here as his mother had never held him. Kristeene taught him what a mother should be, and though she'd always called him her second son, he never believed it. Been afraid or unable to accept it. When you have a son like Walsh Bennett, why would you want a worthless piece of shit like him? He'd never envied Walsh's money or the compounded power that came with the Walsh *and* Bennett names. He'd envied this, though. He'd secretly coveted this goddess who had given birth to Walsh.

Entitled bastard had everything, had *this*, handed to him as an accident of birth, and now Walsh wanted Cam's wife too.

"Kerris came to see me today," Kristeene whispered, making

Cam wonder if he'd fumed so much he had spoken aloud, or if Kristeene's maternal clairvoyance kicked in as it had so many times before.

"She told me."

"She's so special, Cam." Ms. Kris ran her hand over the almost shoulder-length dark hair he'd left hanging loose today.

"Yep." Cam leaned into the gentle stroke like he had since he was thirteen years old.

"Did she tell you I'm going home tomorrow?" Ms. Kris fixed her gaze on the emotion he knew must be soaking his eyes.

"Ms. Kris, I can't—I don't know what I'll do if you…"

"There's no 'if,' baby." A trembling, skeletal hand traced the arch of his brows. "It's gonna happen. This is my last Christmas. I'm dying."

And inside of him, something was dying, too. Something that, early on, had been whipped into a mass of self-contempt, shame, and rage, huddled in a corner when he'd first met this woman. It had healed and come to life under her compassion, love, and acceptance. Cam was afraid it would die with her.

"I have a peace about it," Kristeene said.

I don't!

The denial tolled like a bell in his brain and shook his heart, but he wasn't going to lay his shit on her, the fact that he couldn't deal with a death she already seemed resigned to.

"How can you have peace about death?" His voice sounded hushed and solemn in his own ears.

"I believe in an afterlife, Cam. In Heaven, and I believe that's where I'll be. And I know that I'm leaving this earth with a clear heart. I didn't do everything I wanted, but I did a lot. I paid attention to the things that were most important."

She allowed a small silence to bathe them in contemplation before adding, "And I've forgiven."

Cam stiffened, turning his head to consider her with narrowed eyes. Even sick and near death, she was cagey. There was no way Jo hadn't told her something about what happened with Kerris and Walsh. She would have been curious about why they were never together when they visited; why they avoided each other like hand, foot, and mouth disease.

"Forgiveness isn't always an option, Ms. Kris." He broke the words into bite-size pieces in his mouth.

"When it's your time, *not* forgiving isn't an option. You only ask yourself why. Why would I hang on to that?"

"I know exactly what I'm holding on to and why." Cam slipped off the bed, scooping up his sketchpad and thrusting it under his arm, his movements jerky.

"You'll have to forgive Walsh, Cam." Kristeene's breath hitched with the effort it took to pull herself up on her elbows.

"You don't know what he's done." Cam glared at his Chuck Taylors, the black and white blurring with the rage wetting his eyes.

"He kissed Kerris," Kristeene said, her voice heavy with sympathy.

Cam returned her steady gaze.

"And you think I should forgive him?"

"I think you *have* to. He and Jo are all the family you've got."

"No, I've got Kerris." Cam knifed the air with one long, slim hand. "And no one, not even your perfect son, will take her away from me."

"Did you marry her even suspecting a little bit that there were feelings between them?" Kristeene probed and poked around the thing Cam had barely admitted to himself.

Cam glanced at Kristeene, a battered angel, earthbound and more vulnerable, but fiercer, than he'd ever seen her.

"You think *I* have cancer," she said. "You just keep holding on to that resentment. It'll eat away at you from the inside. It'll spread to everything good in your life and destroy it. Including your marriage."

"He shouldn't have kissed her." The lean lines of his body petrified into stone with no outlet for his hostility. "He had no right."

"No, he had no right. He was wrong, and I'm sure if they could take it back, they would. But they can't, Cam. And you can let that one moment haunt and destroy your marriage and cost you the best friend you've ever had, or you can let it go and move on. Knowing they won't hurt you like that again. Knowing it was a mistake."

"I'm not ready for that." His fingers clawed into twitchy fists at his side, aching to squeeze Walsh's throat. "I keep seeing them together in my head, and I can't stand to look at him."

"You don't hold her responsible at all?" Kristeene raised the skin where her eyebrows used to rest before radiation left it smooth and naked like a baby's.

"I know Kerris, and I know Walsh. I know who made the first move, who initiated this. He's been in love—" He cut himself off, turning away to face the window.

"So you did know."

"I'd have to be blind not to know he felt something for her. At first I assumed he just wanted to screw her like most guys, but then I realized it was more than that."

"More like what you felt for her?" Kristeene pressed. "And you were afraid, if given time, she'd choose him?"

"Who wouldn't choose him?" Cam pressed his forehead against the coolness of the window glass. "He could have anyone. She was for *me*. You know? And I had to lock that down."

"Seems like an honest conversation would have saved us all a lot of trouble." Kristeene slurred her words behind him. "But since that didn't happen, we are where we are. We can't stay here, Cam."

"I don't know where else to go." Cam laid his fist against the windowpane. "I can't give her up, but I can't forget. And I can't forgive Walsh, but I feel like somebody cut off my right hand."

Met with silence, Cam turned to watch Kristeene, who had dropped off practically mid-sentence into a drug-induced slumber. Had he tired her out? What would he do when she wasn't around to talk him off ledges?

Jump.

He leaned over her now-still form. He noticed goose bumps on her thin arms and tucked the sheets around her.

"I'll see you tomorrow." He kissed the silk scarf covering her slick scalp. "Mom."

He'd only dared to imagine calling her that, even though she called him son. The sweet rush of feeling almost brought him to his knees by her bed in a weeping, snotty, begging, incoherent pool of grief. He tightened his mouth, staving it off for now, though he saw it coming like a tsunami, and him its helpless shore.

Cam left Kristeene's room, running his hands over his face in a quick, impatient motion. He brushed away the last of his tears. He glanced at his watch, surprised to see he'd been with Kristeene for more than an hour. He pulled up short on his way to the elevator. Walsh was headed toward him, tall and lean in his gray suit, a preoccupied frown darkening his expression. Cam was prepared to walk right past him, refusing to entertain Kristeene's admonition to forgive.

I ain't forgiving shit.

Walsh had other ideas, stepping directly into Cam's path.

"How was she?" Walsh bypassed the small talk.

"Resting." Cam addressed his response to some point over Walsh's shoulder. He tried to step around Walsh, only to find him blocking his way again.

"Step the hell back, Bennett." Cam spiked the glare he gave Walsh.

"We have to talk about this," Walsh said, obviously unfazed by the barely checked threat written in Cam's fighter's stance.

"What should we talk about, Walsh? The fact that you want to fuck my wife?" Cam's voice was a low blow.

"It was a mistake." Walsh made a quick sweep of their surroundings, looking at the few people waiting in the reception area. "We got emotional talking about Haiti. She was comforting me, and it just went there. It won't happen again."

"You won't get the chance again. What part of staying out of our life don't you understand?"

"The part where you and I aren't brothers anymore," Walsh snapped back, fire in his eyes and words. "Dude, you're not going to throw away years of friendship over one kiss."

"One kiss. You think I was born yesterday."

"What?" Cam saw caution creep into Walsh's eyes.

Cam leaned forward, all aggressive, outraged male. Teeth bared.

"You love her."

Walsh looked back at him, weariness written in every line of his face, in his eyes. And Cam could see that he was tired of the lies, tired of denying what was in his heart.

"Yeah, I love her," Walsh said. "But we can figure this out. I'd never do anything about it."

"Asshole." Cam brushed past him and prowled toward the elevators. "You already did."

WALSH, KERRIS, AND CAM'S STORY CONTINUES IN *LOVING YOU ALWAYS*

About the Author

A RITA® and Audie® Award winner, *USA Today* bestselling author **Kennedy Ryan** writes for women from all walks of life, empowering them and placing them firmly at the center of each story and in charge of their own destinies. Her heroes respect, cherish, and lose their minds for the women who capture their hearts. Kennedy and her writings have been featured in Chicken Soup for the Soul, *USA Today*, *Entertainment Weekly*, *Glamour*, *Cosmopolitan*, *TIME*, *O* magazine, and many others. She is a wife to her lifetime lover and mother to an extraordinary son.

Find out more at:
   KennedyRyanWrites.com
   Tik Tok: @kennedyryanauthor
   Facebook.com/KennedyRyanAuthor
   Twitter: @KennedyRWrites
   Instagram: @KennedyRyan1